For Ie

Happy reunion !!

Flash Mob

Robert O'Connell

Published by Green Chicken Press

Cover design by Robert Burger

For Theresa

she's all I need

Flash Mob

Friday, Dec 7th
~ Boston ~

"Sis, sorry I'm late. My lab ran over, but I bolted as soon as I could. What's wrong?"

Pep Pastor, a college junior, is removing his scarf as he sits down at a café in Harvard Square in Cambridge. He's thin and has his thick, dark hair stylishly flipped up in the front. Pep is barely five foot seven and is wearing a thick hoodie over a cable knit sweater, jeans, and plaid, slip-on sneakers. Across from him at a table for two sits his older sister, Tommy, actually Tommasina. She is wearing a navy blue wool coat, a grey skirt with dark leggings and boots, and a maroon turtleneck. She has medium brown hair worn just past her shoulders and has a dancer's body, albeit a short one, at five feet, two inches. At 26, she is six years older than Pep. Tommy is blowing her nose. Her eyes are clearly red. She slides a paper cup toward her brother.

"Thanks for coming," she says. "I hope this is still hot."

He slugs down half of the cup.

"It's fine," he says. "At this point of the semester, it's simply fuel. Now, tell your baby brother what's wrong."

Tommy puts down her hot chocolate. She takes in a breath and lets it out slowly.

"I finally did it," she says. "I swore I never would, but there it was. I did it."

"Sis, you are typically the rock of the family. You have held my hand through more than I can remember. I have been waiting the bulk of my 20 years for this moment to be there for you, but bear with me. I'm new at this and I want to get it right. I need you to clarify something. What the fuck are you talking about?"

"I used his name," she says, lowering her eyes.

Pep lifts his eyebrows, clearly for effect, but then lowers them in legitimate confusion.

"Pardon?"

"I used Dad's name. I swore to myself I would never do it and out of nowhere, bang, there it was."

"I'd leave out the bang next time you tell the story."

Tommy shoots him a look—no, *the* look. Pep softly puts his hand on hers.

"Sorry, Sis, new at this. Take a breath and tell me the story."

"Okay, you recall that my department was hosting a seminar at the Harborside Hotel this week and that I was in charge?"

"Yes, I vaguely remember you mentioning it. Oh yes, I needed to get a restraining order on Facebook because you wouldn't shut up about it. Ethnobotany, correct?"

She gives him another look, but less severe this time.

Tommy continues, "Everything went great all week until this morning. As executive director, I made all of the arrangements with the hotel. Today was the closing event with the keynote speaker addressing everyone at a luncheon in the main ballroom. I show up at the ballroom this morning and the room was empty of tables and chairs. I immediately ran to the manager, who incidentally was happy to get the booking when they couldn't sell the space. The officious little snot tells me that we have been bumped to a different space."

"Hey, you can't call him that," says Pep, with mock offense.

"Why not? It certainly fits."

"It's just that you have called me an officious little snot so often that I kind of look at it as our thing."

"Sorry, I guess I made a mild effort to stop using that term since you 'exited the closet,' if you will."

"Sis, I did not become gay because you called me an officious little snot. As much as I wish to avoid stereotypes, for all I know, the opposite is the case. I kind of miss it. Besides, according to you, I was the last person on the planet to accept it anyway."

"While it's clear that it was obvious to the other seven billion of us, you know that Mom is still not convinced. I actually stopped calling you the snot thing in deference to her. You seemed impervious to insult, but I could see the pain in her face."

"I've seen it too. Why can't she accept that it's just a quirk of genetics? Our brother is a ginger. You have freckles. Mom went to college for God's sake."

"First of all, if she didn't go to college to find a husband, that still turned out to be the net effect. Also, Pep, she comes from a generation and culture that to some degree looks upon your 'condition' as a reflection on the mother. I know that she knows better in her head, but in her heart, who knows. Give her time."

"Great, pass me the tissues and get on with your story."

"Okay, so I look at the 'alternate space' and it's worse than horrible. It looks like a boiler room in the basement. It's too small, laid out wrong, and forget about the multimedia. I calmly tell him that this is unacceptable and insist on the original room. He tells me that some team from Houston came in town early for the Monday night game against the Pats due to the incoming storm and this shithole was apparently the only thing they could get on short notice. They need the ballroom to walk through plays or something until they can arrange a practice field."

"I assume you had some sort of contract."

"Of course. So I mention that and the fact that we already paid them for the venue. He said he would be happy to refund our money, which really pissed me off."

Pep has witnessed this type of storm brewing in his sister many times before.

"Defcon 4!" he shouts.

"I pull out the contract to show him," says Tommy as she slides down imaginary glasses and looks down her nose, "and this turd says, 'Maybe you should read the fine print. You paid for ballroom space, not a specific ballroom. As you can see, we have placed you in Ballroom F.' I shout back, 'You mean the Ballroom F with the hand-drawn cardboard sign?' And this twerp says, 'Never the less.'"

"No shit!" says Pep. "A Katherine Hep-BURN!"

Tommy slumps her shoulders.

"So I shove the contract up to his face, pointing out my name, and just blurt it out," she says.

In unison, they both say, "Do you know who my father is?"

Resigned, Tommy points her finger at her temple, cocks her thumb and says, "Yeah, BANG!"

"Let me guess the rest," says Pep. "A pause to think, a moment of recognition, blood leaves the face, everything is fixed without a hitch, and you never see the guy again. Something like that?"

"Pretty much. Oh, we also got a shitload of free flowers."

"Yellow roses?"

"Yeah, how did you know?"

"Texans. The Houston team is the Texans. You stole NFL flowers. You are now officially my favorite person."

"No I'm not," she says. "I'm a fucking gangster."

Friday, Dec 7th
~ Newark ~

"Mr. McCall, do we need to go over this again?" says an exasperated Marcellus Truffant, with a furrowed brow.

Scotty McCall is sitting in front of a grey metal desk in the Principal's office at Whitney Houston High School. He is 26 years old with curly, dirty-blond hair. He's wearing khakis, a blue button-down shirt with the sleeves rolled up, and a Cookie Monster tie loosened around an open collar. The desk was not built for comfort, nor was the office, but they were both functional as they have been, accommodating principals since the mid 50's when the school was built.

It was called Southside High School then. Truffant did not love the name change, feeling that Ms. Houston was a mixed role model at best, but the Board of Education was adamant about changing the school names to "inspire" the students. While he was hoping for a scientist or statesman, the finalists came down to Ms. Houston, Ice-T, Shaquille O'Neill, and the actress who played Rudy, the youngest Cosby kid. He shakes his head, thinking, "Reality fucking TV. It could've been worse. Jason Alexander was born in Newark. George Costanza High School…Jesus Christ!"

"Mr. Truffant?" asks Scotty, cautiously. "You look, um, troubled."

The Principal snaps out of his reverie.

"Pardon me, Mr. McCall, but I was thinking about your grandmother," says Truffant.

"Something good, I hope," says Scotty, with a smile.

"Not exactly, young man. Your grandmother was a great inspiration in my life. She was a teacher here when this school opened. She taught me more than I can tell you about fairness, education, leadership, and responsibility. She is, to a large part why I am here today and why, I expect that you have chosen to make a career here as well."

"Well that's seems pretty good so far," says Scotty.

Truffant grunts.

"That is the good part," he says. "The rest is that it is only out of loyalty to her memory that I am not kicking your ass through that door, down the hall, and down the front steps of this building! What the hell were you thinking pulling that stunt at the Pep Rally this afternoon? When you asked me to allow your multi-media students to assist with the Basketball Pep Rally, I was not expecting World War III!"

"World War II, actually, sir," says Scotty.

"This is no time for levity, Mr. McCall."

"Sorry, sir, allow me to explain. When we saw that the Pep Rally was taking place on Pearl Harbor Day, one of the students expressed, um, concern, if you will, that we tend to focus more on sports than on academics at times. I was very careful about discouraging them from making this a referendum on sports vs. academics. Still, I felt that a tasteful reminder of the sacrifice of American soldiers during an assembly of all our students might be appropriate."

"Yes, your grandmother called it 'an educational opportunity,' but that's not exactly an accurate description of what happened now, is it, Mr. McCall?"

"Not exactly, sir, but I did encourage them to study the history, you know, to be as accurate as possible."

"I assume you are referring to the sneak attack aspect of this mess?"

"Sir, that was as much a surprise to me as it was to you. I did find it incredibly creative on their part, however."

"Creative? We almost had a God-damned riot!"

"Yes, I too regret the panic aspect, but look at the bright side."

"Bright side? What bright side?"

"Well, first of all, no one was hurt."

"Thank God for that."

"And probably no lawsuits or negative press either."

"Son, we will have to have a later discussion about your standards for assignment of risk. How the hell did you get an MBA? I'm still waiting to hear how this mess transpired."

"Okay, so once the students decided on the sneak attack approach, they were very careful not to have any actual physical attack. You know, safety first."

"So that's when they decided to simulate the, what do you call it, cyber-attack?"

"Yes, super creative, if you ask me. Their original plan was kind of a nerd vs. athletics thing, but I discouraged that, for the reasons we discussed earlier."

"Saving that for the next Civil War reenactment, are we?"

"That's funny, sir."

"Not really. Continue."

"Well a school with a rival basketball team seemed to fit."

"So using their colors, fight song, and all the rest followed from there?"

"Yes, sir, and you must admit, the quality of the presentation was first rate. The 'sneak attack' aspect, well, clearly nobody saw that coming."

"And the chaos that ensued?"

"Well, the replica of the Arizona that was 'sunk' in front of the exit was there to contain the students, since we didn't want this spilling out into the hall. It actually had a similar effect as blocking Honolulu Harbor during the actual attack."

"Stop! Don't make it worse. Two more questions. First, why not use our true rival school, Central, um, I mean, Queen Latifah High? We battle them for the City Championship almost every year. That seemed the obvious choice. You, I mean your students, picked a school that hasn't beaten us since the two-handed set shot was in vogue."

"That was all the students doing. It was great. I assumed Latifah as well, but they really got into the history. See, they knew that in 1941 we were already at war in Europe and Latifah is like our Germany, if you will. So they looked for an alternative that was more like Japan. Eastside fit the bill perfectly."

"Ginsberg."

"Excuse me?"

"Allen Ginsberg High School, that's the new name for Eastside. It's in the Jewish section of town, so they had more influence over the name. He was born here. At least he's an author and not a singer, actor, or athlete."

"Anyhow, besides the fact that, like Japan, it is in the east, it is also a smaller, weaker, and less expected adversary. Like the actual attack, you wouldn't see it coming. I was very impressed with the students' thought process."

"The students, huh? That brings me to my last question. The last screen on the PowerPoint, that was still on the screen at the end, I assume you are going to lay that on your students as well?"

Scotty breaks eye contact and stifles a smirk with his hand.

"Torah! Torah! Torah! As I live and breathe," says Truffant.

"Sir," says Scotty, straightening in his chair. "I was just trying to inspire the students to apply a creative outlet and to use modern technology to enhance their development and presentation of knowledge."

"Bullshit, son! Although I must admit that when your grandmother Hilda said the same type of thing when I was a student here, I would have followed her to hell and back. Look, Scotty, I appreciate your creativity and there is no doubt that you inspire your students' loyalty as well as their attention. These are no small achievements with today's distractions. Many of your colleagues could learn from you."

"But?"

"But we live in the real world. We are not making great strides, yet, but we have turned the corner, and I can promise you, we *will* make great strides here. Our test scores have been rising for three years straight. I took on the Board and cleaned house of some of the 'less dedicated' staffers we had holding our kids back. For God's sake, son, you know the deal. You run our Media Arts Club. We cannot afford to be on the news, on YouTube, on Facebook, on Twitter, or whatever else is out there."

"I hear you, sir."

"I'm not sure you do, son. There will be NO more incidents of this kind here. Not now, not ever. Not if you expect to continue your good works here. I just cannot risk our success, nor our future, on your, um, *eccentricities*. Do we understand each other?"

"Absolutely, sir," says Scotty. He stands up and walks out of the office thinking to himself, "*...assuming he doesn't hear about the flash mob."*

Saturday, Dec 8th
~ Clifton ~

"Marcus, chill," says Scotty. "It's a beautiful fall day, we just played some great football, and we are killing several sacks of murder burgers. Isn't this the life we always dreamed of?"

Scotty, Carter, and Marcus are at their usual table in White Castle surrounded by several bags and empty boxes. Carter is a tall African-American with a meticulous afro. Marcus, too, is African-American, but is the same height as Scotty, and wiry. His hair is cropped to near baldness. Marcus nods toward Carter.

"Ask Stickyfingers over here," he says, turning toward Carter. "How the hell did you drop that pass? It hit you in the damned chest."

Carter snorts and downs another burger.

"Dude, I told you, I slipped," he says.

"Yeah, 'cause you weren't wearing your spikes, asshole!" says Marcus.

"I told you that I left them at the gym."

"I can't help but notice that you were able to find those new Lebrons you got on. You know you wanted to show 'em off. What did you pay for those things, two hundred?"

"Just doin' my part to spur the economy," says Carter, "certainly more than you cheap-ass motherfuckers. Besides, even Jerry Rice dropped a few balls."

"Jerry Rice didn't need to showboat," says Marcus.

"Scotty, help me out here," says Carter.

"Dude, it was right in your hands," says Scotty. "Anyhow, I want to talk about the flash mob."

"I'm out," says Carter.

"Carter, I haven't even told you about it yet," says Scotty.

"I know it will involve you asking me for the car."

"I won't need the car. Besides, what's the point of having a friend who drives a limo if I can't get an occasional favor?"

"'Cuz I want to keep my job."

"Driving rich white folks around," Marcus interjects.

"Their money is green, and I do recall you both occasionally watching the flatscreen I paid for," says Carter.

Scotty rolls his eyes.

"Can we continue this discussion at another time?" he says. "It's been ongoing for nearly a decade, since we were freshmen, and I don't expect it to end any time soon. Here's what we can agree on. Marcus and I are using our degrees in a feeble attempt to change the world. Carter is not, but makes more than the two of us combined as a mercenary for the 1% who would use him for firewood in a second if it suited them. We share an apartment in Montclair, New Jersey looking for love in a coldhearted world like one big sitcom family. Agreed?"

"I would like to stipulate for the record," says Carter, "that I contend that 20 years from now, I will own my own business and be well on my way to being in the 1% while you two dreamers will still be sharing a dump wondering where it all went wrong."

"If you weren't sitting on your lazy ass watching Law & Order all day, I'd at least consider the possibility," says Marcus.

"But at least I sound good," says Carter.

"So stipulated, asshole! Now pass me the ketchup," says Marcus.

"Please? My problem now?" says Scotty, begging.

Marcus and Carter casually nod in agreement as they each down another burger.

"Good," Scotty continues. "I have volunteered to create a flash mob for First Night in Montclair. It will take place right in the town center, obviously on New Year's Eve. I have no idea how to do this in any capacity, having only seen a few of these on YouTube. Any suggestions?"

"Yeah," asks Carter, "why don't you un-volunteer?"

"He didn't volunteer. His dick volunteered," says Marcus.

"Oh, Robin," says Carter.

"Hey, that's not true," says Scotty.

"Bullshit," says Marcus. "You've been trying to get into Robin Danvers' pants since college. Let me guess. Her father is on the town council. He got her a job running First Night. She batted her eyes at you and you volunteered. That sound about right?"

"No, smartass, her father is the Vice Mayor. Look, Marcus, ass has always fallen out of the trees for you, but Carter and I have to work for it."

Carter protests, "I have never been influenced to do anything with an ulterior motive related to the obtaining of female companionship."

"Oh, please," says Marcus. "You have been going to Toastmasters for the past year. Are you honestly telling me that none of that is motivated by an opportunity to meet women?"

"I am quite honestly offended by your suggestion. I am motivated to better myself and my standing through improved public speaking and presentation. If through this pursuit I find a pleasant side effect, such as becoming more attractive to women of a certain distinction, I see no reason to apologize."

"Marcus, let it go," says Scotty. "He's just being an asshole."

Marcus, taking the bait says, "Screwing white women who think you are 'well spoken?' Have you any self-respect—"

"As a black man?" asks Carter. "I am so tired of that shit. You might be swimming in pussy, but some of the rest of us get thirsty once in a while."

Marcus waves dismissively.

"You know what? Just shut the fuck up!" he says, stifling a laugh.

"Damn," says Scotty, "the Toastmasters is working. Can I steal that 'thirsty' line?"

There is more laughter along with chewing and drinking.

"So what do I do?" asks Scotty.

"Well," says Marcus, "you are going to need dancers and, I suppose, a choreographer, since I've seen you dance."

"Where do I find a choreographer?"

"Gays," says Carter.

"What?"

"Gays. They love that flash mob shit, and make up, I assume, a significant percentage of the choreographers in the world. You're into social media. Post on gay or dance-related websites or blogs."

"Hmm, what about women? I can't have a flash mob of all men and I don't see a tremendous connection between gay women and choreography."

"You don't need to worry," says Marcus. "Most young women today have at least one gay friend in their circle at work. As soon as these gay men read about your flash mob, they will immediately do your recruiting for you among their single female friends. I won't bore you with the psychology, but you will have more than you can handle. Straight guys won't get involved since they don't want to lose their girl to a better dancer, and they're unlikely to hear about it anyway. They won't come even to meet women, because the possibility of getting razzed by their friends is too great. Actually, a dude putting on a flash mob gets the best of everything no matter what their preference—a crowd of single horny people looking to meet a guy. You know what? I think I may be able to assist you with this."

"Damn," says Carter, "you're like the Pussy Whisperer. What the hell. Count me in, too."

Sunday, Dec 9th
~ Glen Ridge ~

"Bella, bella. That'sa fine lasagna!" says Robert Pastor in his best fake Italian accent. "Bravisimo, Ti Amo."

It is a ritual that happens every Sunday at the Pastor home at the end of the traditional Italian family dinner. Robert has thickened somewhat around the middle since turning 56. At the same time, his neatly combed dark hair is thinning. He's in his usual white dress shirt and black slacks, eschewing the jacket and tie in deference to the weekend.

"Thanks, sweetheart," says his wife Ramona, showing a little blush. "Grazie, Ti Amo."

At five feet, eight inches, Ramona is barely an inch shorter than her husband. Her hair is long, dark and lustrous, a credit to Angelo and his team at the salon. She is fit and looks far younger than her 55 years due to a rather intense regimen at the gym five days a week.

"Ugh," Elmo pipes in, "every Sunday, the same bit. Pop, you know this came from Martucci's, right? Mom hasn't cooked a Sunday dinner in, like, ever."

Elmo Pastor, Robert and Ramona's middle child is 25, athletic looking, and at six feet, looks even taller with a shock of curly red hair. They are sitting at an impressive antique table in the equally impressive dining room in an even more impressive Tudor home in Glen Ridge, New Jersey. Everything is tastefully decorated and the table is set as though it is a state dinner.

Robert, looking annoyed, says, "Music, art, dance, and now romance. Is there anything else left for your generation to destroy?"

"I dunno, what else you got?" says Elmo.

"Oh, I forgot to include the English language as well," says Robert.

Ramona wags her finger at her son.

"It's just a little harmless fantasy, honey," she says. "A little romance never hurt anyone."

"If you can get past the gagging," says Elmo.

"Elmo, you could learn a lot about romance from your father."

Elmo covers his ears and shuts his eyes tightly.

"Na, na, na, na! Please, let's not go there."

"Fair enough," says Robert. "Let's clear the table and get the coffee. I sense a great dessert coming."

"Sure, Pop, but we'd use less dishes if we just ate dessert right out of the box."

"Shush!" admonishes Ramona. "Remember, romance—and it's fewer dishes, not less."

Elmo rolls his eyes as he picks up his plate. Robert does the same, but stops to kiss Ramona on the top of her head on the way to the kitchen. She blushes again.

Over coffee, Ramona says excitedly, "I have some wonderful news. Your brother and sister are coming home next weekend and will be here through the New Year."

Elmo shrugs.

"Wait, there's more," she continues. "I want it to be special, so I'm considering doing some actual cooking!"

This gets Elmo's attention and he looks at Robert who is equally taken aback. Elmo decides to change the subject.

"Pop, you gotta call the yard guy to do the leaves."

"What's the rush? There are still a fair amount of leaves on the trees."

"Once they get too heavy with water, it's bad for the lawn. Any money you save now, you'll be paying more in the spring."

"I'm pretty sure dinosaurs walked on this very grass before there were lawn maintenance people and the grass is still here."

"Huh?"

"Robert, don't make fun of him," says Ramona.

She turns toward Elmo.

"Sweetie, I'll call the lawn service tomorrow."

"Kick, save, and a beauty," Robert mutters under his breath.

Ramona narrows her eyes at her husband.

"Excuse me, dear?" she asks.

"Nothing," he says.

"I heard something."

"It was nothing."

"Uh-oh, Pop, you're boned. It's 'The Look,'" says Elmo.

"Watch your language," Ramona says to Elmo, never moving her gaze from her husband.

Resigned, Robert explains, "It's a hockey reference. Any time I raise the slightest issue with Elmo, I become the puck, he's the net, and you are Martin Brodeur. I understand the instinct to protect your young, but I'm his father for God's sake."

"First of all, I am aware of the hockey reference and I know Marty Brodeur. When you fall asleep watching the games in bed, I usually stay up to watch the rest. Second, I will protect my babies from any threat at any time, including from you. Lastly, you are dangerously close to losing your romance points."

He smiles and raises his cup to her.

"A mother who loves her husband, but loves her children just a little bit more, is all I can ask for."

Ramona smiles back at him.

"Thank you, but I still don't like it when you discourage him."

Elmo, sensing an opening, says, "Pop, I want to talk about my future."

Robert braces himself.

"What about your future, son?"

"I want to go into the family business."

"Elmo, we have talked about this. I don't want that for you."

"But what about what I want?"

"Look, my father didn't want me anywhere near the 'family business.'"

"But…"

"Please, son, let me finish. I know I ended up there, but I'll get back to that in a minute. Your grandfather got into the life at a young age. He came here with nothing and did what he needed to do to survive. He moved up fast enough to provide us a better life. How he accomplished this, I don't even know. He was very careful about not discussing his work at home. He made sure I went to the best schools and got a good education. He evened named me Robert to hide any hint of our heritage."

Robert takes a breath and continues.

"He made one mistake. While in grad school, I 'interned' one summer for some of his 'connections.' I was somewhat of a financial whiz and was very successful at solving some, let's say, accounting irregularities. My undergrad degree was in finance. I was in a combined law and MBA program at Seton Hall. They ran some pretty archaic systems and I helped them move into the present.

By the time he realized it, I already knew too much about the inner workings to get out."

"But I'm not looking to work in the office."

"That's the least of my worries."

Ramona shoots him a look, but Elmo misses the dig completely. Robert continues.

"Look, your Mother and I were dating at the time…"

Ramona clears her throat.

"I mean engaged…"

Ramona does it again, louder.

"Pre-engaged?"

Ramona takes a sip of coffee.

"That feels better now," she says.

"As I was saying," Robert continues, "your Mother and I were pre-engaged at the time and I didn't want to keep anything from her, so we discussed our future. She said she was committed to me no matter what."

He takes her hand, and she smiles.

"We decided then to basically do what my father did, to keep any children we had as far from the life as possible. We have been fortunate enough to provide well for you all financially and I think we were pretty loving and involved parents."

"Sure you were Pop, and you, too, Mom, but it's not about money or even love."

"Then what is it, sweetie?" Ramona asks.

Elmo looks back and forth at both of them as though the answer were obvious.

"Respect, Mom. I want to feel important."

"But you are impor—," Ramona begins, but Robert gives her hand a gentle squeeze.

"I understand, son," he says. "Will you allow your mother and me to discuss this in private?"

Elmo looks to Ramona, who has dropped her head, unable to make eye contact for fear of losing all composure. He looks back at Robert, straightens and stands, and simply says in a strong voice, "Yes, sir," before striding out of the room.

After she is sure that her son is gone, Ramona begins to quietly cry.

"Oh, Robert, I can't bear the thought of him—," she says, and fades into gentle sobbing.

He pats her hand.

"I know, baby, I know. We'll get through this. The other two are fine, but Elmo wasn't a good fit for college."

She sniffles.

"I know."

"—or bartending school, or electronics, or construction," Robert says.

"Please don't call him stupid, Robert."

"Honey, I know he's not stupid and, quite frankly, whether he is or is not stupid is irrelevant. The problem is that he makes too many mistakes. In my business, people who make mistakes don't—"

She buries her head in his chest.

"—survive," he finishes, stroking her hair. "We'll think of something."

Tuesday, Dec 11th
~ West Orange ~

Elmo walks into a private room at the rehabilitation and care facility where his grandfather is staying. He's wearing a black suit with skinny lapels and a skinny black tie over a dark grey shirt. He also is wearing shiny black wing tips and carrying a dark grey fedora with a black band.

"Hey, Pop-Pop, it's me, Elmo," he says as he pulls up a side chair.

Tommaso Pastor, old but still strong, with a head of thick silver hair, does a double take and says, "You goin' to some kind of a costume party?"

Elmo laughs and says, "No, Pop-Pop, I'm trying out a new look. Doncha like it?"

"New look? You look like some kinda' cartoon character! That suit's gotta be half a century old for God sakes!"

"Aw, Pop-Pop, I thought you'd like it. Don't you know whose suit this is?"

"Eisenhower's?"

"Who?"

"Jeez, look who I'm talking to. Tell me, Elmo, whose suit is it?"

"It's yours, Pop-Pop! I found it in the attic. Doncha like it?"

Elmo stands and rotates, arms extended. Grandpa squints and nods.

"Well the fit is perfect. Let see it with the hat."

Elmo's smile gets wider as he puts on the hat. He strikes his most menacing stance, but can't stop smiling.

Grandpa thinks to himself, "*Jesus Christ, the happy hitman,*" but senses the kid's excitement.

"It actually looks quite good on you. You just need to pull the sleeves out a little more. That's how we wore them back then. We liked to show off the hardware."

"You kept a gun in your sleeve?" asks Elmo, clearly confused.

"Gun? No you moron. Cufflinks! The hardware was cufflinks."

Elmo is still confused, but now, clearly hurt as well. Grandpa softens.

"See, men didn't prance around in a lot of jewelry back then. Even a crucifix or a St. Christopher's medal was rare. But cufflinks, that's what we used to set ourselves apart, and man, did we love to show them off."

"Cufflinks," says Elmo, thinking. "Yeah. Maybe I'll ask Mom and Pop for Christmas."

"Hey, kid, I got a better idea. I got my old ones back at my place, real vintage stuff, some with diamonds. When I get out of this dump, I'll let you pick out a few sets. OK? How's that sound?"

"Oh, man Pop-Pop, that sounds terrific!" His eyes move to the cane right next to his grandfather's bed.

The cane is a thing of beauty. Onyx, with some ivory inlay near the top, and a polished silver handle in the shape of a wolf's head.

"Elmo, no," says Grandpa, sternly.

"But, I was just—"

"You know the rules. Don't touch the cane. Don't look at the cane. Don't even think about the cane."

"I don't understand."

"I know, but just like it has always been and always will be, it never leaves my side, and no one, including your father, is to touch it. That's all I can say. Can I count on you to respect your grandfather's wishes?"

Elmo, now serious, straightens.

"Yes, sir!"

"Then it's settled. Cufflinks as soon as I am out of this place. So tell me. What brings you here? I know you didn't kill an afternoon dragging out to this dump to show me my own clothes."

"Well, I wouldn't call it a dump. You have a private room, although these plants are a disaster. Don't they ever water them? A little fertilizer would help as well."

"Elmo, they're a bunch of damned plants! Believe me; they'll live longer than I will. Why are you here?"

"I want to go into the family business."

"Elmo."

"I'm serious, Pop-Pop, I want to be like you and Pop. I want to be...important."

"Elmo, have you discussed this with your father?"

"He won't even talk about it.

"Even I have to respect his wishes in this area. He is your father."

"Can you just get him to talk to me about it?"

"That I can do, but it is not as simple as it seems. The business has changed. No more brass knuckles. They use computers now. I'm not sure I would be involved, today. Tell your father I need to see him. I need to discuss something else with him anyway, but I will discuss your wishes with him as well. I promise."

Elmo knows that a promise from his grandfather is as sure as the sun rising.

"Thanks, Pop-Pop. He plans to come here on Saturday."

Elmo is beaming, but sees his grandfather wince in pain.

"Pop-Pop! Are you okay? You need help? You want me to get the nurse?"

"No! NO! and HELL NO! I'm not okay, because I busted my hip and have to stay in this dungeon. I don't need help because I'm fucking Tommaso Pastor. And the last thing I need is that fucking smartmouth, mooly nurse coming in here and giving me shit."

"You rang?" says Nurse Carrie Parker, a robust African-American woman carrying a clipboard. "And that's Nurse Parker or Miss Carrie to you and I ain't no eggplant, so you can shove that mooly shit up your guido ass. Oh, pardon me, we have a visitor and it appears to be Sonny Corleone. Is this one of those stripper birthday gags? Is it your birthday Mr. Pastor?"

Again, Elmo looks confused, but the old man is laughing.

"This is my grandson. He was just leaving. Elmo, don't forget. I need to see your father next week."

"And the cufflinks! I won't forget. Bye, Pop-Pop!"

Elmo heads out the door.

"What was with the suit?" asks Nurse Parker.

"Long story. Does the medical community still use the term 'imbecile?'"

"Not since the work of Drs. Howard, Fine, and Howard, nyuk, nyuk, nyuk."

"I see you are a Three Stooges aficionado. I can respect a devotee of the classics. So, Nurse Parker, what's the bad news?"

"Today, after physical therapy, you will be seeing Dr. Melnick and Dr. Sood."

"Hymie Melnick?"

"Now you listen to me, young man. There will be no heeb, kike, shine, shylock, hymie, or yid talk today, and no dot-head, towel-head, A-rab, bin Laden, or camel jockey, either. These doctors all have boats, but can't seem to afford a sense of humor."

"That doesn't leave me much to talk about. Where did you learn such an extensive list?"

"Nursing school, of course. You just mind your manners around the doctors."

"Party pooper. Hey, I heard a new one."

"Do tell."

"Sand Nigger."

"My, my. Even when you kick an Arab, the shit lands on the black man."

"How's the view from the bottom?"

"Nowhere to go but up, you Snooki motherfucker."

They both laugh.

Monday, Dec 10th
~ Newark ~

Marcus and Scotty are sitting in the back of the Library Resource Room as Carter is being introduced to speak at the weekly Toastmasters event.

"Can you get me the space for rehearsals?" Scotty asks.

A woman, who appears to be acting as the Sergeant-at-arms, glares at them.

Marcus whispers, "Yeah, you can come by and see it on Wednesday. Why are we here again?"

Scotty leans in.

"To support our brother and possibly to mine this for comedic value," he says.

Carter, at the podium begins a story about his childhood in Newark.

"It was cold, that Christmas..."

Marcus moans.

"Oh, man, not the story about the turtleneck."

"You're sure it's no trouble to use the space?" asks Scotty.

"No, it's fine, and better yet, no charge. The rec room is used by the patients during the day, but it's closed after seven."

Carter drones on.

"...and once again, it appeared that Santa had skipped the Stella Wright Projects..."

"Oy vey," groans Marcus.

"Agreed, but look at the audience. They're 90% female and they can't take their eyes off him," says Scotty.

"Some of them are counting 'Ums' and 'Ahs,' but I see your point," says Marcus.

"A nickel says he ends with a quote," says Scotty.

"Bet. Any feedback on the thing?" says Marcus.

"Some, but no choreographer yet," says Scotty.

Carter becomes more animated

"How sharper than a serpent's tooth..." he intones.

Marcus shakes his head in defeat.

"...than to have an ungrateful child," Carter finishes.

Carter winks at Marcus and Scotty to a surprising amount of applause. Marcus shakes his head.

"That line didn't even apply to the rest of the speech. When did he read King Lear?" he asks.

"He didn't," explains Scotty. "He got it from Star Trek. It was featured in one of the cartoon episodes. Shamefully, this is what we do when you're out prowling the streets. Damn, the women are eating this up."

"No shit," says Marcus. "I counted at least 3 orgasms; the big blonde up front, red scarf by the wall, and Whoopi Goldberg."

"Whoopi?" asks Scotty.

"Dreads, on the right," says Marcus.

Carter walks up to them triumphantly.

"So what do you think?"

Scotty taps his fist to Carter's.

"Star Trek? I am impressed," he says.

"The ladies seemed to like it," says Carter.

"Dude, that didn't mean anything remotely related to your dumb story," says Marcus.

"Last minute addition," says Carter, "I was on a roll and it just felt right. And don't knock 'The Turtleneck and the Afro' story. It's a Christmas classic."

"Did Scotty know about the Shakespeare?" asks Marcus.

"It may have come up. Why?" asks Carter.

"Asshole cheated me out of another nickel," says Marcus.

Carter grins.

"Sucker. Anyhow, my public awaits. Don't wait up, gentlemen," he says.

"He might be on to something here," says Scotty as Carter heads toward a group of women.

"He might, indeed," says Marcus, handing Scotty a nickel.

Tuesday, Dec 11th
~ Boston ~

Tommy and her friend Libby squeeze into a corner table in a downstairs bistro on Beacon Street. They order a couple of decaf lattes and take off their coats.

"Ugh! Why do I let you talk me into these things," asks Tommy. "I've never been so embarrassed. Speed dating had to have been invented by bitter unhappily married people to exact revenge on the happily single."

"While happily single may exist somewhere as an abstract concept," says Libby, "happily lonely is an oxymoron here in the mortal realm. Besides, I wouldn't be comfortable going alone, and, of course, it was the funniest experience e-ver!"

"Please explain to me the concept of dragging a companion to find a companion," says Tommy, narrowing her eyes. "And, I fail to see what is so damned funny. Did you even get any nibbles?"

"While I did see some potential, how could I focus on being charming sitting next to you? I couldn't listen to my guys, because I didn't want to miss what was happening to you. You should've seen some of my comments cards. Everything from 'seemed distracted' to 'aloof bitch.'"

"Believe me, I didn't need an audience. I was there, remember? Experiencing every painful moment."

"How about the guy with the alternative music?" asks Libby. "I thought your eyes were going to roll back in your head."

"I know! Were those lyrics, or poetry, or what? He sounded like Chaucer on five Red Bulls."

"I couldn't make out half of what he was saying," says Libby, with a chuckle. "but he was cute; well, cute enough—and he has a job."

"Okay, cute I'll give you, but even if you consider managing at Game Stop a job, I certainly don't consider roadie as a dream career aspiration."

"I'm pretty sure he said band manager and not roadie. What about the developer guy, you know, the techie?"

"Argh, Don't get me started. I can barely tolerate real football, but when they start in on the fantasy crap—"

"I think you're focusing on the wrong senses. Try using less of your ears and more of your eyes. I could barely hear him. I was focused on his chiseled exterior."

"Sure, he looked great, but eventually, you are going to have to speak with them," says Tommy with a shudder. "If it's not sports, it's the gym, or poker, or their music, or their work conquests."

"Tommy," says Libby, "you are aware that they are men, right? That is what we came for. These stereotypes of yours also include Harvard Law, business owner, marketing VP, programmer, accountant, and firefighter. These are at least moderately accomplished individuals."

"I know, and I know that I have too many defenses up, but this process…it's just so…awkward."

"Think of it like clothes shopping. You look at everything, you like some things more than others. On some, you like the pattern, but not the cut. Some, you like the collar, but not so much, the material. Once in a while, you find something worth trying on."

"That may be the creepiest thing I ever heard."

They laugh.

"You've also been known to take three things home to try on, knowing in advance that you'd be returning at least two of them," says Tommy.

"We're still talking about clothing, right?" asks Libby before they both laugh some more.

"Look, everyone has an ego about their 'thing,'" Libby continues, using air quotes. "I've sat politely through you going on about climate change, carbon footprints, and, God help me, ethno botany, until my eyes were ready to cross."

"I suppose, but—"

"But nothing. Your job as an environmentalist is to warn the world about all manner of upcoming catastrophe."

"It's not like that."

"Bullshit, Tommy. If food and water were clean and plentiful, and there were boundless amounts of energy, which did nothing to damage the planet, your field would have no reason to exist."

"That's unfair."

"This is what I'm talking about. Even in my fantasy example of the perfect environment, you're looking for flaws. Look, I'm in advertising. My job is to convince people that in spite of all of the doom-saying of the Tommy Pastors of the world, my product will make it all better."

"Including gasoline, tobacco, sweat shops, factory farming, need I go on?"

"Exactly my point, you do need to go on. Unless you want to spend the next 70 or so years curled up in a fetal position alone, yes I said ALONE, you'd better find a way to alter your standards a smidge."

"All right, all right, I get your point. Should I start with Harvard Law?"

"God no, he was just plain creepy."

They both laugh.

"So what's up for holidays for you?" Tommy asks.

"Mostly work. It's high season in the ad game."

"You mean the pre-Christmas season?"

"No, actually, pre-Super Bowl. We've got a lot at stake this year. What about you?"

"I'm picking up Pep and heading home on Friday. I'm dreading some of the family stuff, but I just need the break."

"I don't even remember what a break is, but what's to dread?"

"Oh, let's see...in spite of my academic success, I have no boyfriend, provided no grandchildren, have no prospects, and my favorite, my Italian mother will be favoring the male children."

"I don't get it. Elmo's kind of a loser and you're nearing your PhD, and Pep is gay, so there's unlikely to be grandchildren from him."

"You know, it's weird. My mom doesn't understand Elmo, and at times almost seems afraid around him, but on the other hand is so bizarrely protective of him."

"I think it's called 'a mother thing.' I assume we'll understand it when we reproduce."

"I'm not even sure we'll understand it, but I suspect we'll be afflicted by it. And Pep, well he's just 'the baby' and that's another pathology altogether. Well, we'd better get going. Too bad you'll be up here alone."

"Alone?" asks Libby, holding up several cards. "I've got 3 dates, bee-otch."

"You ho-bag!" says Tommy with surprise. "Which ones?"

"What difference does it make? I'll be returning them after the holiday, so I can do some more shopping!"

Wednesday, Dec 11th
~ West Orange ~

"Hey," Scotty says to Marcus as Marcus unlocks the door of the West Essex Rehabilitation Center.

"What up?" asks Marcus.

He is putting a wad of keys back in his pocket. Scotty eyes the giant key ring.

"Dude, remember Kindergarten at Twelfth Street? Remember Mr. Thomas?"

"Refresh my memory," says Marcus as they head down a dimmed hallway.

"He was the janitor, an African-American gentleman with white hair."

"Sure, why?" Marcus asks.

"That wad of keys made me think of him. Man, I'll bet 90% of the boys in our class would have been perfectly happy if we would have ended up with that job. He had this giant ring of keys and it just seemed like that would make you the most important man in the school. Even the Principal would need you if he needed to get in a door."

"You dream too small, brother," laughs Marcus, "The first time he came into that classroom with that mop bucket on wheels, that was it for me. I was going to stay in school, do my homework, so I could use that mop squeezing thing."

"Right?" Scotty asks, "Some kid would puke and Mrs. Charles would call for Mr. Thomas. He would wheel in the bucket, dip the mop in the water and—"

Marcus jumps in.

"—and then he'd put the mop in the squeezer. He'd push down the lever and squeeze out the water."

"Oh, and when he put his knee on the lever to squeeze out every drop?" asks Scotty.

"I swear," says Marcus, "you could hear all the boys gasp in unison. Man, if you had to pick a career at 5 years old, there would be no astronauts, firemen, cops, or cowboys."

"Just janitors," they say as one.

They get to the end of the hall and enter a large room used as a recreation area for the patients.

"Here it is," says Marcus. "It isn't fancy, but it should have the room for what you need."

"And you're sure this is okay?" Scotty asks.

"For the tenth time, yes. The room is unused after 7:00 PM. You might have to move some equipment, but just put the stuff back when you're done. I've cleared it with security and the General Manager."

"The one with the ass that you've mentioned, I assume?" Scotty asks, smiling.

"I don't mix business with pleasure, so I'll mind the pleasure, and you mind your business."

They laugh.

"I think we'll just slide the equipment and chairs into the center," says Scotty, "to simulate the Christmas tree, since we obviously can't dance in that space."

"That should work."

"Speaking of work, how's it going here?"

"About the same. I have my regular physical therapy patients, but still do some admin and bookkeeping on the side. Most of the managers are incompetent bureaucrats, whose primary interest is covering their asses."

"Let me guess. They find your 'outside the box' approach threatening?"

"You got that right. But, I'm smarter than all of them, so I can usually find a way to work around them."

"Raises this year?"

"Doubtful; maybe a couple of percent cost of living, but I'm not holding my breath. You?"

"Job's good, students are great. I like the Principal, but he's in a tough spot. It's almost impossible to get anything done with the crappy budget and all of the red tape. At least in the classroom, I feel I can make a more immediate impact. I think he's sorry he left it sometimes. By the way, we *are* going to kick Central's ass this year."

"Bullshit."

"How are the patients?"

"You know, it's tough. A lot of them aren't going to get much better if they even improve at all. We get a lot of diving and motorcycle accidents in here, and they are very up and down emotionally. You know, glad to be alive, but looking at life in a wheelchair. Also, this time of year, near the holidays, we get more depression-related issues. Oddly, the elderly inspire the young ones. Most of them are falls with hip damage. They work harder to get home, even if it's to die in their own bed."

"Interesting psychology."

"Yeah, I actually try to get them together, the old and young. I got this new guy who's a real pisser. Old time gangster or something. Carries a fancy cane everywhere he goes. Fell and broke his hip. He's doing well and should be out in a month, but he's this hilarious, irascible race-baiter who really gets the young ones going."

"How so?"

"Through taunting, believe it or not. I think they want to get better so they can kick the geezer's ass."

"So, what's the difference between a race-baiter and a racist?"

"Not a lot, but this guy's old school, you know, grew up in the streets. Racists try to spread their bile. This guy's will die with him. It's more like watching an episode of 'Good Times.'"

"Well, in any case, I hope I never get to meet him."

"So, what do you think of the space?"

Flash Mob

Scotty nods with approval, and says, "Dy-no-mite!"

Thursday, Dec 13th
~ Bloomfield ~

Elmo is in the passenger seat, cruising up Bloomfield Avenue with Donny Manzetti, his friend and auto mechanic, in a Lincoln Town Car. Donny has a thin Fu Manchu moustache with a soul patch. He wears his black hair slicked back touching the collar of his leather coat.

"Nice ride," says Elmo, "is it from your shop?"

"Nope," says Donny, grinning.

"Well I know it ain't yours, and it sure as hell ain't your dad's, so what's the deal?"

Donny turns to Elmo grinning even wider.

"I stole it."

For a moment, Elmo is stunned. He awkwardly softens his expression.

"You almost had me there," he says. "What is it, your aunt's car?"

"No, asshole," Donny replies, defiantly. "I stole it, just before I came to pick you up."

Elmo tries to be cool, but is clearly nervous.

"Stole it where, from the shop?"

"No, asshole, from the lot by the train station. It was easy. Why the fuck would I steal a car from work? I'd get fired and arrested, for Christ's sake!"

"No way. I don't believe you."

"Do you see a key in the ignition?"

"Shit! And you're just driving it around? What if we get pulled over?"

"First of all, no one gets pulled over at night in Belleville. Second, don't be such a pussy. I can't wait around forever for you to get us in the business. I'm building up my resume, so to speak."

"Hey, that's cool," Elmo replies, anything but coolly, "but, what are you gonna do with it? You got, like, a chopshop or something to sell it to?"

"Nah, you can't get nothin' for a boat like this. They specialize in high end shit or high volume, like Hondas and Toyotas. I figure we'll just take it for a ride and dump it near the river."

"Dump it? It's probably covered in our fingerprints," says Elmo, his voice a little higher pitched than usual.

"Your prints, maybe," says Donny, laughing. "I'm wearing gloves, dipshit. It is winter, you know."

"Holy fuck!" says Elmo, wiping everything he can. "I have no idea what I touched."

"Hey, relax, E. Let's just torch the car."

Elmo is near apoplectic.

"Torch it?" he asks.

"Sure," replies Donny, calmly, "over in Harrison, under the bridge. That's where the brothers do it. They go for a joy ride, and then torch the car."

"How do you know that?"

"Not everyone goes to Immaculate. There are still a few advantages of a public school education."

"But, burn it?"

"I'll be doin' the guy a favor. The busted ignition won't even cover the deductible. This way, the insurance company gets him a new ride. Besides, this one is going to need transmission work soon."

"What, are you going to do to the transmission?"

"Nothing, asshole. It's slipping gears. This baby's got less than 10,000 miles before it needs a new tranny. Double A," he says as he taps the horn twice, "M-C-O," singing the commercial jingle.

"Great, car theft and arson. I thought we were gonna see a movie."

"Look, we could just dump it. Your prints aren't in the system. Besides, if you're scared—"

"Hey, I'm not fucking scared. I just want to think this through, all right?"

"Look, Elmo. You want into the business, and your old man won't help. We're gonna have to make a name for ourselves the good old fashioned way."

"Jeez, I guess you're right. So what's the plan?"

"Stop at 7-Eleven and get something to drink. Stop at the gas station. Use the drink bottles to get some gas. Drive under the bridge, torch the car, and then walk to the PATH station. Piece of cake."

"All right, let's do it."

The process goes pretty much as planned except for the gas station attendant having difficulty understanding Donny asking for 48 cents worth of regular to be put in a Fuze bottle. The attendant was particularly miffed to have to make change for a twenty in the December cold. They head to Harrison and pull under the bridge near the edge of a pond. There are several junked and burned cars in the area.

Even though the heat is blasting, Elmo shudders with a deep chill. He wraps his coat tightly.

"I dunno, Donny," he says.

"Hey, it's time to shit or get off the pot," says Donny. "You wanna be a nobody all your life? You're a Pastor, for Christ's sake. Go big or go home, E."

Elmo sniffs and nods. "All right, let's do it. I ain't no nobody. Just one thing, back up the car about 20 feet."

"What for?" Donny asks.

"The cattails," says Elmo, "you're too close. They'll burn with the car."

"So the fuck what?"

"Just do it, okay?"

Donny shakes his head, shrugs and pops the car in reverse.

"Sure, whatever you say."

They get out. Donny pours out the gas onto the front and back seats and tosses in a match. The car is quickly in flames as they walk toward the road.

"This one was mine," says Donny. "Your turn is next."

"Whaddya mean?" asks Elmo.

"Saturday," Donny replies, "I'll pick you up after the shop closes at one. You're gonna boost your first car."

Elmo does not reply.

Donny adds, "We're in this together now. Don't even think about fagging out on me."

Elmo gives Donny an icy stare. "Dude, watch your mouth!"

"Whaddya mean?" asks Donny.

"Watch the fag reference. You know my brother."

"Geez, E. I've heard you call him a lot worse."

"That's between me and him. We're family, get it?"

"Geez, sure, E. I didn't mean nothing' by it. Sorry, okay?"

Friday, Dec 14th
~ Boston ~

"Yes, Mom," says Tommy into her phone. "I have everything packed, and yes, Mom, I left room for my brother and a reasonable amount of his crap. He may have to limit his shoes…Mom! He must have 20 pair at home! Yes! I'll text when we get on the road. I'm on my way to Cambridge now. No, I'm not driving, I pulled into a parking lot when you called. Love you, too."

Tommy, sighs, exhales demonstratively, and pockets her cellphone. She spots Pep on the street in front of his apartment, pulls into a slushy loading zone and taps the horn. He sees her, grabs his duffel, suitcase, and computer bag, and heads her way. Tommy pops the hatch and looks hopelessly at the space, rather the lack of it.

"I don't think it's all going to fit," she says. "How many shoes do we have?"

"Relax, Sis, as an engineer, this is right up my alley," says Pep.

He starts moving things around.

"Well, you're not an engineer yet, and even a lowly environmental studies major like me is pretty sure that matter can neither be created nor destroyed. Was that Newton?"

"Lavoisier, actually," Pep replies with a grunt, "Law of Conservation of Mass. I'm disproving it as we speak."

"I don't doubt it. Have you considered bringing less crap, baby Bro?"

"Well, I was hoping to have the 4-dimensional hyper car developed by now. Theoretically, there's no limit to what you can put in it."

"It must be great on gas."

"Ion power, baby. There, got it, I think," he says.

He gingerly closes the hatch with one hand while holding the pile back with the other.

"I hope there was nothing breakable in the spotted bag," he says. "I'd hate to douse your car with a lifetime supply of perfume or anything."

"First of all, when have you known me to use perfume? And I doubt there is enough room left for even odors. Still, I didn't think you'd get it all in."

"Spatial relations, baby, it's all about the spatial relations."

They buckle in and head toward the Mass Pike for the 4 hour trip to Glen Ridge, New Jersey.

Once on the highway, Tommy begins, "I must admit that I'm a little nervous about spending nearly three weeks with the family, particularly Elmo."

Pep opens one eye, and yawns.

"Naptime is over, Tommy wants to chat," he says. "You need to relax, Sis. How can you let him get under your skin so easily? You must have 60 IQ points on him."

"I'm not sure, but you're not exaggerating. It's like some sort of allergy or chemical reaction."

"Maybe you should do your dissertation on our family dynamic."

"Ugh, don't mention the dissertation. That's why I'm making this trip. This was by far my toughest semester yet. Between that and the horrible weather this fall, I had to get out of Boston for a while."

"Based on what I've been hearing, you are the star of your department. Granted, environmental studies is about as far as you can get from engineering at MIT, but if anyone can fix the world's problems, my money is on you."

"All flattery aside, why must you be playing with that phone during a conversation?"

"Multitasking, actually, and it's a talent we share. And don't sell yourself short. Who has the best teaching credentials in your department?"

"I do, by far. Most of the others grudgingly teach as a path to research."

"Okay, who is the most talented researcher?"

"Probably me, again, but I sure don't know why."

"Don't ever apologize for having talent. You have the best publications and the highest profile projects."

"Possibly true, but the grad director hates me, and the other students in my cohort REALLY hate me."

"There, that's all the proof you need of your success. Three weeks off, one more semester of coursework, a year on the dissertation and booyah, first doctor in the family!"

"Fair enough. So, Mr. Smartypants. Try these on for size. When did you get so smart? Why are you so nice to me? And how do I handle Elmo?"

"I've always been smart, you just didn't notice because of your six-year head start. As for your other two questions, the answers are somewhat related."

"Continue, Doctor."

"Elmo was born a year after you, and I came 5 years later.

"True."

"Still, in some areas we are even, for lack of a better word, and some not."

"Example?"

"Take our names. They are all equally horrible. You were the first and Dad, for some Italian reason, felt the need to name you after his father Tommaso, thus, Tommasina. Unfortunate at best, but allowing you to take on the rather cool Tommy."

"You think it's cool, but Mom hates it."

"True. Then Elmo comes along and gets named after some Uncle from the old country. Unfortunately for our brother, of course, Dad could have had no idea that a fuzzy, red puppet who can't count past 10 would become one of the most visibly recognizable characters of all time."

"The tragic fact that our Elmo is a ginger with bug eyes is an added bonus."

"My name, Peppino, after yet another ancient relative is usually reserved members of the circus community, most commonly clowns or monkeys. Thankfully, I have been able to live with Pep. Anyhow, none of us can gain enough advantage needling each other about our names as the cost to ourselves would be too great. It's like Russia, China, and the U.S. and a balance of nuclear weaponry."

"When do you have time for homework?"

"I make it up by having no friends or social life."

"Okay, what about the imbalance?"

"Several areas come to mind. You're older, he's younger. He's the oldest male in an Italian family, and you are, well, obviously, not male. You are extremely intelligent, while Elmo is, well, male. These are the types of areas where one of you has the upper hand. No balance equals chaos."

"And how did you escape this?"

"Duh, you! Elmo is strong, athletic, and five years my senior. I was small, annoying, and pretty incapable of defending myself. He took advantage of this by trying to torment me at every turn. And every time, without fail or regard for yourself, you jumped in and saved me."

"Oh come on," says Tommy, wiping the corner of her eye.

Robert O'Connell

"As a child, you were always a hero to me. I honestly can't say that things have ever changed."

Friday, Dec 14th
~ Newark ~

"Mr. McCall," shouts Jamal from the back of the room, "Truffant still in your grill?"

"First of all," says Scotty, "it is Principal Truffant or Mr. Truffant. Second of all, if you and your fellow kamikaze pilots hadn't threatened ritual suicide when questioned about last week's unfortunate incident, he might have been a lot less perturbed at the Multi-Media Club, and at me, for that matter."

"I just want you to know that we got your back, Teach," says Jamal.

A few of the others speak or nod in agreement.

Scotty smiles.

"I appreciate the kind words and your loyalty, but there is a teaching moment in this."

A small uprising of groans is heard.

"Thanks, Jamal!" and "Please, not a half hour before vacation!" are heard from the group.

"Quiet, please," Scotty continues. "Yes, class, even on the eve of your holiday break, we can still learn a few things. And a special thanks to Mr. Davis for reminding me of the opportunity."

He points to Jamal and smiles. This is followed by more hoots from the class and a few wads of paper being directed at Jamal. He slinks down into his chair and behind his desk.

"Class, we do not mock academic contribution, we encourage it," says Scotty. "As such, I award a gold star to Jamal and further ask that you refrain from jacking him in the parking lot after school, so you can all get on with your vacations."

There is a mix of moaning and laughter except for Jamal who puts his head on his desk and covers it with his arms.

"Self-importance," Scotty continues, "is one of the greatest ills in our society, primarily since it should be among the easiest to correct."

"What do you mean?" asks Desiree, who is seated near the front of the room.

"Well, let's stick with my involvement in the Pep Rally 'incident,' if you will," says Scotty. "There were many positives to the event, including applying historical knowledge in a creative way, giving students an opportunity to express themselves, and learning and using technology to teach ourselves to name a few. But at the same time, I chose a venue and a time that was inappropriate. I also allowed the educational message to be diluted in order to add humor."

Donte says, while raising his hand, "But we picked the Pep Rally, and you use humor to make educational points all the time."

"Yeah," adds Shiree, "that's why we like your classes."

"Again, thanks for the kind words," Scotty continues, "but as an advisor, I am responsible for your choices and I was well aware of what you were planning. And while I do frequently use humor in my delivery, I also have a responsibility to take appropriate care that my message does not get lost at the expense of a laugh. I also have a responsibility to my boss, in this case, Principal Truffant, who is entrusting me to educate you safely and properly. I want to be loyal to him as you are to me, and it works both ways. I need his loyalty as you frequently need mine."

"All of these layers of loyalty don't seem realistic," says Rhonda.

"Great point, Rhonda," says Scotty. "It's not completely realistic, but is necessary for a society to work. Earlier, I used the term self-importance. I allowed my ego to override my better judgment, which provided us a good time, but at the expense of others."

Melvin adds, "But no one got hurt."

"Well, Melvin, you have to admit that 'no one getting hurt' is a pretty low standard to reach for. And if you look closely, people were hurt. Whether you agree with it or not, the purpose of the Pep Rally was to promote the basketball players and the program. We certainly denied them that. If we look a little deeper, I hurt Principal Truffant, and as a result, myself, by eroding the level of trust between us. It may seem like a small thing, but small things add up, and it brings me to my point for today."

Melvin mutters, "Here it comes," along with some other comments and much eye rolling throughout the class.

Scotty turns and writes 'Self-correction' across the board in large letters. He turns back to the class.

"Self-correction," he says, "is the most important skill that I can teach you as an educator and as a person. It also is the most important thing you can teach your children, hopefully after you finish college. It allows you to recognize self-importance in others, but more importantly, in yourself. It teaches you to consider the needs of others and the impact on others from all the actions you take. This discussion and our reflection on our actions do not change what happened, but do the next best thing. They allow us to use our understanding to do better, whether doing better includes mending fences, working harder, or simply knowing more."

Jamal pipes in, "Is it vacation time, yet?"

"What's the rush, Jamal?" asks Scotty. "Do you have a plane to catch?"

"Aspen, this year," Jamal responds, deadpan. "Club Med was such a bore last year."

Amid laughter, Scotty says, "Okay, you got me. Sorry for the speech, but I would like you to think about it. I will see you all in a few weeks. Remember, you all promised to try something new. I certainly plan to. Please be safe, make good choices, and have fun!"

The bell rings and the students howl in triumph.

Friday, Dec 14th
~ New Jersey Border ~

"Hey, Pep. Wake up, we just got into New Jersey," Tommy says as she shakes his shoulder.

Pep yawns demonstratively and scrunches lower into the passenger seat. He mumbles unintelligibly.

"Come on!" she says while she pinches his thigh. "You've been sleeping for 3 hours, including through all of the traffic near the Tappan Zee. Would you prefer that I took a nap, here on the Parkway?"

"All right," he moans, removing his headphones. "I took 3 exams this week and I am in a toasty and enclosed space. Sleep was inevitable. Besides, I was having a wonderful dream about sugar plum fairies."

"I assume you were one of them?" she cracks with a smile.

"Har dee har har," he says sitting up. "I expect that sort of lowbrow cheap shot from Elmo."

"Sorry, kid," she says, "I'm pretty burnt as well. Besides the responsibility of transporting you and your sugar plums home safely, I have plenty of additional stress."

"Like what?" he asks while manipulating his phone.

"Well, first of all, the stress of you on your phone while carrying on a conversation," she replies.

"Multitasking, babe," he says while thumbing the keypad at seemingly impossible speed. It's what we engineers do. I've been out of cyberspace for 3 full hours. I can't afford to miss anything."

"God, you can be so—," she says, pausing to find the right word.

"Charming?" asks Pep.

"No, annoying was closer," she says. "That's what I get for trying to find a more colorful adjective."

"Well I have a thesaurus app open now, if you need any more assistance. Here's irksome, vexing, ooh, how about bedeviling?" he says, staring at his screen.

"I've decided to go with asshole. It's a trite old chestnut, but it's so…YOU," she says. "I'm serious, Pep. I'm not used to being home, and certainly not for so long."

"So?" he asks. "I thought you needed a break."

"I do," she continues, "but I don't want to replace one stress for another. I can handle Elmo, and Dad will keep himself occupied with work. You will disappear into tech world, and that leaves me with Mom."

"So?" he asks again.

"God!" she says, exasperated, "two balls, but no clue! You guys have no idea what it's like with Mom's passive-aggressive, no boyfriend, no prospects, why a PhD, let's go shopping, let's get a makeover…Momness!"

"First of all," says Pep, "'Two Balls, but No Clue' would be a kick-ass title for your dissertation. Second, give Mom a break. She's new to the empty nest thing and what's wrong with a spa day for relaxation? I'd love it."

"Then you go," she says. "Would you like some guilt with that mud pack? Last time I was home, she actually asked me, "What are you doing, or not doing, with your hair? UGH!"

"And she offered you a free salon visit with all of the extras. Just go with it," says Pep.

"You and I clearly have a different definition of the word 'free,' little brother," Tommy adds.

"Well," Pep continues, "if you can convince her that a 'girls day out' is not exclusive to girls, I will happily step into your place. All you need to do is to find another project."

"Project? For who?" asks Tommy.

"For you, as a commitment breaker," says Pep. "You know, 'Oh, I just remembered. I have that *thing* this afternoon. I won't be able to make it to the spa after all. Why don't you take Pep?' Something like that."

"You are quite disturbed," she says.

"Wait, I just saw something that would be perfect for you," he says, followed by more key-thumbing. "Here it is. It's perfect."

"What's perfect?" she asks suspiciously.

Pep reads aloud, "Choreographer needed for a Flash Mob to be performed at First Night, Montclair. Minimal experience needed. Obviously, your discretion is requested.

For more information, Contact Scotty McCall at blah, blah..."

"Flash Mob?" she asks, looking confused, "What possible interest would I have in that?"

Pep looks away from his screen for the first time since waking and says, "Are you kidding me? You took dance for, like, fifty years. You taught and choreographed for years in the Summer Arts Program. I was in your class, remember?"

"Oh yeah," she sighs, "Mom implied that I would make you gay, yet another cross I must bear."

Pep ignores her and continues, "You love the genre. You've sent me YouTube links to about a hundred flash mobs. It fits your time period exactly and, best of all, it's away from where you live, so even if you embarrass yourself, no one gives a shit. You might even meet someone. It's perfect!"

"Meet someone?" she asks raising an eyebrow. "Wait, where did you find this?"

"What do you mean, where?" he asks innocently.

"You know what I mean," she says. "What site did you find it at?"

"Some forum," he says sounding a little evasive.

"A gay forum?" she asks accusingly.

"So what?"

"So, this Scotty and his troupe are very likely gay, is what," she says curtly. "Who am I supposed to 'meet' that way?"

"All right," he says. "You're probably right about Scotty McCall, but so what? Gay people do have straight friends, occasionally. So maybe the master plan needs a little more analysis."

"Forget it, genius," she says dismissively. "I'll take my chances with Mom."

As they pull into the driveway, Pep says, "Oops, I already texted you the link."

Friday, Dec 14th
~ Glen Ridge ~

"Ooh! My babies are home!" squeals Ramona as she hears the car door close in the driveway.

She runs to open the front door. Tommy and Pep are loaded down with bags and suitcases. They bring them inside and hug their mother.

"Robert! Elmo! They're here!" she shouts toward the kitchen.

"I missed you, Mom," says Pep as he sniffs the air, "but I may have missed Martucci's almost as much."

He slides out of his coat and heads toward the kitchen.

"Pep, we're in the dining room tonight, honey. I got all of your favorites!" says Ramona.

She turns toward Tommy, sees her hair and drops her smile for about a half-second. The smile returns and Ramona says, "My poor baby. You must be so…busy."

Tommy rolls her eyes and says, "I love you too, Mom," with a little more ice than she originally intended.

Ramona protrudes her lower lip ever so slightly.

"Oh, Tommasina," she says, "I'm sorry, I didn't mean—"

"No, I'm sorry, Mom," says Tommy. "I just spent four and a half hours in the car and I was wearing a hat. I will be sure to 'freshen up' before dinner."

Tommy strokes her mother's arms.

"I don't want you to think that pursuing a PhD is so intense that I don't have time to brush my hair."

Ramona smiles.

"Well, Pep always kept that awful poster in his room."

"Awful?" says Pep from the dining room entrance. "Mom, it was Albert Einstein, one of the greatest minds in human history."

"Well he may have been a great mind, but I can tell a lot more about his mother based on the way he wore his hair," says Ramona, hanging up the coats. "Let's eat."

Elmo bounds down the stairs as they move through the living room.

"Hey, big Sis," he says toward Tommy. "Hey, little Sis!"

He directs this toward Pep. Elmo seems pleased with himself.

"Seriously, Elmo?" says Tommy, getting her dander up.

"Hey, did you park at the end of the driveway?" Elmo asks no one in particular. "You should move it. The sycamore tree drops sap that will ruin your paint job."

Pep ignores his brother, takes Tommy's hand and leads her to the dining room.

Robert enters from the kitchen, puts down his glass of wine and comes over to give Tommy a big hug.

He says, "Welcome home, baby."

He turns to Pep and embraces him.

"It's good to have you home, son."

"Yeah," says Elmo, "he screwed up the DVR again."

"Don't listen to him," says Robert. "I'm glad you're here, and not for your tech support skills."

"It's okay, Dad," says Pep, pulling out his chair. "When is the Giants game?"

Robert smiles while sitting down.

"Sunday at 1:00, in Atlanta," he says. "I also have a few laptop issues, if you don't mind."

"Don't worry," Pep assures him, "I'll get to it all before kickoff."

The table is beautifully set with an Italian feast. Plates are being passed in what appears to be an elegantly choreographed pattern. Pep digs out a piece of eggplant from the bottom of a dish.

"Hey!" Elmo shouts. "Stop taking from the bottom!"

"Sorry, big Bro," says Pep, "I'm just trying to avoid the cheese. I've determined this semester, that I have inherited Mom's lactose intolerance."

"I have pills for that," says Ramona. "They work pretty well if you don't go overboard. Let me get you one."

"Thanks, Mom, but no," says Pep, trying to avoid an argument over the propriety of sharing medication. "I'm trying to control it through diet for now."

Tommy turns toward her father and smiles.

"Dad, you haven't asked Pep or me about school, yet. Don't you want to know where your tuition money is going?"

Robert makes an almost imperceptible glance toward Elmo before replying, "This meal is a celebration. We'll deal with that later."

Tommy realizes her dad's point and responds with a quiet, "Sure, Dad," feeling slightly embarrassed with herself.

Elmo, seeing a moment of weakness turns to his father and looks at him sharply.

"Any news for me, Dad?" he asks.

Robert returns an icy look as if to say, "not here, and not now."

"I am going to see your grandfather tomorrow…as I promised."

Tommy and Pep look at each other in mild confusion, but shrug and continue eating.

Elmo picks up the water pitcher and pours himself a glass. Pep makes eye contact and holds his glass out to Elmo.

"A drinkie for the twinkie," says Elmo, as he fills Pep's glass with a wide grin.

Tommy shoots Elmo a dirty look, but Pep does not take the bait.

"Thanks, El," says Pep, calmly, "but I believe the term you are looking for is 'twink,' not twinkie."

"Huh?" says Elmo, confused.

"If you consult the Urban Dictionary," Pep continues, "you will find that I am in no way a 'twinkie,' which is a slur toward certain Asians. And, while 'twink' may be more accurate, it typically implies a lack of intelligence which also would hardly apply in my case."

"Can we not discuss such things at the table?" asks Ramona, although it's clearly not meant as a question.

Everyone keeps eating, but only Elmo remains confused.

"I am so glad to have everyone home," says Ramona. "I have made plans for a wonderful vacation together. Even your father has agreed to take some time off."

All three Pastor siblings immediately stop in mid-chew and look up. Tommy swallows hard and asks hesitantly, "What kind of plans?"

Pep, gives her 'the look' and Tommy secretly wishes that she had inherited the diplomacy gene from her father as Pep seemed to. If Ramona heard any negativity, it fails to dampen her excitement.

"Well, besides the Christmas festivities, family pictures, and church," she says, "I've planned to reconnect with my children, of course."

She looks lovingly at Tommy.

"First of all," says Ramona, "I plan to make a real family breakfast for all of us tomorrow. Be here at the table at 9:30."

Tommy looks at her brothers for help. Receiving only panicked stares, she enters the breach.

"Mom," she asks, "can you please clarify your use of the verb 'make?'"

"I mean exactly what I said, young lady," says Ramona indignantly, "I'm going to *make* a special breakfast. I am quite capable of handling myself in the kitchen. Then, I am going to treat my daughter—"

"Which one?" Elmo cackles.

This is immediately met by a laser stare from his father. Elmo shrinks deeply into his seat.

"Tommasina and I have a spa day scheduled for tomorrow afternoon, for the works!" says Ramona, with glee.

Caught off guard, Tommy is in full panic. She looks to Pep, who offers nothing in return.

Tommy blurts out, "Oh, Mom, that sounds great, but I have a conflict."

"Already?" Ramona asks doubtfully, "You just got here a barely an hour ago."

"It just came up," says Tommy, flailing. "I have to meet someone about a choreography gig."

Ramona turns toward Tommy with a look of both shock and hurt.

"It was Pep's idea," Tommy barks out, in a panic, "He asked me to do it!"

Pep shoots Tommy a look. Ramona shoots Pep a look. Elmo sees what's happening and shoots his father a look, albeit somewhat delayed. It's a typical family dinner at the Pastors.

Finally, Pep speaks up.

"Don't worry, Mom. I'd love to go with you."

He still manages to give Tommy the stink eye.

"Thanks, baby," says Ramona.

She also is giving Tommy the same dirty look.

Tommy turns on her phone to open the link sent to her by Pep.

Friday, Dec 14th
~ Montclair ~

Marcus is filling the dishwasher in the kitchen of their Montclair apartment, while Scotty is at the table writing something. Carter is bringing Marcus the last of the dishes.

"You never compliment my cooking anymore," says Carter. "You've become so cold and distant."

"Shut the hell up, asshole," Marcus shoots back. "Maybe you should try to expand your repertoire. Every time it's your turn to cook, it's Steak-umms and Tater Tots."

"I made scrambled eggs last time," says Carter.

"…with Tater Tots," adds Marcus. "What about a salad or some vegetables? We have a game tomorrow morning, and I'd prefer not to shit myself, if possible."

"It is my understanding that potatoes *are* vegetables," says Carter, apparently serious.

"The starch is bad enough," says Marcus, "but to deep fry them in grease, and then you cover them in salt."

"That's three food groups in one shot, Brother," says Carter, "and with the roll and the Steak-umm, you're completely covered. You know, next time, I'm gonna put the Tots on the sandwich. I think I've invented the perfect food."

Marcus turns to Scotty.

"Are you listening to this fool?" he asks.

"Huh?" Scotty mutters, still looking at his paper. "Actually, no, but I think I have something here."

"More plays?" asks Marcus. "Our offense is already too complex for flag football."

"No," says Scotty, "I think the key is less plays against these guys."

"I hope this is better than Carter's 'Perfect Sandwich,'" says Marcus, sitting down at the table. "What's the idea?"

"All right," begins Scotty, "we're playing Park St. Baptist again. They killed us, primarily because we couldn't keep that kid, the track star, out of our backfield. He kept moving from side to side and I was running for my life most of the time."

"Yeah," says Marcus, "because your 'safety valve' here would never turn around for the short pass."

He jerks his thumb toward Carter.

"Go big or go home," says Carter, not looking up from his newspaper.

"Agreed," says Scotty, "Oh, with you, not Carter."

"To hell with you both," says Carter, still not diverting from his paper.

Scotty and Marcus ignore him and continue with their game plan.

"We call a play that goes either to the left or the right," says Scotty, "but, after the huddle, their star kid LT Junior lines up and disrupts the play. The rest of their team is pretty mediocre. What if we just use one or two plays, but audible at the line to always go away from the kid?"

"You mean allowing everyone to adjust to the kid's position, instead of just the quarterback?" asks Marcus, getting the idea. "Not bad, I like it. If we just take the spread play, and the sideline play, tweak them to have a right and left version—"

"—and run away from the kid's pursuit on every down," says Scotty, finishing the thought. "It will be like 7 on 6 if we execute it right."

"We need an audible that they won't be able to figure out after the third play," says Marcus.

"How about odds for the left side and evens for the right?" asks Scotty.

"You mean numbers instead of words?" asks Marcus, "How is that different?"

"Random numbers," Scotty explains. "It doesn't matter what they are. Like when we were kids. Just call out a random sequence of numbers, like '22, 13, 54,' and when the kid picks his side, just call the last number using an odd for left and an even for right to run the play away from him, followed by 'hut.'"

Marcus nods approvingly.

"I like it," he says. "One problem. What if we have a teammate who's too stupid to know the difference between odd and even?"

"Fuck you," says Carter.

This time, he looks over his newspaper. They all laugh. Scotty's phone bleeps, and he picks it up to check his messages.

"Hey, I got a hit on a choreographer," he says. "I was starting to panic. He wants to meet tomorrow in the early afternoon."

"He?" asks Marcus.

"Well, I assume so, since his name is Tommy," says Scotty. "Not my first choice, but the clock is ticking. He seems to have both choreography and dance teaching experience. I'll arrange to meet him at the Town Center at 1:00."

"Dude," says Marcus, "our game is at 11:00."

"Yeah, I'll just go straight from the game," says Scotty.

"No shower?" asks Marcus.

"Dude, it's a dude," says Scotty, "and probably a gay dude at that. No need to lead anyone on."

"A needless precaution," says Carter. "What makes you think that you would be any less off-putting to gay men than you have proven to be to straight women?"

"Fuck you," Scotty and Marcus say in unison.

Saturday, Dec 15th
~ Glen Ridge ~

Pep runs into Tommy at the top of the stairs on his way to breakfast.

"Hiding out, I see," he says as she turns toward him.

"I just don't need to get into it with Mom, after her shameless attempt to get me in for a makeover today," she says. "She's so transparent."

"Did it ever occur to you that she just wants to share something with you, possibly something that she likes?" he says, "and you get a free makeover in the process. It wouldn't kill you, you know."

"Do you honestly believe that?" she asks. "And what about her making a 'special' breakfast? I can't even remember the last time she cooked anything."

"Well, it's obvious to me that she's going through a rough time, and it can't hurt to be supportive and open minded."

"God," says Tommy, shaking her head. "Who are you? You used to be such an insufferable twerp. We'll see how you feel after your spa day."

Pep tilts his head and says, "I'm actually looking forward to it."

"And breakfast?" asks Tommy.

"Not quite as open minded about that one," he says, grinning.

At that point, Elmo roughly shoves past them, wearing all black. He heads down the stairs without looking at them.

"Whoa!" says Pep. "What's eating him?"

"Maybe he got an advanced peek at the breakfast menu," says Tommy, as they head toward the dining room.

Again, the dining room is beautifully set and everyone is seated except Ramona, who has apparently banned everyone from the kitchen.

Robert clears his throat and speaks.

"I assume that I do not have to tell you that we are all going to not only eat, but are going to enjoy our breakfast today."

The siblings all make shuddering faces, but nod in agreement.

"Dad," asks Tommy, "is everything okay with Mom?"

"I'm sure it's nothing," he replies. "She is having a little trouble adjusting to you all being out of the…"

He glances at Elmo and catches himself. Elmo's scowl gets deeper as Robert continues.

"Er, growing up," he continues. "She's looking for purpose, you know, where she fits in."

"Aren't we all," mutters Elmo, not completely under his breath.

At that point, Ramona comes in wearing a frilly apron and carrying a tray holding a carafe of coffee, a pitcher of orange juice, a pitcher of water, and all manner of sweeteners, creams, and jellies. Robert rises to help her, but she stops him by speaking in a sing-song voice.

"No, no. I have it. This is my special breakfast!"

She leaves and everyone pours his or her coffee and juice. They all cautiously smell and taste everything but it all seems in order. She returns with a large tureen and places it in the middle of the table and lifts the lid.

"Ta-da!" she shouts.

It appears to be Eggs Benedict, and it looks quite impressive.

"Wow, Mom," says Pep, "very Martha Stewart."

"It looks wonderful, dear," adds Robert. "What is in the crock?"

"Oh, that's oatmeal, for me," explains Ramona, "you know, lactose. Oh, my! Peppino, I guess you won't be eating the main course either. I'm so sorry."

"It's okay," he says, somewhat relieved, "there looks to be plenty of oatmeal."

"Well," says Robert, steeling himself, "let's dig in."

Ramona gives Robert, Elmo, and Tommy each a healthy portion, and waits for them to try it. Robert takes the first bite and smiles. His left eye droops almost imperceptibly as he tastes the concoction. He continues to chew and swallow showing rather remarkable restraint. He nearly blows it by reaching for the coffee too quickly, but he lets out a big "aah!" at the end to seal the deal. Ramona is beaming. Elmo and Tommy follow his lead and give equally adequate performances.

"This is just perfect!" Ramona exclaims, with a tear in her eye.

As the meal moves along, Ramona asks, "So, what are everyone's plans today? Pep and I are going to the spa."

She shoots a brief look at Tommy.

Tommy takes yet another long swig of coffee before speaking.

"Yeah, sorry about that, Mom. I need to meet this guy about choreographing his event."

Upon hearing the word "guy," Ramona immediately switches gears.

"Oh, what sort of 'guy' are we meeting?" she asks.

Pep jumps in with, "Probably not the kind you're thinking about."

"What do you mean?" asks Ramona.

"He means that I am possibly going to be choreographing a flash mob and that there is a high likelihood that the 'guy' is gay."

"What is a flash mob, and how does that make him gay?" asks Ramona, confused.

Elmo jumps in.

"Mom, a flash mob is one of those things where a bunch of people just bust out dancing in a mall or train station. That should answer both of your questions."

"More specifically," explains Tommy, "it is a seemingly spontaneous expression of movement to music in an unexpected place, by apparently random people."

"It sounds like fun, but if it's random, how do you know if anyone is gay or not?" asks Ramona.

"It only is set up to look random for the audience," says Tommy. "You know, people of different ages in different clothing. That's where the choreography comes in. If it's not choreographed well, people just jump in doing their own thing, which takes away from both the audience and performers' experience."

"Definitely gay," says Elmo.

Ramona looks toward Robert. He tilts his head and nods in agreement. Everyone looks at Pep.

"Hey," he adds, "My money's on gay."

Ramona shrugs and moves on to Robert.

"So, you're going to visit your father this afternoon?"

"Yes, honey," he replies, glancing at Elmo, "we have some things to discuss."

"What about you, Elmo?" asks Ramona.

"I'm going to get on with my life," he says stoically, looking at his father rather than his mother.

After the meal, Pep is loading the dishwasher while Ramona brings in the dishes. He gets a strange whiff of something and makes a face. He smells the tureen and turns to Ramona.

"Mom," he asks, "did you taste the Hollandaise?"

"Heavens, no!" she says. "You know I can't eat that. The calories alone would kill me. Why do you think I go to the gym every morning?"

"Well, not every morning," he says. "Today you were making breakfast."

"No, honey, I had Pilates this morning," she says.

"Then when did you make this?" he asks. "I'm no gourmet chef, but I understand that Hollandaise sauce is cooked for a relatively long time at a low temperature. Was it pre-made?"

"Pep! How could you?" she admonishes him. "I made everything from scratch, just as I said I would. I knew I had to be at the gym this morning, so I just made it last night."

"Last night?" he asks, confused. "Didn't it get wrecked in the refrigerator?"

"I didn't put it in the refrigerator, silly," she says, proudly. "I left it in the oven. With the pilot light, it was just warm enough to keep it just right!"

Pep sniffs the tureen one more time and shudders as he puts it in the dishwasher.

"This can't be good," he whispers to himself.

Saturday, Dec 15th
~ Upper Montclair ~

Scotty, Marcus and Carter are walking toward the field for their flag football game. Their shirts have a logo of clasped hands and have Essex Youth printed above. Marcus and Scotty are local youth advisors and Carter helps out when the others twist his arm. Marcus turns toward Carter.

"You got your spikes today, right?" he asks.

"Yes, Mom," says Carter. "I have my spikes. Damn, it was just one time."

"Yeah," says Marcus, "one time for the spikes, and before that, it was your jersey, and before that—"

"So you admit that it was just one time with the spikes. I'm glad we could agree on something and put this matter to rest," says Carter, interrupting.

"Damn," says Scotty, "the field looks pretty muddy. Maybe I should have left time for a shower. At least it may slow down the kid."

Marcus waves to the rest of the team, who have already arrived.

"Gather up, gentlemen. We have a new game plan."

There are some moans.

"What does 'baby Belichick' have for us today?" asks Billy, nodding toward Scotty.

"Actually," says Marcus, "we are going to simplify the plan for today."

They all they huddle together except for Carter, who is watching something on the next field.

The game begins with George Lutz, the new Park St. Baptist Church Pastor calling heads as the coin flips through the air. It comes up tails. The referee looks at Marcus, who is pointing to his chest.

"We'll receive," he says.

Marcus takes the kick and is quickly stopped. If anything, the kid is faster than the last time. He darts down the field and grabs one of Marcus' flags practically before he catches the ball. Marcus makes eye contact with Scotty and shakes his head. Scotty winces back and says, "Yikes!"

Scotty calls the play in the huddle and reminds everyone, "Odd, left, and even to the right."

Marcus elbows Carter who seems to be watching a young lady on the sideline.

"I got it, dude," says Carter, never taking his eyes off of his prey.

"27, 14!" calls out Scotty as the kid runs up to the line on Scotty's left.

"Seven, HUT!" he shouts, as the center tosses the ball back to him.

Scotty immediately breaks to his right as planned, but the kid has crossed the line and is closing the gap quickly. Marcus, who was playing end on the far right, is running toward Scotty, like on a reverse, but to the inside. Just as the kid reaches for Scotty's flag, Marcus stops him dead in his tracks with a clean, but brutal block.

Scotty continues to roll to the right, pump fakes a pass to freeze a defender, and lofts a soft pass to Carter crossing to the right. Carter cradles the ball and lopes untouched into the end zone for a touchdown. He calmly tosses the ball to the referee and winks at the young lady on the sideline.

Scotty turns back to see Marcus helping the kid up and gently pushing him toward his teammates. The kid is still shaking the fog out of his head.

"Is he okay?" asks Scotty.

"For now," says Marcus. "I see our system worked."

"For now," says Scotty.

After stopping Park St. Baptist on downs, Essex Youth goes back on offense, this time with Marcus at quarterback and Scotty lined up behind him in the backfield. Again, the kid runs up on the left side and Marcus calls out, "Five, HUT!"

Marcus takes off to his right, with Scotty behind him. He fakes a pitch to Scotty and turns up field. The kid again is in hot pursuit, but Scotty cuts back behind Marcus and plows the kid, who is focused on Marcus' flags, off of his feet. Marcus continues on for a touchdown.

This pattern continues for most of the game until the Pastor mercifully sits the kid down for the last quarter of the game. The score is well out of reach at this point, and the team is having a good time even though everyone is covered in mud. Everyone except Carter, that is.

"How the hell do you stay so clean?" Scotty asks Carter.

Instead, Marcus answers.

"By avoiding contact and playing like a punk," he says.

"We're up by 30," says Carter, seemingly taking no offense. I have contributed 2 touchdowns—and, it appears that I may be taking my new lady friend out after the game."

He gives a dainty wave to the girl on the sidelines.

"Didn't she come here with someone from the other field?" asks Scotty.

"All's fair in love and football," says Carter.

"You disgust me," says Scotty.

"Hell," says Carter, "even *I* disgust me, but I *am* a dude, and to the winner goes the spoils."

After the game ends, they are having a brief chat with their opponents. Marcus is talking to the kid who still is clueless as to how the game plan was used to completely nullify his speed advantage.

"Nice kid," says Marcus. "We'd better start working on our game plan for basketball, assuming he plays for them."

Marcus, Carter, and Scotty head back toward the car.

"I get the shower first," says Carter. "I gotta meet the new girl for lunch at 1:30."

"Just make sure you leave your cleats outside," says Marcus. "Last time, you tracked mud in the house. And don't take all day. I want to go into the office this afternoon for some paperwork."

"Well, why don't you take the car and drop me off downtown so I can meet this Tommy person?" asks Scotty. "I'll have to shower later. I have my house key and I can walk from there."

"Hey, maybe you'll get a date with Tommy," says Carter. "You want to double?"

Too tired to speak, Scotty just flashes Carter the bird. Carter and Marcus laugh.

Saturday, Dec 15th
~ Bloomfield ~

Elmo hears Donny's horn and heads down his driveway. He is getting a little headache behind his right eye, but dismisses it as stress. He's wearing a black leather jacket over a black t-shirt and black jeans. Donny is driving a 1969 Chevy Nova. Donny has been restoring it during downtime at the garage where he works. It is painted a bright cobalt blue. Elmo gets in the passenger seat.

"The car is coming along great," he says.

"It oughta," says Donny. "It costs me more than a girlfriend."

Donny puts the car in gear but spins the tires on the wet leaves by the curb.

"God dammit!" he shouts. "I'm so tired of these fucking leaves all over the place."

"I dunno," says Elmo, buckling his lap belt, "I kinda like 'em."

"You like wet, festering garbage?" asks Donny, making a face.

"I like the idea of renewal," says Elmo.

"What the fuck are you talking about?" asks Donny, incredulous.

"Renewal," Elmo explains. "Deciduous trees lose their leaves to make room for new growth."

"Leaving a fucking mess in the street," adds Donny.

"I actually started composting most of ours in the back yard," continues Elmo, who is finding that he seems to be generating too much saliva.

"All right," Donny snarls, "let's drop the fucking leaves. We're heading to Wayne to the mall. We're gonna bust your cherry by boosting a car."

Elmo is feeling a little queasy, but is still convinced that it is just nerves. He rolls down the window and spits to empty his mouth.

"Hey, watch the fucking paint job!" shouts Donny. "What is wrong with you today?"

"I'm fine," says Elmo, quietly.

He is starting to sweat and he loosens his jacket. They pull into the mall parking lot and start cruising, looking for a car for Elmo to steal. The lot is gigantic and is completely packed with Christmas shoppers.

"We're looking for an older car, since they have less security," says Donny. "We went over the hot wiring instructions, but if you can't get it to start, you should be able to pop the lock with the tool I gave you and use the screwdriver to start it. I'll hit the horn if anyone is coming. If you hear it, calmly get out of the car, close the door and walk through to the next row and head toward the mall. I will drive around and pick you up. No running, and don't look back at the car. Those will get you busted."

Elmo nods his head in assent, but his head is pounding at this point. He has been swallowing a lot and is sweating profusely. After about twenty-five minutes of cruising the parking lot, Donny slows down.

"There," he says. "See the maroon Toyota over there? It's perfect. Far from the mall, no security and the guy just left it. Best of all, it's a '95. The pre-'96 Camry is the easiest car to steal short of someone leaving their engine running. Okay, you got all the tools in your pockets?"

Elmo opens his door a crack and is met by a wave of exhaust fumes. Elmo turns 3 shades of green and turns toward Donny. Donny looks at Elmo and sees that he looks terrible. He hesitates for a moment and then says, "C'mon, E. It's time to shit or get off the—"

Before Donny can finish his go-to line, Elmo releases a projectile stream of saliva, coffee, and rancid Eggs Benedict. Donny sees the stream frozen momentarily in mid-air, but can do nothing. He and much of the interior of his car are covered.

"Fuck!" Donny screams. "You fucking fuck! My seats! I just redid this interior! Oh, fuck! It's in the fucking console!"

At this point, Elmo is hanging out of the car door finishing the purge of his breakfast. He slumps back into his seat, glassy-eyed and holds his stomach. Miraculously, other than a thin stream of drool, Elmo has missed himself completely. This is not lost on Donny, who is practically in tears with rage.

"You fucked my car, you fuck!" he shouts. "It took me three months of work to pay for this interior. You're gonna pay me back for this, every fucking dime!"

"Sorry, man," croaks Elmo, as Donny puts the Nova in gear and squeals toward Route 23 and home.

Saturday, Dec 15th
~ West Orange ~

"Hey, Papa," says Robert, to his dad as he walks into his room.

Robert sits in the side chair and takes off his jacket.

"They sure keep it warm enough in here," he says.

"I don't feel warm," says Grandpa. "So, to what do I owe this visit?"

"I need to talk to you about Elmo, Papa."

"Direct. I've always respected that about you, son. Most people would give me a song and dance like, 'Can't I just want to see my old man?,' but not you. Right to the point."

Robert nods to accept his father's compliment.

"Of course, I still am interested in how my 'old man' is doing," says Robert, with a smile.

"I've been better," says Grandpa. "There is progress, but it's slow, and I don't have the energy I once had. I can't believe I was chasing widows just a few weeks ago."

"Stay focused on that and you'll be out of here in no time."

"I hope so. I'm starting to feel old."

"What about the treatment here?"

Robert rolls up his sleeves and begins mopping his brow.

"Surprisingly good, I have to admit. Very professional. There's this colored kid, physical therapist, but he does other things as well. He's a natural leader, keeps everyone in line."

"African-American, Papa, or at least, Black."

"Yeah, whatever, who can keep up. In any case, if they were all like him, the Family would be out of business. You'll probably run into him. He seems to always be around. How about you, son? I hear that all the kids are home."

Robert rubs the back of his neck as if it aches.

"Yep, it's great to have them home, particularly for Ramona. She's been having a tough time of late with the 'empty nest' syndrome."

"Syndrome. Everything's got a name, now. Rotator cuff, turf toe, syndromes. Probably all made up by Jew doctors."

Robert ignores his father's mini-rant.

"And, of course, there are the usual 'women issues' at her age," he says.

"Your mother, God rest her soul, never made it to that stage. I expect that she would have never said a word to me about any of that and that was fine with me. Shouldn't that be over already?"

"Who knows?" says Robert. "Pre-menopause, peri-menopause, menopause, post-Menopause, and who knows what else. Every time she reads an article, it adds two years to the process. Yet she works out every day and looks great."

He shrugs and holds his hands out to the sides.

"How about the kids?" asks Grandpa.

"Mostly great," says Robert, loosening a button on his shirt. "Tommasina is getting close to her PhD. Ramona would rather she had a boyfriend, followed closely by some grandchildren, of course. She is a little high strung, so I suppose some male attention wouldn't hurt."

"And Peppino?"

"20 going on 50," says Robert. "He's obviously a smart kid, but he also has a level of…what word am I looking for? Wisdom, I suppose. He's very sure of himself."

"And the queer thing?"

"Gay, Papa, we don't use queer anymore."

"I don't get it," says Grandpa. "They can call each other 'queer,' and the blacks call each other 'nigger.' If someone ever called me 'guido,' 'wop,' or 'dago,' I would kick their ass, no questions asked, but if I got that from another Italian, the beating would be twice as bad."

"You know, it's funny, Papa," Robert continues. "I was worried that it would affect our relationship, I mean the whole family, but nothing has really changed. He is who he is and we love him unconditionally. It might even be better with no unspoken 'thing' hanging out there."

"Good. Now, what about Elmo? You know he came to see me recently."

Robert looks surprised.

"Really? Tell me about it."

Grandpa raises his bed slightly, mostly so he can more comfortably use his hands while speaking.

"Well, first of all, he comes in here dressed like Al Capone, wearing one of my old suits he found in your attic. By the way, why are they even up there? Shark skin is not coming back."

"Continue, Papa," says Robert, squirming in his seat.

"Hey. You don't look so good, son," says Grandpa.

Robert waves him off.

"So, basically," Grandpa continues, "he tells me he wants in to the family business. I didn't encourage him and I didn't discourage him. I told him he needed to discuss it with you."

Robert rubs his stomach.

"I have to find a way to keep him out of it, Papa."

"Why?" asks Grandpa. "I know it's not your first choice, but it has provided well for both of us and our families."

"I can't. I promised Ramona. I promised myself."

"You think that your mother and I didn't have the same plans for you? But, it happened. It was unplanned, an accident."

"C'mon Papa, it was different for me. I work in an office building, and I was smart. What kind of work is there for Elmo? He'd be eaten alive!"

"Maybe it will make him a man. Ramona has to let him go at some point. He's 25 years old, for God's sake!"

Robert stands and shouts, "He doesn't have what it takes!"

Grandpa points at his son and shouts, "You didn't have what it takes! I knew that you'd never have the stomach for what I did!"

Suddenly, Robert bolts to the bathroom stall and falls to his knees, vomiting.

Grandpa looks mildly surprised. He gathers himself and calls to Robert.

"I meant that as a figure of speech, you know."

Saturday, Dec 15th
~ Montclair ~

Tommy is sitting on a bench in front of the Christmas tree in the town center of Montclair. Not surprisingly, every possible religion and persuasion is represented. All of the flags hanging from the streetlamps are appropriately neutral. She is watching the people, trying to guess which one is going to turn out to be Scotty McCall. Although she agreed to meet him in a desperate attempt to dodge her mother's equally desperate attempts to 'fix' her, she is now getting excited about the idea of getting back involved in dance.

She sees a nattily dressed man, balding, in a gabardine coat and stylish scarf standing alone. He has horn-rimmed round glasses and reminds her of a slightly smaller Stanley Tucci. She is about to get up to greet him when a rather large woman walks out of the Toy Shoppe and brusquely hands him an armload of packages. He sneers and follows the woman down the street. Tommy then sees a rather unkempt young man walking around the tree, no doubt looking for a handout. She shudders when she realizes that he appears to be covered in mud as well. She is about to move to a farther bench when she hears him ask a fellow passerby, "Excuse me, are you by any chance Tommy?" He holds out his hand as if to shake. The man stops suddenly, reaches into his pocket and places a dollar bill into Scotty's outstretched hand.

Tommy lets out an audible gasp, and turns to walk away, completely giving up on the flash mob idea, but not before she and Scotty make eye contact. This freezes her, and during this pause, Scotty tilts his head to one side.

"Tommy?" he asks.

Still frozen, she stammers out, "Uh, yes. Are you Scotty?"

This comes out sounding more like "are you Bigfoot?" Scotty smiles and walks toward her with his hand extended when he realizes he is still holding the dollar bill. As shocked as he is to find that Tommy is a woman, and a rather cute one at that, he is lucid enough to figure out that to her, he appears to be a homeless panhandler. He quickly stuffs the bill in his pocket.

"Oh, my," he says, "wow, this did not go as planned. Here, let's sit down so I can explain, okay?"

Tommy realizes that at least he can speak, so she lets down her guard enough to nod and sit.

"Sure, why not?" she says.

Scotty also sits and lets out a breath.

"Okay," he says, "My name is Scotty McCall and I posted the note about needing a choreographer for a flash mob that will be taking place at this very spot at the First Night celebration in Montclair, obviously on New Year's Eve. I am caked in mud because I play in a flag football league in town and I had to come directly from my game in order to meet you on time."

Tommy is nodding and feeling safer as well.

"You know," Scotty continues, "you really threw me for a loop being female, um, based on your name I mean."

"Is that a problem?" asks Tommy.

"What? Is what a problem?" asks Scotty, perplexed.

"The fact that I'm female."

"I don't get it. Why would that make a difference?"

"Well, based on where you posted your ad, and the fact that you seem surprised that I'm a female..."

"Oh, no!" Scotty blurts out, making a mental note to strangle Carter. "I'm not gay! I just figured it might be a good way to find dancers. No, wait, that's not what I mean."

Tommy laughs and puts Scotty out of his misery.

"I get it," she says. "You're not homeless, perpetually dirty, or gay, and you were not expecting a girl named Tommy. My given name, believe it or not, is Tommasina, so you can see why I go by Tommy."

"Well it's a pleasure to meet you, Tommy. I must admit, I can't recall a more awkward first meeting."

At that moment, Tommy gulps, runs over to the closest potted topiary, and heaves her breakfast into the pot.

Ramona and Pep are in lounge chairs at the Gentle Strength Health Spa in Caldwell. They are both in fluffy robes and their faces are coated in a greenish paste. Both have their eyes covered by a mask filled with some sort of soothing gel. Their hands are soaking bowls of a frothy liquid.

"Sorry that Tommy couldn't make it here with you today, Mom," says Pep.

"Don't be ridiculous," she says. "It's her loss, and quite frankly, it's my gain."

"Thanks, Mom, but I'm sure she would have come if not for her meeting," he says, unconvincingly.

"Please, she would have used any excuse to avoid this, and besides, she'd have spent the entire time complaining. Part of the spa experience is the relaxation. Neither your sister nor I would be relaxed right now."

"Well, I for one could get used to this," he says. After a pause, he adds, "Don't be too hard on Tommy. This isn't exactly her thing."

"Of course it's not her thing. I know that. But couldn't she give it a try? I'd expect a little more open-mindedness from her. Besides, she's a little high-strung these days. A little relaxation might do her some good."

"I guess this kind of thing makes her more stressed as opposed to less so, although this is pretty sweet."

"I think we both know that it's me that is causing her stress. She's so defensive around me."

Pep shakes off his right hand, wipes it on his robe and gently scratches his nose. He places it back in the bowl.

"She's just a little sensitive to, um, your approach to, um, how should I put this?"

"Delicately, I would recommend."

"Well, her hair, for example," says Pep, cautiously.

"Is it so much for a mother to want her daughter to look her best?" asks Ramona.

"No, but I have noticed a somewhat, um, heavy-handedness about your approach, Mom."

"I suppose, but it's just hair."

"*Welllll,*" says Pep, stretching out the word.

"Well, what?" asks Ramona, defensively.

"Well, there might also be a slight issue with a few other things."

"Such as?"

"Possibly make-up, clothes, boyfriends, grandchildren—"

"Grandchildren?" Ramona blurts out. "You make me sound like some sort of controlling monster!"

"No, no, Mom. I don't mean it like that. It's what, oh, damn, what's the term she uses? Oh, yeah, passive-aggressive. It's very common between mothers and daughters in particular. She feels a certain subtle pressure to be what she thinks that you want, no, not want, what you expect her to be."

"Nonsense," says Ramona, curtly.

"Mom, I don't mean it as a bad thing. It's completely normal. Dysfunctional, but normal. Take Dad, for example. He obviously loves both Elmo and me—"

"Equally," interjects Ramona.

"Of course, but he doesn't always treat us the same. Elmo was a not only athletic, but regularly performed as an athlete. I have a minimal interest in sports, at best. On the other hand, Dad and I process information the same way, while Elmo doesn't. We have a similar sense of humor. We just *get* each other."

"Well, I don't see what the big deal is about a girls' day at the spa."

Pep realizes that he probably should have not pursued this conversation and changes the subject.

"Forget it, Mom. I'm having a great time, aside from the 'girls' day' reference. How have you been?"

"You know, while you are both wise and insightful, beyond your years, you still have the tact of a 20-year-old male. All right, quite frankly, I'm bored."

"Bored?" he asks.

"Yes, dreadfully and stultifyingly bored; bored with the gym, bored with book clubs, bored with the house—just bored."

"I guess your life has changed with your kids grown."

"Well grown is a relative term, but yes. I have no more involvement with the school. I'm less involved at the church. I don't spend 5 hours a day chauffeuring you all around. There are no more games, concerts, recitals, or even family meals."

"I guess it is like losing your job."

"It wasn't just a job," she says.

"It was an adventure?" asks Pep, smiling.

"No," she says, missing his joke, "it was a passion."

Pep is about to yet again say something tactless, but is saved by a gentle gong indicating the next phase of the treatment. A young woman comes in and removes their eye masks. Given an extra moment to gather his thoughts, he turns to Ramona and mouths to her, "I love you, Mom."

Saturday, Dec 15th
~ Glen Ridge ~

Robert, Tommy and Elmo are all in their pajamas and robes sprawled across the chairs and sofas in the den. Tommy and Elmo have wastebaskets nearby for emergency purposes. They all look rather dazed and lethargic.

"All right," says Robert, "it appears that the crisis has passed and we all might live. Let's get our story straight."

Tommy and Elmo both moan, but are unable to form any coherent protest.

"We all came down with some sort of bug," Robert continues, "a 24-hour thing."

Tommy, painfully and slowly, turns toward her father.

"How is that even possible?" she says. "Pep and I have barely been home for 24 hours, and I assume that neither he nor Mom have gotten sick."

"Have you got a better idea?" asks Robert.

"I've got one," says Elmo, a little angrily. "How about the truth, that Mom poisoned us?"

"We don't know that, for sure," says Robert, "and besides, I see no reason to make your mother feel badly."

"You mean badly like us?" asks Elmo.

At that moment, Ramona comes into the den.

"Oh, my God!" she says. "What happened to you?"

Pep follows her into the room and immediately realizes what transpired.

"I guess we all picked up some sort of stomach virus," says Robert, immediately.

Pep makes eye contact with Tommy and they both roll their eyes.

"Well, I feel fine. What about you, Peppino?" asks Ramona, turning toward her baby.

Pep smiles at Tommy.

"Actually, I feel great," he says. "I just had a three hour spa treatment."

Tommy tries for a comeback, but is unable to lift her head to speak. She does manage to direct a half sneer his way. Suddenly realizing what happened, Ramona cups Elmo's face in her hands. She then moves to Tommy and does the same looking into her glassy eyes. She looks at her husband.

"Oh my God!" she wails. "I did this to you!"

They all expect her to burst into tears, but no one has a clue of how to stop the impending breakdown. Ramona covers her face and appears to be sobbing, but they all quickly realize that instead, she is laughing hysterically.

They are momentarily stunned and then look at each other as if to confirm that they are all seeing the same thing. Pep picks up Tommy's legs, sits next to her on the loveseat and places her legs back down on his. Ramona, still intermittently laughing and gasping for breath, plops down on the couch next to Robert and hugs him.

"You sweet man," she gasps, between laughs. "I can't believe that I made all of you sick, and you are still trying to protect my feelings. Oh, God, you're such a sweet, sweet asshole!"

"I'm sorry, but did you just call me an asshole?" asks Robert, even more confused.

The others look at each other, also confused.

"Yes, I believe that I did," she says, loosening her grip on him. "Have I become so fragile that you would still think to lie to me after I *poison* my family? Oh, my. I'm terribly sorry. Elmo, baby, please tell me what happened."

Elmo looks toward Robert. Robert shrugs and waves his hand to let Elmo know that it is okay to proceed. Elmo shrugs and tries to sit up, unsuccessfully.

"Pretty standard, worst day ever," he says. I was in Donny's car, with the brand new interior."

Ramona puts her hand over her mouth and gasps.

"Oh, it gets worse," says Elmo. "I felt it brewing, but didn't realize what was coming as I have never had food poisoning before. Suffice it to say that neither Donny or his car fared well. Dad was kind enough to give him a hundred bucks to get his clothes cleaned and sent his auto detail guy to clean the car on his dime."

"Oh, I feel awful," says Ramona, snickering.

"No you don't, Mom," says Elmo. "You hate Donny."

"No, sweetie," she says, giggling, "I mean that I feel awful for not feeling awful."

At this point they are all laughing, although some of them are doing so through abdominal pain.

"Well, I at least made it to a bathroom," says Robert. "I was visiting Papa. He was quite amused when I told him that you had prepared us a 'special breakfast.'"

He looks at Elmo and continues.

"I'll have to go back to finish our conversation," says Robert.

Elmo tries to show indifference and shrugs.

"What about you, Sis?" asks Pep.

Tommy stares at the ceiling.

"Worst day ever, plain and simple," she says. "Let's see…meet gay guy, turns out to be straight. Looks homeless, turns out to be cute, smart, and nice."

"Ooh!" says Ramona, before being shot down with a look from, well, everybody.

Tommy continues.

"Oh yeah, then there's me yakking into a potted tree in the middle of downtown Montclair."

Ramona gasps.

"Yep," Tommy continues. "I'm not sure that it's possible to reach a deeper level of embarrassment."

"Oh, babe!" says Ramona, unable to contain her amusement.

All except Tommy start laughing at Ramona's inability to stop laughing. Finally, she composes herself.

"What happened next?" asks Ramona.

Tommy, seeing that no one else was jumping in, continues.

"He was actually quite nice about it. He held my hair while I was heaving my guts up. He sat me down with my head between my knees, which was fine, since eye contact was out of the question. Obviously, I didn't want to stay there drawing a crowd. He walked me to his apartment to get his car and mercifully drove me home. My car is in a lot, so it's safe overnight. I'll go pick it up with Elmo or Pep tomorrow, assuming we are ambulatory. Dad and Elmo were already here, near death, when I arrived. I made some tea with mint leaves and we were able to keep it down. I think the crisis has passed…literally."

"Mint leaves?" asks Ramona.

"It was his idea," says Tommy.

She shrugs and points her thumb at Elmo.

"He claimed it settles the stomach. It seems to have worked."

"So you say this young man was both straight and cute?" asks Ramona, unable to contain herself.

"Arghhh!" shouts Tommy, covering her head with her pillow.

Sunday, Dec 16th
~ Montclair ~

Scotty comes out of the bathroom in a pair of lounging pants and a t-shirt from a Juvenile Diabetes Walk. His hair is still damp from the shower. Marcus is in the kitchen preparing some breakfast. Carter is standing in his underwear in front of an ironing board. He is watching Sportscenter while he irons a white dress shirt.

"Dude," says Scotty, with a grimace, "put on some pants."

"In a minute, side job today," says Carter, absently. "Damn!"

He is focused on the television.

"The Jets?" asks Scotty. "You know their season has been over for quite some time."

Carter pays no attention and continues ironing. Scotty moves toward the kitchen and directs his attention to Marcus.

"Smells great. Need any help?"

"No, I got it," says Marcus, not looking up from his cutting board. "Omelets today."

He continues to cut up a variety of items.

"Western?" asks Scotty, leaning on the door jamb.

"Western Newark, maybe," says Marcus. "It was time to clean out the leftovers. This should be interesting."

"Belgian toast," says Scotty.

"What's that?" asks Marcus, while buttering a frying pan.

"My grandmother made me breakfast every morning before school. You know, hot breakfast, most important meal of the day."

"She was right," says Marcus, swirling the egg around the pan.

"French toast was a favorite of mine," Scotty continues, "but every so often, she would make it from a different country using a different kind of bread. While we were eating it, she would tell us all about the country, you know, the capital, the geography, the history."

"A teacher, 24/7," says Marcus, sprinkling the hodgepodge of chopped leftovers onto the egg.

"Of course," says Scotty, "but here's the funny part. I was in college, in the cafeteria getting breakfast. They're serving French toast. All of a sudden, out of the blue, I realize, there's no such thing as Belgian toast. I think I actually said it out loud."

Marcus is smiling and is sliding the omelet onto a plate warming in the oven.

"Let me guess," he says. "She was out of white bread, and used whatever she had and covered up with the geography lesson."

"So well that it took me about 10 years to figure out the scam," says Scotty.

"So what was it?" asks Marcus, working on the next omelet.

"What was what?" asks Scotty.

"Belgian toast, what kind of bread was it?" asks Marcus.

"Hot dog rolls, if you can believe it," says Scotty, laughing.

Marcus laughs as well.

"Well, that makes you pretty gullible, but in honor of your grandma, we will call this concoction a Belgian omelet," he says.

They bring the food to the table and call over Carter who has added a sleeveless t-shirt to his ensemble, as well as a worn pair of gym shorts. Marcus gives him a disapproving look.

"Jesus," he says, "put on a robe. You look like the black Stanley Kowalski."

Carter falls to his knees, thrusts out his arms and in a minimally passable Brando, and shouts out "Shaniqua!!"

Scotty and Marcus roll their eyes and they all sit down for breakfast. Carter takes a bite.

"Not bad, Brother," he says.

Marcus nods as they continue eating. Scotty turns to Carter.

"What type of side job?" he asks.

Carter takes a drink of what appears to be Kool-Aid.

"The usual," he says, "driving rich white folks around. In the City, usually means good tips."

He takes another bite and continues.

"I am not fond of working on Sundays, but besides the cash, it's a good way to learn the business and meet clients for when I start my own company."

"You may also want to consider saving some of that cash," says Marcus.

"One time, dude," Carter protests. "One time I ask you to float me on the rent. It was for 3 fucking days."

"I'm just saying," says Marcus, with a wink. "Scotty, how did your thing go yesterday? Was the dude gay or straight?"

"Oh, yeah," he says. "You guys both got in late last night. It wasn't a dude at all."

Both Marcus and Carter look up.

"You mean Tommy?" asks Marcus.

"Yup; Tommasina, apparently," says Scotty. "Actually, she is a rather cute young lady who is neither gay nor male."

"Do tell," says Carter.

"Well," says Scotty, "if you ignore the parts where I was caked in mud and funky, and when she thought I was gay, and homeless, and finally when she serially vomited in the bushes, I'd say there might have been a connection. I guess I'll find out more if she shows up to rehearsal tomorrow."

Marcus looks stunned, but Carter keeps eating.

"Cute, huh?" he asks, nonchalantly, "how's her ass?"

Sunday, Dec 16th
~ Montclair ~

Tommy and Pep exit the bagel store in downtown Montclair. They came to pick up Tommy's car, but as soon as Tommy saw the bagel shop, she insisted on going in. She draws a deep breath from the bag.

"Oh, God, how I missed these," she says. "They're still warm."

"Jeez, they're just bagels, Sis," says Pep.

"You live in Boston. Have you found a decent bagel there? Because I haven't. You know, for a city in the Northeast, you'd think you could find a decent bagel—"

"Or pizza," Pep adds. "Actually, I'm surprised you can even think about food after yesterday."

"Are you kidding?" she says. "I'm famished. My rib cage, however, feels like I got hit by a linebacker."

"Hey, is that the scene of the crime?" asks Pep, pointing toward the Town Center Christmas tree.

"Ugh, don't remind me," she says, with a shudder. "Over there, to the right. I hope somebody hosed it down."

"Luckily, it didn't freeze last night," says Pep, holding out a finger as if testing the temperature.

"Gross," says Tommy. "This is where the flash mob will be. I expect there to be a lot of movement around the tree. For safety reasons, no one will be dancing on the surrounding ring, but we can do a sitting and kicking thing."

"Wait," says Pep, surprised, "you're still going to do it, after the 'incident'?"

"Sure, why not?" she asks. "I've been to the first circle, so to speak."

"Dante?" he asks.

"No, Solzhenitsyn. Of course he wasn't referring to the first circle of embarrassment," she says. "Ironically, I'm thinking of using the Trans-Siberian Orchestra piece, Sarajevo something or other."

"Yeah, but it's called Christmas Eve/Sarajevo," says Pep, "and your thing is on New Year's Eve."

"I considered that," she says, "but we're doing it in front of a giant Christmas tree. You think it makes a big difference?"

"I do," he says. "Most people are pretty sick of Christmas by then, and it is based on the Carol of the Bells."

"It's just that there really aren't any New Year's songs that come to mind, except, of course, slow and sappy stuff. Most are also rather depressing," she says.

"What about that new thing, by Mandy-Sue Martin or something?" asks Pep. "You must have heard it. It's been playing everywhere for the last few weeks. It's called New Year's Hayride, if you can believe it; a crossover rockabilly thing."

Tommy shrugs.

"I guess I was focused on the end of the semester, she says.

While she is speaking, Pep is manipulating his phone.

"Here," he says, handing her the phone. "Here's the video. It's catchy, timely, and people are flipping out over it. I guarantee that it will be stuck in your head for at least half of the day."

She takes the phone and listens. You can tell she is already blocking out steps.

"Hmm," she says, "not bad. This might work."

"And I may have saved you from further embarrassment," he says.

Tommy gives him a punch in the arm and returns his phone.

"I thought we agreed never to mention that again," she says.

"That's where you've lost me," says Pep. "I still can't believe you're going through with it."

Tommy is envisioning dancers with the music playing in her head, already working on the choreography.

"I said," Pep repeats a little louder, "I can't believe you're going through with it."

Absently, Tommy says, "I made a commitment to him."

"Him?" asks Pep, with reality dawning.

"Him what?" asks Tommy.

"You said," says Pep, pointedly, "'I made a commitment to *him*,' just now."

Tommy, catching herself, quickly responds.

"It," she says, "I made a commitment to *IT*. You need to remove your earmuffs."

"Whatever you say," he says with a wry smile.

"Let's get the car," she says, in a huff.

Sunday, Dec 16th
~ Glen Ridge ~

The Pastor family is once again at the dinner table. This time, there are several cardboard containers from Panda Gardens.

"I see you all have your appetites back," says Ramona.

She picks up the container of steamed dumplings and quickly puts it back down.

"Finish it, Mom," says Elmo.

"No, I shouldn't, really," she says. "Here, you have it."

She pushes the container toward him.

"Mom!" he says.

"Son, she's contractually obligated to not take the last of anything," says Robert, smiling. "It's part of the Mother Code."

"Oh, stop it," she says.

She gently smacks Robert's hand.

"How about we split it?" asks Elmo.

"Fair enough," she says.

She cuts the dumpling far from evenly, giving Elmo at least 80 percent. Elmo looks toward his father. Robert shrugs and mouths the words, "Mother Code." Elmo shakes his head and pops the rest of the dumpling in his mouth.

"Great job on the Christmas tree, Elmo," says Robert, as he rises to clean up from dinner. "Blue spruce?"

Elmo looks at him like he has three heads.

"No, it's a fir," he says, as though this were evident. "The spruce drops too many needles. Mom hates that. The pines are the best for that, but aren't as full."

Tommy and Pep look at Elmo with mild shock, but they let it go.

"Well I appreciate you thinking of me," chirps Ramona. "After cleanup, it's time to decorate the tree."

She is clapping her hands together, but the children are somewhat less enthusiastic.

"I was going to see a couple of high school friends tonight," says Pep, sheepishly.

"And me and Donny got a thing tonight, too," adds Elmo.

Tommy, with no escape plan, glares at them both.

She stammers, "I was uh, hoping to, uh…"

"Enough," says Ramona sternly. Immediately after cleanup, we will *ALL* put up the lights, and everyone must put on at least one ornament. Only then are you excused. Your father and I will complete the rest."

They all nod in agreement and proceed with the cleanup.

Soon, they are all in the living room. There are some minor kerfuffles with the lights, but with some jiggling and teamwork they complete the task.

"Nice job," says Tommy.

Ramona squeezes Robert's arm and puts her head on his shoulder. She sighs.

"Beautiful," she says.

They each place one or two of their favorite ornaments on the tree. Pep and Elmo slip out quietly. Before they make their escape, Tommy makes eye contact with each of them long enough to stick out her tongue at them.

She is engrossed in putting up ornaments, when her father slides over and whispers to her.

"Didn't you have some reading to do?" he asks.

"What?" she responds, turning toward him.

Ramona is next to him simply aglow with the spirit of love and possibly a little Christmas. He gives Tommy a conspiratory nod toward the stairs. She is about to stick her finger in her mouth to signify the international symbol for barfing, but remembers the physical and emotional pain of yesterday too vividly. She rolls her eyes and heads toward the stairs muttering.

"Time for research, big paper due on the mating rituals of the elderly," she says.

Robert smiles as she heads up the stairs.

"Remember this one?" asks Ramona.

She holds up an ornament made of Popsicle sticks.

"Elmo, Cub Scouts," says Robert. "We must have re-glued this a dozen times."

"I just love this time of year," she says. "I miss the kids so much."

"They're here now, baby," he whispers.

"I know," she says. "Even when they fight, I love having them around. Did you get anywhere with your father yesterday?"

Robert is somewhat taken aback by the sudden change in the direction of their conversation. He recovers and answers.

"Not really. I, um, took ill before we got very far. I'll go see him this week."

"Good," she says, turning to hold him. "I hate to see Elmo in pain."

She puts her head on his chest.

"It'll be all right," he says, and after a pause adds, "I promise."

Ramona turns to look at Robert and brightens. She switches to her best Jersey Shore voice.

"Yo, Bobby, dint I see yooz puttin' up some mistletoe or somethin' aroun' hea?"

Robert smiles and says in his best street lingo, "Yo, babe, I gotchya mistletoe right hea."

He grabs his crotch.

She pulls him close and they kiss passionately. She slides her hand below his waist.

"Ooh, bada bing!" she purrs.

Monday, Dec 17th
~ West Orange ~

It is ten minutes to seven as Tommy walks into the Recreation Room at the Rehab Center. She is wearing an outfit that can be used for going out, but also is clearly functional for dance. She has a bag over one shoulder and is carrying a boom box in the other. There is a good crowd, and she sees Scotty in the middle of a cluster of people directing them as to where to move the chairs. They appear to be creating a circle to simulate the downtown Christmas tree. She is happy that the group seems organized, but her smile indicates that something more is pleasing her. Marcus and Carter are on the side of the room and see Tommy arrive.

"Uh-oh," says Carter, directing his head toward Tommy, "check it out, Bro."

"I see, and don't start," says Marcus.

Carter, looks offended.

"What kind of a pig do you think I am? I heard the way he talked about her yesterday. I'm more loyal than you give me credit for. Besides, look at her, she has Scotty written all over her," he says.

"She's definitely his type," says Marcus. "I can see why he called her cute."

"At Toastmasters, I believe we would use the term 'adorable,'" says Carter. "Anyway, I have a date this week with Cherisse, from the game the other day."

"I don't want to tell you or 'Little Carter' your business," says Marcus, "but that Cherisse is trouble, and this one is off limits."

"I read you, Captain," says Carter, with a salute, "but, charming is as charming does."

"I'm not playing," says Marcus, sternly.

He makes eye contact with Carter as they move to greet Tommy.

"Hello, you must be our choreographer," he says, extending his hand. "I'm Marcus and this is Carter."

They shake, while Carter nods pleasantly.

"I work here and provided the space," says Marcus. "We are Scotty's roommates."

"It's a pleasure to meet both of you," says Tommy, smiling. "I'm really looking forward to this. Um, where might I be able to plug this in?"

She holds up the boom box.

"Allow me," says Carter.

He takes the box from her hand and holds it up to his ear like it's 1980. He does his most ghetto saunter toward the outlet.

"This way, Sistah," he says, in his most Ebonics dialect.

Marcus shoots him a look and turns to Tommy who is a little taken aback.

"Please ignore him," he assures her. "He thinks he's funny."

Marcus walks Tommy over to Scotty who lights up when he sees her.

"Hello again," he says. "I'm glad you could make it."

He pauses awkwardly and sees Marcus give him a nearly imperceptible nod of encouragement.

Scotty, stammers, "Oh, um, I guess you met Marcus."

"And Carter," she says.

She points her thumb in his direction.

"It looks like a good crowd," she adds.

Her eyes shift and focus on a group of about ten somewhat elderly people in patient-like garb, most with canes and walkers.

Scotty follows her gaze and says, "Oh, don't worry about them. They aren't doing the flash mob. They're here to kibitz along on the sidelines. They may attempt a few steps, but they'll be outside the range of our dancers. Marcus thought it would be fun for some of his more ambulatory patients to get out of their rooms for a little while."

"Oh, that's nice," says Tommy, although she feels a very slight wave of discomfort, but can't put her finger on why.

Scotty, not noticing, continues, "Other than a slightly disproportionate number of 30- to 50-year-old males, we seem to have a perfect group. I assume it's a result of the places I posted the flyer. The best news is that there appear to be no divas."

"Well, thank goodness for that," she says. "Shall we get started?"

Scotty calls everyone together. There are about 60 people, although that includes the patients. He introduces Tommy and Marcus. He reminds everyone to complete their liability waiver from the township, a requirement of participation. He turns the floor over to Tommy and moves with Marcus to the back of the room, where Carter is waiting at the boom box for his cue.

Tommy stands on a chair to better be heard.

"Welcome, and thank you again for coming," she says. "Obviously, we are not professionals, but I hope to help you to look like professionals, but most of all, to have fun. The good news about a flash mob is that it is not terribly physically demanding, nor does it require any real dance experience. It is about choreographed movement, so you will need to practice, but the main hook to the audience is surprise. First, I'd like to play the music to give you an idea of what you will be hearing."

She waves to Carter with a flourish. He hits 'Play' and the music begins.

Scotty turns to both Marcus and Carter and asks, "So what do you think?"

"Adorable," says Carter.

Scotty gives him an odd look.

"Don't listen to him," says Marcus. "She's great, and seems as smitten with you as you are with her."

"You think so?" asks Scotty, clueless.

Marcus and Carter both shake their heads in mild disgust.

"Just don't screw it up," says Marcus.

Carter demonstratively puts on his Jets cap.

"I'm off," he says. "I'll see you at McGinty's as soon as you're done here."

He pokes Scotty in the chest and heads out.

"Are you kidding me?" says Scotty. "I seriously have to babysit him at another Jets game? Can't you help a brother out? I want to get to know her."

Marcus shakes his head.

"Sorry, Brother, no can do. First of all, it's for your own good. You need to pace yourself, and your next rehearsal is in two days. You have a habit of 'peaking too early' in a relationship. Also, I went with him to the Ice House last week and we nearly got thrown out. I have to work early tomorrow and I am not about to get dragged into any fights."

The song ends and Marcus turns off the device. The crowd is murmuring and Tommy claps her hands for attention.

"Okay, team," she says, "the whole effect is the selling of the spontaneity of the dance. We will discuss more about this later, but just to set the stage, everyone will basically be dressed as themselves. We'll have some shoppers, some party goers, and mostly regular First Night participants. It will be cold, and you may need to dance in your heavy outerwear, so plan on something you can move in. The song is just under 4 minutes so we won't be running a marathon here."

At 9:00, Tommy and Scotty are near the main doors, thanking everyone for coming. Scotty is collecting waivers from participants and everyone looks happy. Scotty watches Tommy laughing with the last two gentlemen, a middle-aged set of identical twins.

"Don't worry about telling us apart," one of them says.

The other pipes in, laughing, "Yeah, even our mother gave up after a few years. After 50 years together, I'm not even sure that we can tell the difference!"

The first one, also laughing, adds, "Just call us Lew and Stew Jew!"

They both howl hysterically as they wave and head through the double doors. Scotty is smiling.

"Whew!" says Tommy, grabbing the back of a chair for support. "That was intense."

"It was wonderful," says Scotty. "You were great. Everyone had a great time, and the dance looks great."

"Oh, please," she says, catching her breath, "How could you tell? We barely blocked out the basics."

"I could tell," he says. "You had them eating out of your hand. You know, you're quite a natural at this."

At this point, Marcus walks in after getting the patients back in their rooms. He sees them, hesitates for a moment, but sees the time and continues in.

"Sorry to interrupt," he says, looking at Scotty, "but I think you need to be somewhere."

"Oh, crap," says Scotty. "Carter."

"That's right," says Marcus. "Kickoff was 40 minutes ago. He might be dead already."

Tommy looks confused.

Scotty turns to her and says, "Sorry, I have a prior commitment, um, babysitting. I'll have more time on Wednesday. You were great tonight."

He turns to Marcus, points to the mass of chairs.

"You got this?"

"No problem," he says, "go."

Tommy blurts out, "I'll help him clean up!"

She immediately realizes that she sounds like a smitten schoolgirl. She blushes, but Scotty is already trotting toward the exit and his car. Marcus notices and smiles.

She recovers and says, "So what can I do to help?"

"I really can handle it, if you need to go," he says.

"Absolutely not," she says. "You've been kind enough to provide us the space and I have nowhere else to be. I assume the chairs go around the tables against the wall over there?"

"Yes, but the tables stay near the wall," he says. "Bridge and Gin Rummy are a big part of the recreation here. I appreciate your help, but I sense that there might be something else on your mind."

"Is it that obvious?" she asks, with more blushing, "Or are you unusually perceptive?"

Marcus smiles. He is pulling the tables away from the wall, while Tommy slides the chairs underneath.

"Maybe a little of both," he says. "My radar is always up when it comes to Scotty, and besides, I find it quite charming."

"Well it's nice to meet a true diplomat," she says with a curtsey, "How long have you known each other?"

"That's kind of a story," says Marcus.

He puts the last chair in place.

"Come with me," he says, "and I'll treat you to a hot chocolate, compliments of the Center."

"It's a deal," she says.

She picks up her bag. Marcus scoops up the boom box and locks it in a closet. They head for the door. He hits the lights, locks the door, and leads her down the hall. Marcus unlocks an office suite and motions for Tommy to sit down at the conference table. She puts down her bag and sits. He moves to an alcove with a counter. He fills two mugs with water from the sink and puts them into the microwave for a few minutes.

"Marshmallows, or not?" he asks.

"Not, I think," she replies. "Even that little bit of dancing reminds me how out of shape I've become."

Marcus continues making the drinks, brings them to the table, and sits across from Tommy. She thanks him.

"I met Scotty when we were four years old," he begins. "He grew up with his grandparents in Newark, over in the predominantly Jewish section; at least it was forty-plus years ago. Most of the Jews had moved out, but his grandparents didn't. His grandmother was a lifelong educator in Newark, while his grandfather taught in Montclair. His grandma, Hilda Gold, ran a pre-school program for underprivileged kids near the projects where I grew up. My mother worked in the cafeteria in her school and Mrs. Gold always looked after her. I ended up going to the program."

Tommy, who has been nodding, suddenly asks, "Jewish? Scotty McCall sounds, well, Scottish."

"Yeah, Scotty's mother was very young when she had him," says Marcus, "I think, like, 15 or 16. She married a guy named James McCall. His father was out of the picture before Scotty was born. I don't even think Scotty has ever met him. They moved back with the Golds and that was that. Scotty's mother was never quite all there from what I understand. I've only met her briefly a few times. I think she lives on a commune somewhere out west. His grandparents were great people, though, and he lived with them until college. They've both since passed, so it's pretty much just me and Carter to look after him."

"Oh, is that what you were referring to earlier, why he had to leave?" she asks.

"Exactly," he says. "We all look out for each other. Carter gets a little crazy when it comes to the Jets. He also likes to watch the games in a public place, but can get a little overly enthusiastic. One of us typically goes along to rein him in."

"And tonight is Scotty's turn," she says.

"Yeah, but in the spirit of honesty, I could have covered him."

"So why didn't you?"

"Two reasons. One, I could tell by listening to him that he was, how should I put this... 'intrigued' by you. He is not as experienced in these matters as, say, I am, and I didn't want him to come on too strong."

"And two," she interjects, "is that you wanted to vet me first, I'm guessing."

Marcus smiles sheepishly, giving himself away.

"I'm impressed with your loyalty to each other," she says.

He holds up his cup, nods in thanks.

"I value loyalty even more than honesty," he says. "So, going back to pre-school, I had never even met a white child except for TV. To me, white folks were cops, doctors, business owners, but not children. Scotty didn't see color at all, even though most of the black kids shunned him. We played all the time and we just, um, *connected*. Even at four, you could just tell."

"You were both pretty young," she says. "Racial bias is a learned behavior."

"Maybe in the suburbs," he says, "but in Newark, it's natural law. I'm not saying it's biological. It's more like gravity; it just…is."

Tommy looks away, slightly embarrassed.

"I'm sorry, I didn't mean to—"

"Nothing to be sorry about," he says. "That's my point. Some things, you just need to experience to understand. I have had hundreds, no thousands, of white friends and associates. Scotty is the only one who has met my mother, the only one who has been to my house in the projects, the only one who has met my family. Scotty hasn't just walked in my moccasins. He's lived in them."

"Oh, my God, I can't believe I call myself a liberal. I feel like such a fraud," says Tommy.

"Sorry, I got on my soapbox," he says. "You seem smart enough to learn and smart enough to know that it's never too late."

"No, it's worse than that," she says softly. "When I met you, you were talking about the patients, and I realized that you were a doctor or a physical or occupational therapist at least. I felt something inside, like a wave of something negative. I finally realized what it was. When I saw you from a distance carrying around the key ring and being in the rec room, I assumed that you were with maintenance or security. It never occurred to me that you might be, um, *more*, I guess. I felt guilt and embarrassment and didn't even know why. I guess I failed the vetting, but in the spirit of honesty—"

"Nonsense," Marcus assures her, smiling. "Your honesty alone would pass any test. You obviously have a good heart and are also quite capable of learning. You might just have to learn some different things than you expected. Scotty is my brother in every sense of the word. As such, I'm probably over protective. He's sweet and funny and probably the best person I know."

"Just curious, then," she says. "What did you mean earlier about him possibly 'coming on too strong?'"

"Scotty can be a little like Peter Pan," says Marcus, thoughtfully, "He can be naïve and he has had a few less-than-pleasant relationships in the past."

"Oh?" she asks.

"Nothing crazy or anything," he continues. "He dated this girl Delia, for a while. To be honest, she was kind of a self-centered bitch, and not a good fit for Scotty, and of course, he was the only one who didn't realize it."

"Marcus, I wouldn't want you to betray a confidence," she says.

He waves her off and continues.

"No, it's nothing like that. She would refer to him as a 'free spirit,' but would hiss it through gritted teeth, you know, filled with bile. Well, it's one of his best qualities, and to him, she might as well have been singing it with a smile."

"Did you help him dispose of her?" Tommy asks, smiling.

"I'm a diplomat, remember?" he says, returning the smile. "Let's just say that Carter and I were there to help him get through it."

Tuesday, Dec 18th
~ West Orange ~

Marcus walks into Tommaso Pastor's private room. He is perpetually looking things over for anything that needs attention.

"Good morning, Mr. Pastor," he says.

Tommaso is watching the television. There is a courtroom-based reality show on consisting of mostly shouting. Tommaso shakes his head with disgust. He is shaking the remote and pushing buttons, which is having no effect.

"Here, do me a favor, kid," says Tommaso. "Shut this thing off for me…and then throw the TV and the remote into the ocean while you're at it."

Marcus smiles. He takes the remote and tries to shut off the television, but nothing happens. He walks over and turns it off manually.

"Sorry," he says, "I'll get you some new batteries."

"Don't bother," says Tommaso. "In another minute I was about to destroy 2 weeks of rehabilitation and go over there myself to kick in the screen."

Marcus' smile widens. The old man has moxie, and Marcus respects moxie.

"I wouldn't advise that. You'll just extend your therapy."

"Believe me, the therapy is less painful than the crap they show on television. Who watches this garbage?"

"Too many people, that's for sure. Did one of the nurses or staffers turn that on without asking you?"

"I'm an old man, what do I know?"

"Apparently, plenty. I know who you are, Mr. Pastor, and I've been around you enough to know that you know pretty much everything."

"Then you know that I don't rat, flatfoot."

Marcus feigns surprise and they both laugh.

"Anyway, it takes one to know one," says Tommaso. "You've got this place wired as far as I can see. You seem to pretty much run the place. Let me guess. Your bosses have no idea, right?"

"Half of them. They're too busy focusing on not doing their own jobs. The other half of them know, but are afraid of getting shown up, so they don't acknowledge anything."

"In other words...management. But you notice things, like the help coming in and watching television while supposedly doing their job. So how do you handle that?"

"Am I on a job interview?" asks Marcus, smiling. "The problem is that half of them work slower because of the TV, but the other half might not come in at all if not for the

TV. It's the workforce of today, unfortunately. I'm…hmm…formulating a strategy."

"Thoughtful, not impulsive…kid, if you were interviewing, you'd be doing very well."

Marcus rubs his hand against his cheek.

"You mean until I walked in the door," says Marcus.

Tommaso laughs.

"Okay, you got me. It's Marcus, right? I'm Tommaso Pastor."

He extends his hand and Marcus shakes it.

"So what do I owe the honor?" asks Tommaso. "My therapy isn't until later, so I assume you wandered in for a reason."

"How do you know I didn't come in to see Divorce Court?"

Tommaso ignores the bit.

"You said you knew who I was. Since I already know who I am, you must have had some agenda."

"Okay. This may seem odd. I met a young woman named Tommasina Pastor last night."

He fills Tommaso in on the flash mob and the use of the rehab hospital. It takes a few minutes to explain the concept of a flash mob to an 82-year-old who has never used a computer and rarely watches television.

"I didn't make the connection immediately, because she didn't mention having a relative here. Anyhow, I did some research and found out about you."

"Don't believe everything you read in the papers."

"Well, I used the internet, but if anything, that information is less reliable."

"God damn computers! They'll be the end of my...um...business. Let's assume that she is related to me. What is your interest. It can't be romantic because if you know who I am, you certainly would know better than to tell me about it."

"Well, you're close. My best friend Scotty, who is white, completely white, is the guy running the flash mob event. He appears to have a possible romantic interest in Miss Pastor."

"And you are very protective of your friend?"

"Very."

"Shouldn't a man be able to handle his own issues?"

"He can. He's no less fierce than you or I, but in a different way. He's not naïve exactly but...what's the right word?...idealistic. I grew up in the streets, not unlike you from what I understand."

"I respect your loyalty to a friend."

"That's what makes him special. He knows that I would have his back in a fight, but he's never been in a fight. Actually, he wouldn't hurt a fly. But, I know that if someone jumped me, he would be on top of them without hesitation."

"Okay, I'm intrigued. Let me do some inquiries about this young woman and see what is what. You are a good friend."

"And you seem to be one tough customer. Your injury and therapy is quite painful, and I've never heard a whimper from you. You are making remarkable progress, at least compared to the average patient."

"From what I've seen, most of your patients will be lucky to get home to die in their own beds. They're weak."

"Unlike you, they're weak because they are frightened."

"Don't kid yourself, Marcus; they're frightened because they're weak."

Wednesday, Dec 19th
~ West Orange ~

Tommy walks into her grandfather's room and sees that he is reading a newspaper. She gently taps on the open door. He looks up and grins. He folds his paper and reaches out for a hug.

"Grandpa," says Tommy, "I'm so sorry. I was actually here on Monday, but had no idea that this was the place you came for rehab."

"Don't be silly, sweetheart, I figured it was something like that."

"Wait, you knew I was here? How is that—"

"No, no, I found out yesterday. You think I don't hear things?"

"But, still…how could you have found out? Mom or Daddy didn't even know where I went."

Grandpa smiles.

"I have spies everywhere. For example, I hear your mother cooked breakfast the other day."

"Ugh, don't remind me. My ribs are still sore. That I know you heard from Daddy."

"That's true, but I assume you are here for another rehearsal. Do you have time to sit with an old man?"

"I came early just for that very purpose, Grandpa. I have about 30 minutes before I need to be downstairs."

"Well, let me look at you, then. Move over there so I can get a good look at you."

Tommy goes past the foot of the bed. She removes her coat and spins around. She is wearing a leotard under a dancing outfit. She comes back by the bed sits in the side chair."

"So what are you in for?" she asks, with a smile.

"I fractured my hip, as you know. I have at least few weeks of therapy before I can return home. It's painful and annoying and I'm bored out of my mind."

"The story I heard was that you fell changing a light bulb in the bedroom of a neighbor...a female neighbor."

"Something like that."

Grandpa breaks eye contact momentarily before regaining his composure. Tommy lets this go and fills him in on school and her life in Boston as Grandpa nods politely.

"I can see that I'm boring you," she says.

"Well I must admit that I'm a little foggy on the research that you are doing. I just read in the paper here about a government study saying that overweight people need more exercise. Jesus, who doesn't already know this? Yet they won't let kids play dodgeball because it might damage their self-esteem. From what I can see, most of these kids should have low self-esteem. They don't do anything to get esteemed about."

"Calm yourself, Grandpa. I hope to do meaningful research to solve meaningful problems, but mostly, my goal is to teach."

"Sorry, Tommasina, you must indulge a cranky old man. I really am interested. It's more that I don't understand the world these days."

"Nonsense, you have a greater understanding of human nature than anyone I know, certainly more than any of my professors."

"You flatter me, sweetheart. Now, tell me about Scotty."

Tommy is stunned.

"What?... how did…Jesus, Grandpa."

Grandpa laughs and says, "I told you that I have spies."

"It was Pep, wasn't it?"

"I swear that I have not heard from Peppino since he has been home. Incidentally, please let him know that his grandfather wouldn't mind a visit. Anyhow, what is your interest in this Scotty?"

"Jeez, Grandpa. I just met him. Who knows? It's too early to have him 'taken for a ride' if that's what you're asking. You're freaking me out, to be honest."

Grandpa is clearly pleased with himself.

"I'm sorry, sweetheart. I didn't mean to pry. Go to your rehearsal and have a good time. And thank you for brightening an old man's day."

Tommy stands and gives her grandfather a kiss. She looks at him with awe as she heads for the door. Tommy heads for the recreation room for rehearsal. She tries to focus on the task at hand, but her thoughts keep creeping back to Scotty. She enters the Rec Room and is pleased to see a full crowd. Many are in dancewear and are stretching. She does not see any of the residents, nor does she see Marcus or Carter. Lew and Stew spot Tommy and race over to greet her. They are breathlessly sharing their ideas on the choreography when she sees Scotty across the room. He is sliding chairs toward the center to simulate the First Night venue.

"Pardon me, gentlemen," she says. "Let me get set up and we'll talk in a few minutes."

She walks toward Scotty, but the twins continue as though she is still there.

Scotty sees her approaching and says, "Hey! We seem to have a pretty good crowd. It looks like this is going to happen."

"I'm glad," she says. "Where are Marcus and the residents?"

"I'm on my own tonight. Marcus has a Youth Group meeting at his church and Carter is out looking for trouble. "

"Trouble? It can't be another Jets game already."

"No, he's on a date with, well, let's say the girl comes with some baggage. Anyhow, I set the music up over here.

I think you'll get better sound. Just give me the cue and I'll hit the buttons."

Tommy shoots out two fingers and winks.

"Okay then, let's get the party started," she says.

As she turns, her eyes immediately roll back into her head and she is mentally kicking herself for that gesture and comment.

"Oh, my God," she mutters to herself, "who talks like that?"

During the first half of the rehearsal, Tommy is going over the steps with the group. It is a slow process, but does not require the music, so Scotty is sitting in the back of the room watching her. A woman stops outside of the glass door to the Rec Room and watches for a minute. She spots Scotty, who is still transfixed on Tommy, and comes in and moves toward him.

"Scotty?" she says.

She says this in a breathy tone as much for effect as for not disturbing the rehearsal. Scotty is startled to see Robin Danvers standing next to him, a little too closely. He stands up clearly caught by surprise.

"Robin! I didn't see you there."

"Then I guess I'll have to return this dress."

She shows the pouty look. She is wearing a skin tight red dress showing an impressive amount of cleavage. Scotty looks back to Tommy to see if she has seen Robin. Tommy seems to be engaged with a small section of the group.

"No, no," he stammers, "not at all. I was just, um, I didn't want to miss my music cue. What…um…brings you here?"

Robin is surprised, but doesn't show it. She can't remember ever having to go to her cock-teasing arsenal a second time with Scotty. She switches to the come-hither look.

"Officially, I came to see the how the flash mob was going, but I really wanted to see you."

"Oh, great, the rehearsals are really going great."

Scotty glances again at Tommy. Robin follows his gaze and gets a clearer picture, but has no intention of letting Scotty's insult go. Incensed, she switches to the salacious look.

"Well, I hope you are coming to the City Hall Christmas party tomorrow afternoon. I'll be there…with bells on."

Robin says the last part in a deep throaty whisper while leaning in so close to Scotty that she could be breastfeeding him. He can smell her perfume, which momentarily knocks Tommy out of his head. Tommy finally glances over and witnesses this exchange.

Absently, Scotty replies, "Sure, I…um…maybe I'll see you there."

Robin switches to the self-satisfied look and heads toward the door. The fog lifts and Scotty looks back toward Tommy. She is frantically trying to cue the music. Reddening, he rushes to hit the play button.

"Shit," he says.

The rest of the rehearsal goes quite well as the steps are pretty easy and go well with the music. Tommy gets back up on the chair and addresses the group.

"You are all doing great," she says, "I think this is going to be a great experience for all of you. Many of you are asking great questions and I appreciate those of you who are helping the others. Don't be afraid to ask me, particularly if you have a question about the steps."

Lew and Stew both immediately raise their hands and wave them vigorously. Tommy holds up a finger in their direction and continues.

"You may be wondering why everyone is learning the entire dance, when some of you will be starting at different times."

Lew and Stew look at each other and give each other a high five while giggling.

"I want you all to know the entire number. We will be working on the entry points at the next rehearsal on Friday. This way, if anyone does not show, we can move people around without panic. I look forward to seeing you then and don't forget to stretch before and after practice."

Tommy would normally encourage them to help rearrange the furniture, but is hoping to spend some time alone with Scotty. The room gets cleared more quickly than expected and Scotty is locking the boom box in the closet with Marcus' key. Tommy slides the last of the chairs into place and moves closer to Scotty.

"I thought it went pretty well," she says. "What did you think?"

"Oh, I thought it was great. The group is really into it."

"So who was the woman who came to see you?"

"Woman?" asks Scotty.

His brain is firing out a warning...DANGER.

"The one in red," says Tommy. "She was hard not to notice. Is she friend of yours?"

"Uh, no, no. She was just looking for her, um, grandmother's room."

More alarms go off. Scotty is wondering why he is lying.

"Wait," he says, "forget I said that. Her name is Robin...Robin Danvers. Her father is on the town council and she's on the First Night Committee. She just stopped by to see our progress."

"Interesting, and the grandmother? What was that all about?"

"To be honest, I'm not sure. I assume it was a guy thing. It felt somewhat...primeval."

"How about I treat you to a hot chocolate and we can talk about it? Marcus showed me where."

Scotty locks up the Rec Room and they head for the office. Scotty finds the key and opens the door. They head into the breakroom and Tommy begins making the drinks.

"So you were saying?" she asks. "Primeval? I take it you have a past with Robin?"

"No—I mean, yes. Oh God, kill me. Okay, yes, we have a past in that we attended college together, and no, we do not have a romantic past. In the interest of full disclosure, there may have been some lust on my part at various times over the years, but no actual, um…you know, I'd rather you just kill me."

Tommy brings over the cups and they sit down. She is smiling broadly. Scotty is digging her smile. Another alarm—dude, focus!

"Let me guess," says Tommy. "She's a bit of a tease."

"To put it mildly. Was it that obvious?"

"Women have primeval instincts as well. We can be as catty as men can be deceitful. While I will admit to having some fun at your expense, I actually found your stammering to be quite flattering."

Scotty reddens, but is smiling.

"If I'm not mistaken, you're a female," he says. "Maybe you can explain to me someday how some men can get away with the most ridiculous lies and others, myself apparently included, are completely transparent."

"If I knew that, I'd probably be running a bank or a law firm. If I had to guess, I'd say that you wanted to get caught, something having to do with guilt or punishment. The psychology can get quite disturbing, which is why I choose to be flattered. Clearly denial is my thing."

"Wow, creepy. Is that what you're studying?"

"God, no. Actually, my area focuses on the environment."

They continue to talk, covering all of the basics such as family, education, and favorite foods, before the security guard pops his head in and they realize that they've been at it for a couple of hours. They lock up and head for the parking lot. There is a dusting of snow on the ground and there are light flurries illuminated by the lights in the lot.

"I'm over here," says Tommy. "The Prius, no surprise there."

"I'd like to continue our conversation," says Scotty, "possibly over dinner tomorrow."

Tommy turns and leans on her car door.

"I think I would like that."

"Hey, I have to stop in at the Town Hall Christmas party in Montclair tomorrow afternoon. Why don't you come with me, so I can introduce you to some of the event organizers? Now that you're part of the team…"

"Are you sure it will be okay?"

"Absolutely. If we get there at 4:30, we can stay for an hour and walk to one of the restaurants downtown."

"What should I wear?"

"I believe the invitation said casual."

"What kind of casual?"

"What do you mean?"

"You know, there's business casual, smart casual, leisure casual…"

"You're kidding, right? Is this a woman thing?"

"No, it's a fashion thing. My mother and brother Pep are the experts."

"Well, I'm going with business casual since it's City Hall. Khakis and a button down shirt, which I would wear regardless of which casual we're talking about."

"Well I'll go with that, but I expect you to call me if you find the invitation is drastically different, like semi-formal or full costume. And, I'd like to meet you there, since I will be downtown with my Mom doing some shopping in the afternoon anyway, assuming you can offer me a ride home."

"Absolutely. I'm really looking forward to this. I will meet you in the foyer of the Town Hall at 4:30."

"You know, it might just be the hot chocolate talking, but I'm looking forward to it as well."

Tommy then leans forward, grabs the lapels of Scotty's jacket and gives him a firm kiss on the mouth. He is so surprised that he barely gets prepared in time. Tommy hops into her car, starts it, hits the lights and wipers and pulls away. Scotty stands motionless in the snow for another 30 seconds or so before snapping out of it and fishing his keys out of his pocket.

"Yowzah," he says.

Wednesday, Dec 19th
~ Glen Ridge ~

Elmo is sitting on the sofa watching TV. Pep is sideways on the love seat, but seems more interested in his computer than the episode of Dexter on the screen. Ramona walks in while on the screen, Dexter's sister Debra is having a typical meltdown including some extremely foul, yet colorful language. Elmo laughs out loud when the character uses the term "Fuck nuggets."

"I cannot imagine how you can watch this violent show," says Ramona, "and the language! Does anyone really talk that way?"

"You'd be surprised, Mom," says Pep. "Most people talk that way, these days. At least the young people do."

"Well I don't see the need. It's vulgar, especially for a woman."

Elmo pauses the DVR.

"C'mon Mom," he says, "how did you talk with your friends in high school and college?"

"I don't know, Elmo," says Pep. "I think Mom was born 50."

Ramona sits on the arm of the couch, but somehow makes even this casual act seem regal.

"Well first of all," she says, "I was raised to be a lady, something that was already falling out of fashion even then. I will admit, however, that I was somewhat more casual around my peers than around my parents and out in the world at large."

"Let me guess," says Elmo, "you said 'darn' and 'drat' and 'fiddle-dee-dee.'"

"And I'll bet she danced in her underwear to Elvis, or the Beatles," says Pep, grinning. "I'll bet you were into Paul—no, George—the 'quiet one.'"

"Laugh it up," she says. "Grace, manners, and decorum are all lost arts. You could learn a few things from the past."

Elmo grabs the remote.

"You're right, Ma," he says, "I think we have 'Tombstone' on demand. That was in the 1800's, I think."

"Wait, look for 'The Tudors,'" says Pep. "That goes back to the 1500's. There'll be no debauchery there."

"Okay, you win," says Ramona, "but if you must know, I was into John, the 'smart one.' I also was into the Monkees and David Cassidy, later James Taylor, and believe it or not, I had a brief fling with Ted Nugent."

"The gun nut?!" both Elmo and Pep shout nearly simultaneously.

"This was pre-gun nut," she says. "I was overcome by the…um…Cat Scratch Fever."

They are all laughing when the front door opens and Tommy walks in. She sees her mother laughing hysterically and looks at Elmo and Pep, who are clearly laughing more at her than with her. She is about to ask what is happening when Ramona looks up and sees her.

Ramona shouts, "Fuck nuggets!!" and howls with more laughter.

After a start, Elmo and Pep are roaring as well. Tommy is gaping at her mother with mock offense. Finally, the laughter subsides enough for her to speak.

"Have any of you seen my mother? She was here when I left."

Ramona gasps for breath holding her chest.

"Oh, I haven't laughed like that in a while. Sorry, honey, I was hoping to catch you before I went to bed, so we could plan tomorrow. You look so flushed. Did it get much colder?"

Tommy just smiles. It's Elmo who picks up on her reaction.

"Who's the guy?" he asks.

They all look at him, surprised, but Pep is particularly shocked that it was Elmo who picked up on this before he did. Elmo can tell this by the dumbfounded look on his face.

"How did I know?" Elmo asks. "You don't have to be a faggot to be sensitive."

"Elmo! Stop it!" shouts Ramona. "We don't talk that way in this house!"

"I was calling him a faggot," says Elmo, "long before he was a faggot."

"Maybe that's what confused him," says Ramona.

She closes her eyes and immediately regrets saying such a horrible thing, but before she can even turn to apologize, Tommy diplomatically jumps into the fray.

"Okay! We've obviously all had a long and emotional day."

She puts her arms around her mother and leads her to the stairs while Elmo and Pep alternately flash each other the bird.

"Shopping tomorrow at 10:00," says Tommy. "I need to be done by 4:30 as I am meeting someone downtown. You should get a good night's sleep. Where's Dad?"

Ramona responds absently, "He was up in his office doing some work. I expect he's in bed by now."

"Good, get some sleep. I love you, Mom."

Tommy returns to the den. Elmo is watching his show and Pep is back on his computer.

"What is wrong with you two? And what the hell was going on with Mom? 'Fuck nuggets?'"

"Forget all that," says Pep. "Who's the guy?"

"It's Scotty, the guy running the flash mob."

"Sounds gay," says Elmo.

Tommy and Pep ignore him.

"Tell me the best thing that he is," says Pep.

Tommy thinks for a few seconds.

"Sweet," she says.

"Strike one," says Elmo.

Pep rolls his eyes.

"Tell me the best thing he's not," says Pep.

This time Tommy responds almost immediately.

"Self-absorbed," she says.

"Strike two," says Elmo.

They continue to ignore him.

"I kissed him!" she says.

This gets Pep's attention and he turns to face her completely.

"Tell me how he kissed you," says Pep.

"No," she says, "*I* kissed *him.*"

Elmo throws his fist in the air with his thumb extended.

"Strike three!" he shouts.

Tommy looks at Pep, confused.

Pep shrugs and says, "He's out?"

Wednesday, Dec 19th
~ Montclair ~

Marcus is emptying the dishwasher when Scotty comes in.

"Hey," says Scotty, "how was Youth Group?"

"Fine, the kids missed you. I told them you'd be back in a few weeks, and I told them about your show. Some of them might come. I told them not to show up without parents, but I also told them how to go about asking their parents about taking them. I was able to…uhh…obtain about 20 First Night badges from a benefactor. I'll only give them out with a signed note from their parents. It might get a few of these parents more involved in their kids' lives."

"I assume Carter is still out with…um…be-donk-a-donk?"

"Yeah, looking for trouble again. The grass is always greener for him."

At that moment, the door opens and Carter walks in. He sees the others and breaks into a wide grin.

"I take it that things went well with…Cherisse, I believe it is?" says Marcus.

"You got that right, Brother. T-minus and counting," says Carter.

"What are we counting down to?" asks Scotty.

Carter mimes having a headset and radio.

"Four-Three-Two-One-Ignition. We have Pants-off!!"

"Houston, you have a problem. Isn't she currently with Gerard?" asks Marcus.

"If Gerard can't keep his woman, that's his problem. Besides, what's that little punk gonna do to me?"

"Gerard has friends, and besides, Cherisse has a big mouth," says Marcus.

"She might just be trying to make him jealous," says Scotty.

"Nonsense!" says Carter. "And she won't be the first to brag about sex with 'Carter the Magnificent.'"

"I think that was more of a public service announcement," says Scotty. "Just be careful…and while you're at it, try to be less of a pig."

"Oink, motherfucker," says Marcus. "What were you up to tonight?"

"Youth Group for me," says Marcus, nodding toward Scotty, "and rehearsal for him. Oh, and I emptied the dishwasher for your lazy-ass self."

"Hey, I'd have done it. I didn't have time between work and duding up for my rendezvous," says Carter.

He changes the subject by turning to Scotty.

"How was your thing?"

"We kissed."

This gets both of their attention.

"My man!" says Carter. "It's about time you took some initiative."

Carter holds up his hand indicating the need for a high five.

"Actually, she kissed me."

Carter pulls his hand down.

"Excuse me?" he says.

"We talked over hot chocolate, walked outside in the snow, and she grabs my coat, pulls me in, and kisses me."

"Jesus," says Carter. "If you are a representative example, the white race is doomed to extinction."

"Shut up, asshole," says Marcus. "Good for you, Scotty."

"And thanks for showing her the coffee room," says Scotty. "I wouldn't have thought of it. I'm assuming your time with her didn't end the same as mine."

"No, just laying the groundwork for you, Brother."

Marcus holds up his hand.

"Now that's worthy of a high five," says Scotty.

He gives Marcus a gentle slap.

"There is something I have to tell you, however," says Marcus.

He goes over to the kitchen and brings back three glasses, a half-full gallon jug of milk, and a bag of Fig Newtons. He drops everything on the table. Marcus distributes some napkins while Scotty pours the milk.

"Well," says Scotty, "let's have it."

"Her grandfather is a patient of mine," says Marcus. "His name is Tommaso Pastor. Ring any bells?"

Scotty shakes his head. Carter wags a finger.

"Wait, Pastor," he says. "Mob lawyer. Robert, I think. Yeah, Robert Pastor."

"Bingo," says Marcus. "That's her father. The grandpa was a big time gangster before our time. He was called Tommaso the Wolf."

"Tommy the Wolf sounds better," says Carter.

"Apparently that would get you an all-expense paid trip to the Meadowlands, one way only, from what I was able to find on the internet," says Marcus.

Scotty is dumbfounded.

"Tommy? Gangsters? Mob lawyers?" he mutters.

"Wait, hang on," says Marcus, "The dad is apparently clean. He's some brilliant accountant and lawyer who has represented the mob in several high-profile cases."

"Yeah," says Carter, "when we were kids, there was a big RICO trial in Newark. It was supposed to clean up a shitload of mob activity, you know, put dozens of high-level gangsters in jail."

"And," Marcus continues, "this young lawyer, Robert Pastor, basically makes monkeys out of the Feds and the entire Justice Department. He used some modern accounting techniques to beat their brains in. He got all of them off. They tried to profile him in Time magazine, but the mob closed ranks and he kind of disappeared from public view, but his name pops up from time to time when there is a mob trial. He's like their go-to super consultant."

"Apparently, the Feds are still afraid of him," says Carter. "Maybe you should be, too."

Marcus shoots Carter a look. Scotty still looks stunned and is holding his head in his hands. Marcus puts his hand on Scotty's shoulder.

"Relax, Brother," he says. "This doesn't change anything. I just thought you should know."

"But, I have a date with her tomorrow," says Scotty. "We're meeting at the Town Hall Christmas party and then getting dinner."

"I recommend Italian," says Carter, grinning.

"Will you please shut the fuck up?" yells Marcus.

He turns back to Scotty.

"It's fine. I spoke to both her and her grandfather. You'll be fine. Just store it away in the back of your mind."

"Jeez," says Scotty, "first Robin and then this."

"Robin?" asks Marcus.

"Uh, yeah. Robin Danvers showed up tonight. She claims she was just checking out the rehearsal, but she was dressed like a pole dancer. Nothing happened, but I was sufficiently distracted between, well, everything, to know what was going on."

"Well she's going to be at the party tomorrow for sure," says Carter. "Marcus and I will both be at work so we can't provide a diversion. We need to give Scotty a plan. She is the biggest cock tease in the free world."

Carter looks at Marcus who shifts his eyes to avert his gaze.

"Yeah, we need a plan," adds Marcus.

"Well, I'm too shot, at the moment," says Scotty. "I'm gonna shower and get some sleep. Let's reconnoiter in the morning, okay?"

Marcus nods absently. Carter waves, but continues staring at Marcus. After Scotty leaves, Carter lowers his voice and speaks.

"You fucked her!"

"Don't ever mention this to Scotty."

"Dude, I would never do that to him or you, but you gotta admit, this is earth shattering news."

"Look, it was way back in college, probably before Scotty even knew who she was and certainly before she made him her guinea pig for her bizarre cock teasing experiments. She didn't know we were friends at the time either."

"So it was just the one time?"

Marcus looks down.

"Are you kidding me?" asks Carter.

"Look, a few times, when Scotty was interested in another girl, I took one for the team and 'distracted' Robin. She really gets off on screwing up Scotty's relationships."

"Okay, I've seen her in action, including that particular peccadillo, but taking one for the team? Seriously? When I 'take one for the team,' it generally involves working a double shift or helping someone move a sofa. It has never involved fucking a hot white chick."

"Can we just drop this?"

"Just promise me that I can be there when you ask your boss for a few hours off to go to a Christmas party so you can fuck the hot babe who is trying to cock tease your friend out of a potential relationship with a mafioso's daughter."

"Shut the fuck up. I'm begging you."

Thursday, Dec 20th
~ Glen Ridge ~

It's nearly 8:00 AM and Robert is sitting on a barstool at the kitchen counter drinking coffee with his right hand, and reading the Wall Street Journal with his left.

"The eggs were great, Ro," he says, "thanks."

"Notice anything different?" asks Ramona.

He puts down his paper.

"I don't know, maybe a little lighter? Did you use less love?"

He is smiling. Although Ramona is in a robe and apron, she is still the most beautiful thing he has ever seen. She looks at him sardonically.

"No, but I tried Egg Beaters instead of real eggs. Your doctor said—"

"Please, not the cholesterol again," he says. "They were slightly thin and slightly bland."

He walks around the counter and pats her on the behind.

He leans in and whispers, "Nothing a little hollandaise sauce wouldn't fix."

Robert kisses her on the neck.

"Oh, stop," she says. "Look at my hair. You were working awfully late last night. I was hoping you'd get some time off for the holidays."

"I'm trying, Babe. There is something brewing at the bank. I don't think federal regulators have families."

Elmo walks in and asks, "Is there anything I can do to help, Pop?"

"Only if you have a Master's in finance."

Robert immediately regrets the way this came out.

"Sorry to disappoint you again, Pop," says Elmo.

Ramona immediately moves in to change the subject.

"I gave you Caprese salad for lunch, so remember to put it in the refrigerator. I sprinkled extra basil on it for you."

Robert kisses her and tries to think of something to say to Elmo.

"See you later, son," is all he can manage.

"Why don't you grow your own?" asks Elmo.

Ramona looks around to see if anyone else is in the room.

"Grow my own what?"

"Basil. Why don't you grow your own basil? It's a hundred times better than that crap in the spice cabinet."

"Well, for one, I'm not a farmer. You also may have noticed that it's about 25 degrees outside."

Elmo is pouring a bowl of cereal.

"No, inside. It's easy. You can use the sunroom."

At this moment, Tommy walks in wearing a plush robe and fuzzy slippers. Ramona is happy for an opportunity to change the subject yet again.

"Good morning, sweetie. Can I fix you something for breakfast?"

"Please tell me we have some bagels. Boston has its charms, but making bagels is not among them."

Tommy opens the breadbox, finding only some extreme bran loaf.

"Crap," she says.

"Have no fear, Mommy's here!" squeals Ramona.

She reaches deep into a low cabinet and brings out a plastic bag containing the forbidden carbs.

"I have to hide these from your father. Now tell me, was I dreaming, or did I hear something about some kissing last night?"

"Yes, you heard correctly, and you may also recall that I am meeting him at the Montclair Town Hall Christmas party at 4:30 and we are going to dinner afterward."

"Ooh! I'll buy you a new outfit today."

"Mom, I have plenty of clothes. I'm more concerned with what I was thinking, or rather not thinking."

"What do you mean?"

Elmo, who has been reading the sports page, says, "*She* kissed *him*."

"Oh, my," says Ramona, "that does seem a little forward for you."

"I know things are different from when you were young, but it almost felt like I was watching someone else, you know? In any case, I have no idea why I would get involved with someone here when I am only in town for a couple of weeks."

"Well it sounds like you had a spark, and that can happen anytime."

"It's just not *me*."

"Look, honey. You're talking to a person who goes to Rite-Aid, and then across the street to CVS, to buy chocolate and tampons separately so the cashier won't judge me. Keep an open mind."

"Gross," says Elmo. "I'm still here."

"Well, in that case," says Tommy, "I'll be open minded about the outfit as well. Oh, and Pep will not be joining us. He was up late watching half a season of Buffy the Vampire Slayer. He's going out with his band geek friends for dinner tonight."

"I won't be home for dinner either," says Elmo. "I'm going to visit Grandpa and then go out with Donny."

Elmo rinses out his bowl and heads upstairs.

"Looks like it will just be your father and me for dinner. Maybe I'll meet him downtown. In any case, let's get in the shower so we can go SHOPPING!"

She takes Tommy's hand and looks at her nails.

"And maybe we can squeeze in a manicure."

Thursday, Dec 20th
~ Montclair ~

Ramona and Tommy are walking past the stores on Church Street. Tommy is wearing a new outfit. It is a mid-length dress in a hounds tooth print. It is appropriate for winter, but is light enough to have some movement. It is both professional and stylish with a slight 60's modish look. She is wearing a red patent leather belt and dark grey, suede, short boots. Her nails are freshly polished in a red matte finish with gloss red French tips. Ramona grabs her by the arm and ushers her into a boutique.

"I must admit that your saleswoman is quite the diplomat," says Tommy.

"Well, I suppose we probably should have discussed the 'fashion vs. function' issue before we walked in," says Ramona. "She seemed a little distressed there for a while."

"She recovered nicely. I have a hard time buying an outfit just for show. It goes against my personal philosophy."

"Think of it as plumage. If birds had your philosophy, they'd all be extinct."

"Well, I must admit, I'm happy with the result. I just didn't count on all of the accessorizing. It's exhausting."

"I'm just getting warmed up. Of course, I've spent the past several years building up my shopping muscles. Tommasina, if you learned anything today, please let it be that Gor-Tex is only fashionable if you are romancing a Sherpa. Oh, wait! There it is—the finishing touch."

"Mom, no more touches. You've spent over $200 already."

But it is too late. Ramona has already run into the store. She reaches and picks up a red beret from a rack sitting on a display case.

"Here, put this on," she says.

"A beret? Don't you think that's a bit much?"

Tommy looks at the price tag.

"Whoa, it's actually too way too much," she says.

"Just put it on. Oh it's perfect. Here, look in the mirror."

She drags Tommy to the full length mirror. Tommy is impressed. It actually does make the outfit.

"No, I can't let you spend any more money. Besides, how often am I going to wear a red beret?"

"It's like they say about the atomic bomb. If you use it right the first time, you won't need to use it again."

"What? Mom, please tell me who says that. You need to stop hanging around with people like that. Besides, I just don't need a hat."

"It's not for you, it's for *him*."

"Him? Who, him?"

"Your date. You said his name is Scotty?"

"Why am I buying Scotty a hat? I'm confused."

"Ugh! No wonder I have no grandchildren. It's not *for* him, it's FOR him."

"Please kill me."

"Let me explain. This hat sets the outfit apart. It sets you apart. And when he sees it for the first time, all of the outside distractions disappear. It creates the illusion that you are all for him. It has a very powerful effect on a man."

"Mom, you're delusional. Did this work on Daddy?"

"It works on all men, believe me. Your father is no different. He gets horny when I give him the largest pork chop."

"I'd hurl if I hadn't already done that in front of Scotty."

"Sorry, but the point is that he won't even know why he feels like more of a man. It's a powerful tool."

"Got it, berets and pork chops, powerful tools. Who needs a PhD, anyway?"

"I've often wondered the same thing, honey."

Tommy shoots her a look before realizing that she's been had. She laughs and they buy the hat. Ramona is pleased with herself.

"Okay Mom, I'm off to City Hall for my date. I'll let you know how it goes with the hat."

"I'd wish you luck, but you won't need it. I'm going home to drop off our packages and then I'm meeting your father at Merola's for a romantic dinner."

Tommy smiles and hugs her mother.

"Pork chops, no doubt," whispers Tommy.

Thursday, Dec 20th
~ West Orange ~

Marcus walks into Tommaso Pastor's room and gives it the once-over. Tommaso is reading a newspaper and puts it down when he sees Marcus.

"Marcus, to what do I owe the pleasure? Our session is not until 3:30."

"I'm just making the rounds, eye-balling things."

"Bullshit. You do that every morning."

Marcus smiles.

"Okay. I hear you haven't been eating."

"I'll make a deal with you. If you eat this shit, I'll eat it."

"Sorry, Mr. Pastor, you're not the first to make me that offer. I didn't last one meal, so I feel your pain. It's simple biology. The stronger you get, the sooner you leave."

"I can't argue with that. I have another question. When is the next rehearsal?"

"With your granddaughter? Tomorrow evening. I'm afraid I cannot not permit you to dance, however."

Tommaso ignores the joke.

"I'd like to be there, to watch."

"You mean to check out Scotty."

"I promise I won't kill him, and I'm pretty sure he can outrun me at this point. Can I go?"

"Well you're not ambulatory—"

"Marcus, no jargon, yes or no?"

"Wheelchair, only if you can do it without pain. I'll tell you what. I'm on lunch now. Let me take you for a walk. I'll get you something substantial at the commissary, and we'll see how you feel. If you're still feeling good by our session this afternoon, I'll take you to the rehearsal myself."

"Fair enough. Is the food better there?"

"Nearly disgusting. I think you'll find it to be a significant improvement over what you have been eating, or rather, not eating. I'll be right back with a wheelchair."

Marcus brings the chair and carefully maneuvers Tommaso into it.

"Okay so far?" he asks.

"Don't treat me like an invalid."

"As long as you don't try to be a hero."

"Fair enough. Wait, not without the cane."

"Is it okay if I touch it, Your Majesty? You are aware that a cane is for walking and not riding, right?"

He hands Tommaso the cane and they head out the door. The commissary is open to the lobby, separated by a row of tall potted plants. They pick out the least vile looking food options and move to a table by the window.

"Well, it may look awful, but at least it smells like shit," says Tommaso.

"Stop complaining. We just got raised to no stars by Zagat. May I ask about the cane?"

"Why not? I think we understand each other. Of course this is just between us."

"Certainly."

"Okay, you said you've read up on me. Let me guess, 'notorious enforcer for the Pizzoli crime family. Right hand to Godfather Enrico Pizzoli himself. Later became a master fixer and Consigliere.'"

"I don't believe that it said *master* fixer, but that's pretty much it."

Tommaso smiles and gives Marcus a conciliatory nod.

"You're funny, Marcus, but not quite so funny as you think you are. Anyhow, that description is not entirely accurate."

"How so, if I may ask without getting…I believe the term is 'made?'"

"This is a good example. Allow me to digress. Traditionally the term 'made' referred to being fully initiated into the family, if you will. It was about an oath, an honor, a commitment. Later, between the movies and some particularly violent factions, it became generally assumed that it involved a murder."

"That would be my understanding."

"And not just any murder. Murders for personal reasons don't count these days."

"I get it. This is a common practice now in gangs where I'm from, where my mother still lives. It didn't used to be that way."

"Exactly. Animals, and not just the gangs—my people as well."

"No value for human life."

"True, but the real problem is no value of honor. I've known you long enough to know that you are a man of honor. Honor to your friends, your family, your patients, and most of all, to yourself."

"Thank you."

"Now, of course, I couldn't consider you 'made' based on this, but it allows me to cultivate trust, so you might even get 'made' based on a preponderance of actions."

"But doesn't murder, or at least some other high crime, lock me in, you know, as a co-conspirator?"

"That's the problem. It was a shortcut to try to replace the long-term building of trust. The worst part is it makes people desperate. If they do get caught, they have no choice but to rat because they all have something to offer. Then, there's more killing to shut people up. Once the paranoia starts, everyone is at risk, including the innocents, which just brings more scrutiny."

"I wish you were teaching some of my business courses in college. I actually would be running this place."

"Start with fixing the food."

"Done. Okay, explain this to me. Doesn't the trust system leave you more vulnerable to infiltration by, I don't know, undercover operatives?"

"Good question. Actually, no. First of all, murder makes the front page. Managing a criminal enterprise gets much less hassle when it stays out of the headlines. You have no idea what a RICO investigation costs the taxpayers, let alone a trial. We could have colonized Saturn by now. Second, it's actually a lot easier for an undercover to fake a murder than to truly gain trust over time. No one can keep up the act long enough."

"Interesting. So how does the cane fit in?"

"I wasn't 'made' by killing anyone."

"Ever?"

"Never. I can't say that I never made a management decision that led to a death or two, but how's that different from Lee Iacocca? He was the main force behind the Ford Pinto, for God's sake."

"I never looked at it that way."

"No one does, and I'm sure he sleeps like a baby, just like the insurers, the lawyers, the pharmaceutical makers. Need I go on?"

"It's something to think about."

"Okay, the cane. I came to this country in 1942. I was 12 years old. I stowed away on a merchant ship, didn't eat for

10 days. I end up in Hoboken with no papers, no people, no nothing. I lived in the street, and spoke minimal English. When I found people speaking Italian, I found that they were looked upon as dirt here, something I'm sure you can relate to."

"So they were forced to resort to crime."

"Forced, I'm not sure, but yes, a criminal culture. I was young and looked younger. I picked pockets, participated in small cons, and scammed the child service system."

"No school?"

"For what? I was smart and was taken under the wing of Roberto Pizzoli, the younger brother of Enrico. Of course Enrico wasn't Don, yet, not even close. Roberto was brilliant. He understood business and human nature. He could have done anything if Italians weren't discriminated against. Again, I know you understand. Enrico, on the other hand was as ruthless as Roberto was intelligent. He didn't like Roberto keeping me around so much."

"I'm assuming Enrico preferred the more...um...concrete exhibition of trust."

"Exactly. You know, Marcus, it is a pleasure to converse with someone who doesn't need everything repeated or explained. Sadly, it's rare these days."

Marcus nods.

"Anyhow, Roberto convinces Enrico to give me more responsibility. He puts me on a protection detail since Enrico is in a war for control of most of North Jersey, but, he sticks me out in the back entrance of the tenement where the family is based. I'm carrying a gun that's nearly as big as I am and have no idea how to use it, and I'm stationed with an oaf who is on the same detail because he is mentally incapable of anything but punching. Of course, he has a gun as well."

"Great story, but don't stop eating. We have a deal."

"So a rival family attacks the house. This is a major breach of protocol, even during wartime. I hear some movement in the alley behind the house. We keep a spare car there for emergencies, but otherwise the alley should be empty. I tell Dominic, the oaf, to take a defensive position on the stoop, while pointing up the alley. He immediately walks into the alley and takes one to the face. At the first shot, I hear all hell break loose out front. I sneak behind the six foot retaining wall between the house and the alley. I know there's some stone blocks in the corner, so I climb to the top of the wall. I can see that there are three guys in the alley almost near the house. I figure that the Pizzolis' only chance of escape is the car in the alley, so I run across the top of the wall toward the entrance. At this point, Enrico and Roberto burst out of the back door, but the three guys see me first, so they are looking at me. The second guy picks up his gun to shoot me, but I dive down on the first guy, to stop him. The second guy fires, and creases my scalp right here."

He points to a spot just above his left ear and continues.

"I land on the first guy and club him with my gun and he's out. Enrico shoots the second guy, but doesn't see the third guy coming around the corner. I want to save Roberto, who is kind of frozen, and rush to get between him and the third guy. I'm right in front of Enrico when the guy shoots. He blows up my hip, which effectively saves Enrico. Enrico then kills the third guy. Mind you, there's still shooting like crazy in the street. Enrico heads for the car, but Roberto won't leave me. After a brief argument, Enrico helps Roberto drag me to the car and we make it out."

"Damn. Wait, what about the guy you knocked out?"

"Oh, Enrico emptied his gun into him before he ever considered saving me."

"Ah, family. Good times. This is when Enrico took over, I assume."

"Oh, did he ever. The war ended quickly, primarily because Enrico pretty much killed all of the competition. He took over as Don and the Pizzolis have run things ever since. Well, it turns out that Roberto took a bullet inside the house, in his side. We both survived, but my hip was shattered and I needed many months of recovery. Roberto insisted that I recover in the family compound so I could have the best care. Since Enrico had to admit that I had saved his life, he agreed. Roberto was not so lucky, however. He had infection problems and could never beat them. He lived for several months, but eventually died from his wound."

"I'm sorry. Roberto. Your son?"

"Yes, named in his honor, but Robert, not Roberto. That comes later. Roberto took me under his wing while we, or at least I, recuperated. He taught me proper English, accounting, but mostly, how to solve problems. After he died, Enrico needed to keep me around. I kind of assumed Roberto's position as a fixer. I also had the highest status since I took a bullet for the Don. The story got more heroic over the years, but was essentially true. I later fell in love with Enrico's daughter and married her, which separated me even further from potentially violent actions. Since my hip never fully recovered, he gave me this cane as a wedding present. It represents the she-wolf that suckled Romulus and Remus."

"But it also came to represent the brutality of the Pizzoli family and made your reputation as an enforcer."

"Ironically so. Unfortunately, it also cast a shadow upon my son and now possibly his children."

"Things are never as cut and dried as they seem."

"Well, I hope they will be soon. I have reached a point in my life where I need to make some changes."

"You're going to recover."

"No, Marcus. I'm not having a great awakening, nor am I preparing to die. But, I do have one regret in life and I need to fix it before it gets worse."

Tommaso explains to Marcus how he and his wife desperately tried to keep Robert out of the family business and how it is potentially affecting the next generation.

"She was the love of my life and I let her down," says Tommaso. "Thankfully the cancer took her before Robert got involved in the business. I still feel an obligation to her."

"I'm sorry."

"Here's the thing, Marcus—and this, my family doesn't even know. No one knows."

"Are you sure you want to do this?"

"I am, and I need your advice."

At this point, Elmo walks into the front entrance. He sees his grandfather at a table facing away from him talking to an African-American in scrubs. He is about to go into the commissary, but decides to wait. He takes a seat by the plants separating himself from the two of them. He finds that he can hear their conversation.

"There is a safety deposit box in the First National Bank in Montclair," says Tommaso.

"I know the place. It's right downtown, actually a few blocks from my apartment," says Marcus.

"Well, I got a box there years ago, under an assumed name. No one else knew. Not my wife, my son, the bosses. I have something in there that is very personal and could shake some things up. Not a smoking gun or evidence on anyone. It's really about me."

"So what's the problem?"

Elmo is curious why his grandfather would share this with a stranger, let alone a black stranger, but his wandering attention span keeps him from focusing too deeply on this. He absently sticks two fingers in the dirt inside the planter box. He removes them, rubs them together, and looks at them. He shakes his head in disgust. He refocuses on his grandfather's conversation.

"Three problems. Number one, I can't get to the box. Not only am I stuck here, but also, I took out the box before I was known. People know my face. Now they even have software to find you on the camera."

"Do you really think anyone is looking that carefully? You could leave that cane in the car, you know. You'll be walking in there within a month."

"That's problems two and three. They're always looking at high ranking crime figures, even those of us who are lucky enough to make it to 82. If the Feds catch me using an assumed name, they can get a warrant for the box contents. What's worse is that the bank has been purchased by one of our interests."

"You mean the Family?"

"Not precisely, but close enough for the Feds to be nosing around."

"Can your son help?"

"That's the worst part. His office is in the bank building now. The whole point is to remove him from scrutiny, and this could be very bad for him."

"Hmm, what about problem three?"

"The timing. I wanted to get the contents by the 31st."

"That is a problem. Even with the remarkable progress you're making, it's less than two weeks. You won't be released by then. Your previous damage to your hip is going to be an issue. Why the deadline?"

"New banking regulations take place on the second of January. I have it on good authority that the Feds are planning something ineffective, but potentially damaging. I should have handled this sooner, but I didn't expect to break my hip."

"On the other hand, it appears that your accident was the catalyst for making the move."

"Tell me what I don't know."

"Okay, I need to get back to work. I'll think about this and we can discuss your dance rehearsal when I see you at therapy. I appreciate you confiding in me."

"Why not, you've seen my balls."

"I'm serious, Mr. Pastor."

"I know, and no thanks for lunch."

Elmo gets up and leaves before his grandfather is turned around. He heads for the door and to his car. Marcus cleans up the table and brings Tommaso back to his room.

Thursday, Dec 20th
~ Montclair ~

Tommy walks to the City Hall complex. She checks her reflection in the window and opens her coat to best show off her outfit. At the last moment, she shakes her head, adjusts her beret, takes a deep breath, and heads inside. Scotty is at the east end of the foyer near the Council Room where the party is being held. Upon seeing Tommy, he actually stops breathing for a moment. Scotty is wearing dark brown dress pants and a pale yellow dress shirt. He has on a sharp beige jacket with an elegant print tie and a brown silk pocket square. He's glad that he dressed up, or more accurately, that his roommates dressed him up. Tommy turns his way and smiles. He hesitates and then moves toward her, possibly a little too fast, and nearly runs into her.

"Oh, sorry, I mean, hi."

Tommy is smiling, both at his reaction and about how pleased her mother will be when she hears about her latest triumph. Scotty exhales.

"Whew," he says. "What I really meant to say is, wow! You look spectacular."

Tommy figures she may as well give her mother the full report.

"How do you like the beret? I thought it might be too much."

"Too much? God, no. It's perfect. I felt like Tony in West Side Story, when he sees Maria for the first time. Everything else fades into a blur."

"It could also be a sign of a stroke."

"What?"

"The blurred vision. Sorry, never mind. It was just a feeble attempt at humor."

Tommy thinks to herself, "That didn't take long. Note to self: Way to blow the big entrance. Save the dry wit for later. Try keeping your mouth shut."

She says, "You look very nice as well. What happened to the casual look?"

"Well, let me take your coat and I'll try to explain."

He takes her coat, drops it off in the makeshift coatroom, and they head toward the party.

"First of all, I wasn't thinking that I would have an escort when I originally planned my wardrobe. Most of all, my roommates made me upgrade."

"It's nice that they look out for you."

"You don't know the half of it. The shirt, socks, and underwear are mine. The jacket and pants belong to Marcus, and the shoes, tie, and pocket square are Carter's."

"That's sweet. Do they always dress you?"

"No, just on special occasions, or when I am clueless about what looks good. They are both snappy dressers, particularly Carter. He even irons his underwear."

"Really?"

"I'm serious. If I spill cocktail sauce on his tie, I'll have to join the circus."

"Well, they have good taste."

"They definitely know how to dress."

"I meant that they have good taste in friends."

Scotty looks at her and grins. Tommy takes his arm and thinks, "Bam! Now we're finding our groove."

Scotty stops by the table verifying that he is on the guest list and gets a nametag for himself and his "plus one." He also is handed two drink tickets.

"Do you mind if I don't wear the name tag?" says Tommy. "I think the adhesive might be bad for this material."

Scotty bows and with a flourish waves his hand toward the party.

"As you wish, m'lady," he says, in some sort of an unidentifiable accent.

Before he even finishes the flourish, Scotty imagines that this action will brand him as the biggest douchebag on the planet. There is a makeshift bar in one corner of the room. In order to quickly change the subject, he asks Tommy if she would like something from the bar.

Tommy rarely drinks, but doesn't want to come across as prudish. She mentally matches all possible drink options against the expected male reaction, also factoring in the alcohol content and its effect on her small frame and empty stomach.

"I suppose a white wine would be nice."

He brings her a white wine and has what appears to be a cola for himself. Tommy is mentally kicking herself. Her analysis failed to consider that he wasn't drinking. Rookie mistake. Maybe he has rum in his coke.

"I have an extra ticket if you want another one," he says.

Tommy begins to feel sweat under her beret. She makes a mental note to kill Mom before cutting her wrists later. Deciding that it may act as a depressant and slow her heartbeat, she takes a larger than normal slug of the wine.

"Nothing for you?" she asks.

"No, I don't drink. I have no moral objection. I just never developed a taste for it."

"So no drunken orgies at your bachelor pad?"

"Nope, Marcus doesn't drink at all. Carter likes an occasional cocktail, or a beer at a sporting event, but I think he mostly likes the look."

"What do you mean?"

"If he read in Esquire that it was suave and debonair to drink paint, he'd be at Benjamin Moore buying a six pack right now."

Scotty is acutely aware that he needs to steer the conversation away from his roommates and toward himself.

"I'd introduce you around, but I know very few people here personally," he says.

Tommy is relieved as nearly everyone here knows of her father and she'd just as soon remain anonymous, at least until they've had a few more dates, or possibly after their wedding. "Yikes," she thinks, and takes another gulp of wine.

"McCall!" someone calls out, from halfway across the room.

Scotty turns and sees Dale Hankins. He suppresses a wince and waves to him. Dale walks over. He's wearing a cheap looking sport coat and tie.

"Scotty, I thought that was you. What brings you here? I thought this was for the connected people. I'm guessing he's with you," says Dale, turning toward Tommy. "No nametag. I'm guessing you're one of the new office temps."

"No, Dale," says Scotty. "I'm here as part of the First Night event. This is my escort. Tommy Pastor, meet Dale Hankins. We went to school together through high school."

Tommy was hoping that Scotty would not use her last name. Her douche meter is already off the charts with Dale.

"It's a pleasure to meet you," she says.

She slugs down the last of her wine.

Dale ignores her and turns back to Scotty.

"I guess you heard? I made Detective, youngest ever in the history of the squad."

"You must be good," says Tommy. "You had me pegged as an office temp right away."

Scotty nearly chokes on his soda. Tommy decides to dial it back.

"Good for you," says Scotty.

"Yeah, I plan to really shake up this department. We got a lot of dead wood here."

"I'm sure you had to put a lot of people out of commission to get there," says Scotty.

"I took down my share."

"I think he meant your co-workers," says Tommy.

Scotty looks at Tommy with mild shock. Fortunately, Dale is so full of himself that he misses or at least ignores, the crack.

"Yeah," says Dale, "this is my uniform now, strictly jacket and tie."

"Nice," says Tommy. "Is that from the Lenny Briscoe collection?"

Tommy cannot figure out why she is having so much trouble controlling herself, but Scotty is very impressed. She may be the one.

Dale sees Alex Gersten nearby and seizes the opportunity to suck up to him.

"Hey, Alex, let me introduce you to a couple of people."

Alex sees no immediate escape options, and comes over. He is impeccably dressed and extends his hand to Scotty. Alex acts as though he is the host.

"Welcome to the party. My name is Alex Gersten. I'm the Assistant Prosecutor for the County. It's a pleasure to meet you."

Before he can move on to Tommy, Dale jumps in awkwardly.

"This is his friend Tommy…um…Tommy…"

Tommy is pleased to catch a break. One benefit of Dale being a lousy detective and all-around tool is that he can't remember her name.

"Pastor, Tommy Pastor," says Scotty, clueless.

Unlike Dale, Alex immediately knows who she is. Alex extends his hand. She knows that he knows.

"Ms. Pastor, it's a pleasure to meet you."

"Charmed," she says. "Scotty, I think I may need some more wine."

"Um, sure," he says. "Nice meeting you, Alex, and congratulations, Dale."

They move toward the bar. After watching to see that they are out of earshot, Alex turns to Dale.

"How do you know them?"

Dale is pleased that Alex is interested enough to keep talking to him.

"I went to school with him. Her, I just met. He's here because of the First Night thing."

"You know who she is?"

Dale gives him a conspiratorial wink.

"No, but I saw her first. I think she's a new temp."

"I'm not interested in her, you idiot, at least not for that. And she's no temp, either. Her father is Robert Pastor."

"Who's that?"

"Jesus Christ, Hawkins."

"Er...*Hankins.*"

"Whatever. How did you make detective? Robert Pastor, the mob lawyer? He's been beating our brains in for years."

"Oh, yeah, him."

Alex raises an eyebrow.

"Look, kid. Beating Robert Pastor would be my ticket to...well, I could write my own ticket. You'd be doing yourself a favor if you kept an eye on them."

"I read you loud and clear, sir."

Tommy is halfway through her second wine and is wondering what else could go wrong.

"Your friend Dale seems like a credit to the force," she says.

She wonders if that sounded too harsh.

"Oh, I wouldn't call him a friend. Assuming I read your sarcasm accurately, you are correct about him being a bit slow on the uptake. We sat next to each other in band for the entirety of our freshman year of high school. I played first alto and he played second. Saxophones, I mean. He wanted to fight me, literally, every day. He said to meet him beyond the bandroom after school."

"And?" she asks, "Did you give him the beating he deserved?"

"No, I never showed up. To this day I don't actually know if he was ever there waiting. It got to be kind of a joke among the other people in our section."

Tommy smiles. She likes this. She likes him. She might even forgive him outing her to the Prosecutor. Suddenly, it's Scotty's turn to panic. Robin Danvers is approaching. She's wearing a black cocktail dress that appears to be painted on. She is wearing a Santa hat and red high heels at least 6 inches long. She clearly got an early start at the bar.

"Yoo hoo!" she squeals. "I've been looking for you."

She gives him a far too friendly hug and hangs on for several seconds too long. Robin is swimming in perfume and now Scotty is as well.

"Robin, hey," he says, "I'd like you to meet someone."

"Oh, this is the dancer, from last night. I'm Robin. I picked Scotty to do the flash mob. I *sooo* enjoy working with him."

"Don't we all? It seems that you and Scotty are good friends."

"Oh, the best! We went to college together. Fun times, right Scotty?"

Scotty is looking for a hole to jump into.

"Why don't you two catch up for a minute," says Tommy. "I need to powder my nose."

Scotty's eyes widen in panic as she moves toward the hallway. Moving across the room she notices Dale Hankins following her with his eyes the entire way. In the restroom, Tommy dabs her forehead and the back of her neck with a damp paper towel. She looks in the mirror and wonders why she had the wine. She wonders what that ho-bag Robin is up to. Most of all, she wonders if her father's business is going to doom her to become the cat lady, or some other spinster character. She decides to suck it up and make this date work.

She reenters the Council Room and sees Robin dragging Scotty toward a rear doorway in the room. Tommy immediately sees the mistletoe hanging from the door jamb. Robin takes Scotty by the lapels and plants a big wet open-mouthed kiss on him. By the time he pushes her off, he already knows that Tommy has witnessed this. He can feel it.

"Thanks a lot, Robin."

He walks toward Tommy, already knowing what's coming.

"Any time, big boy," says Robin, after him.

Scotty approaches Tommy feeling like his head will explode. At least she won't see him cry.

Tommy says quietly, "I think you'd better take me home."

Other than giving directions, they ride silently to Glen Ridge, neither of them knowing what to say.

Scotty pulls in front of Tommy's house. Tommy holds up her hand when Scotty moves to get out of the car. She gets out of the car and turns to close the door.

"I'm sorry," she says.

Robert O'Connell

She heads up the walk.

Friday, Dec 21st
~ Montclair ~

"Sorry, Bro," says Carter, "I wish I could've been there. I'd have intervened."

Carter is at the table dressed for work, finishing a bowl of cereal. Marcus is sitting across from him looking over some paperwork and Scotty is making some scrambled eggs.

"I don't know what you could've done," says Scotty. "It all happened kind of fast."

"Still, I'd have liked to slap that bitch," says Carter.

"What's done is done," says Marcus. "It might not be that bad."

"I don't see how," says Scotty. "She looked mortified. You want cheese, Marcus?"

"Sure, whatever. What I mean is that it makes a difference about why she was embarrassed."

"Oh, here it comes," says Carter. "Dr. Phil is on."

Marcus ignores him.

"If she was embarrassed by you, I agree that you're probably screwed, but she may have been embarrassed by her own behavior."

"I don't see the distinction, nor do I see how it makes a difference," says Scotty.

He brings a plate to Marcus and sits down with his own.

"Jealousy, Brother. I know she digs you. If she was jealous when she saw Robin's stunt, she might be embarrassed about that, and that could be recoverable. It's good that you didn't overreact and handled it like a gentleman. Sometimes people are looking for an excuse to test a relationship early by subconsciously torpedoing it."

"You are out of your fucking mind," says Carter.

"If you had an ounce of sensitivity, asshole, you and Mr. Pete down there might get a second date once in a while."

"Oh, thank you Imperial Groove Master. Please teach me. How can I start?"

"You can start by rinsing out your bowl properly."

Carter gets up and bows.

"Yes, Sensei. Wax on, wax off."

"Can we get back to my problem?" asks Scotty. "I don't even know if she'll show up to rehearsal tonight."

"She'll show, and I'll be there."

"What if Robin shows up?"

"Unlikely, but if she does, I'll take care of her."

Marcus shoots Carter a look as he says this.

"Dear me, look at the time," says Carter. "I must be off to work."

Marcus turns back to Scotty after Carter leaves.

"God, she looked so beautiful," says Scotty. "You should have seen her."

"Focus, Scotty," says Marcus. "There might also be something else at work here. Tell me exactly what happened with the detective and the lawyer."

Friday, Dec 21st
~ Glen Ridge ~

"I'm sorry, Sis. Can you run through this again? I don't want to get it wrong in my memoir," says Pep.

Pep and Tommy are in his bedroom. He's rolled up in his covers and she's curled up at the foot of his bed.

"A cautionary tale?" she asks.

"It would make one hell of a blog."

She repeats the highlights of the story.

"At least he wasn't an asshole about it," says Pep.

"No, he was a perfect gentleman. It would be easier if he were a jerk. He seemed more concerned about my feelings than his."

"Don't you just hate that?"

"No, what I mean is that I've dated a few jerks in my time. The one saving grace is that the breakup is a relief. Sometimes it's actually the most enjoyable part of the relationship."

"See? That's another blog post, right there. It could be the new disorder, binging and purging relationships."

"You're a disturbed individual, baby Bro. I just wished she hadn't kissed him like that. She was a real piece of work."

"Jealous much?"

"You should have seen his face. He was so embarrassed. I almost felt sorry for him."

"Then why did you bail?"

"I was already reeling from the episode with the prosecutor. The cop was an idiot, but this guy knew who I was. I wasn't ready to get into that with Scotty. The wine didn't help, either."

"That's not gonna go away, you know. The 'who you are,' not the wine, I mean."

"My life sucks."

"Yeah, but the good news is that the humiliation will soon be forgotten. You have another rehearsal tonight."

Tommy grabs one of her brother's pillows and whacks him over the head.

At this point, Ramona walks in wearing her robe. She sits on the bed beside Tommy.

"So, I take it that things didn't go so well yesterday," she says, stroking her daughter's hair. "You came home quite a bit earlier than I expected."

"First off, I must tell you that you were spot on about the beret, but it was pretty downhill from there. I'd have told you about it, but you and Dad were apparently up here getting ready for your dinner."

"Yes," she says, looking away, "that's exactly what we were doing."

Pep covers his head with his pillow and shouts, "I'm blind!"

"Oh, gross," says Tommy. "Why would you mention that?"

Ramona gives Tommy a little shove.

"Why is it romantic for you, but gross for me?" she asks.

"Tell her, Sis," says Pep.

Tommy turns to Ramona and says, "Think of it as *your* parents naked."

Ramona shudders.

"Okay," says Ramona, "I see your point. So what happened?"

"Basically, I'm probably too smart for my own good. Either that or I actually have a physical need for mortification. In any case, I'd be shocked if he ever looked at me again."

"Don't be so sure," says Ramona. "Boys have a way of filtering out a lot of noise when there is a girl involved."

Pep peeks out of his pillow at his mother. Tommy shakes him off and he slides back into his nest.

"I hope so, Mom," says Tommy. "I really hope so."

Friday, Dec 21st
~ Bloomfield ~

Donny is in the back of the garage in front of a large utility sink. Elmo is sitting on a stool next to a desk covered in work orders. Donny grabs a handful of white glop out of a can and rubs it vigorously on his hands. The glop turns gray as the grease cutting solvent works its chemical magic.

"I wish this shit didn't stink so much," says Donny. "I'd almost prefer the grease."

"You should try mint leaves," says Elmo.

"What?"

"Mint leaves, it gets the smell off your hands. Parsley works, too."

"What the fuck are you talking about?"

Donny rinses his hands and dries them and then checks his fingernails.

"God, I hate this fucking job. This shit's never coming off," he says.

He gives his hands a sniff. Donny then grabs a scented pine tree shaped air freshener off of a pile on the desk. He uses his teeth to rip off the cellophane and spits the wrapper onto the floor. He then rubs the air freshener on his hands. He crushes the pine tree and tosses it at Elmo.

"Here, have some fucking mint leaves. Let's go."

They get in Elmo's car and head out onto Bloomfield Avenue.

"Where you want to eat?" asks Elmo. "Hooters okay?"

"Nah, I had tits for lunch. Let's go to Shorty's. We can shoot some pool after."

"Works for me."

Elmo hits his turn signal and heads toward Clifton.

"You talk to your grandfather yet?"

"I went to see him today, but didn't talk to him."

"Come on, E, I'm going fucking crazy in that shop. They give me all the shit jobs. The owner, Hoosmanian, he's got two sons and like a million fucking nephews. None of them know shit, and none of them do shit, but they're all ahead of me."

"Wait, Donny, lemme finish. I overheard him talking to some doctor. He's got some big secret in a safety deposit box in the bank in Montclair, the one where my Pop works."

"So?"

"I don't have all the details, but he needs to get in it before January, and he can't 'cause of his hip."

"So why can't your dad do it?"

"Lemme finish. There's a whole bunch of complications, between the Feds and the Family. I don't get it all, but I was figuring that it might be a good way to show him that I, or I mean *we*, can, you know…handle a job."

"Running a fucking errand? E, you think too small. Nobody makes their bones like that."

"Jeez, sorry Donny. That's why I gotta find out more about it."

Donny looks again at his fingernails.

"Just hurry the hell up. One way or the other, I gotta get out of that fucking grease pit."

Elmo turns into the parking lot at Shorty's.

Dale Hankins pulls into a space across the street.

Friday, Dec 21ˢᵗ
~ West Orange ~

Nurse Carrie Parker is helping Tommaso Pastor out of his bed and into a wheelchair.

"Are you sure you shouldn't have some help doing this?" he asks.

"I figure I've done this about ten thousand times, and I haven't lost a patient yet, Mr. Pastor. Besides, I've carried five children and two ex-husbands, so you should be a piece of cake."

"It wouldn't surprise me if you carried them all at once, Ms. Parker. I must say, that's a delightful cologne you're wearing."

"Do you like it? It's a combination of witch hazel, iodine, and soframyicin. I deal with a lot of bedsores here. And I must say, you do not exactly smell like a gentle spring rain, honey."

"You don't need to tell me. At this point, I'd drink Old Spice."

"All, kidding aside, Mr. Pastor, you've got to let me know if you're not getting a sponge bath every day."

"I'm getting them, but you might want to tell management that they should do them after physical therapy rather than before."

"Well I can tell *management* if you would like, but you've been here long enough to know how effective that will be. I recommend mentioning it to Marcus. He'll be here to pick you up in a few minutes. You two seem pretty tight."

"Maybe he'll assign you to wash me if I ask him real nice."

"You two ain't that tight, you dirty old man. Besides, if I gave you a sponge bath, you'd bust your other hip."

"Is that what happened to your first husband?"

"Both of them. Number two is two doors down. Now, I suggest you calm yourself, before your heart gives out."

"Knowing that you are single has given me a lease on life."

"Lease? Honey, I ain't no rental. You apply for a mortgage and we'll talk."

Marcus walks in at the end of their exchange and smiles, shaking his head.

"Here's your ride Mr. Pastor," she says, "Enjoy your rehearsal and don't forget to mention that thing to Marcus."

"Thanks for getting him ready, Ms. Parker," says Marcus, "and have a nice weekend."

"I hope to see you in church on Sunday, honey. My baby Ranisha has a solo. And, give your mama my regards."

"I will, and I'll be there for sure."

Carrie holds the door while Marcus wheels Tommaso down the hall.

In the Rec Room, Scotty is setting up the space when Tommy walks in. She is immediately swamped by the dancers with a myriad of questions, ideas, and complaints. Lew, or quite possibly Stew, races to the front of the line and is breathlessly sharing his latest idea for a new intro. Marcus wheels Tommaso in and begins heading toward Tommy., but Tommaso holds up a hand and points toward a corner of the room. Marcus gets the message and takes him around the outside of the chaos. Tommaso says something briefly to Marcus causing him to scan the room. He sees Scotty, turns back toward Tommaso, and jerks his head in Scotty's direction. Tommaso nods, and dismissed Marcus with a flick of his fingers. Marcus wanders over to Scotty, who is watching Tommy intently.

"Chill, Brother," says Marcus.

"Huh?"

"She's not going anywhere. Relax. Let her breathe."

"But what if—"

"She's still interested. Trust me. We...well, you, just need to take a step back."

"But what if—"

"If Robin shows up, I'll handle her. I promise that she won't get near you or Tommy."

"But what if—"

Marcus looks at Scotty. He holds out his hands, waiting.

Finally Marcus asks, "What if *what*?"

"Nothing, I was just testing you. You were two for two so far. I didn't want you to get overconfident."

"Well, there is one more thing. The gentleman in the corner is her grandfather."

"The gangster?"

"Shh! As far as you're concerned, the gentleman. He's here to check her out, but he's also here to check you out, so be cool."

Scotty rubs his temple.

"What's a stroke feel like?"

"Stop being an asshole. Just stay back here, look busy, hit your cues, and smile…but not too much. I'll be around."

"Can you see? Are my ears bleeding?"

Marcus shakes his head and leaves.

After a productive half hour, Tommy spots her grandfather in the corner. She smiles and he waves. In another ten minutes she calls out to the troupe.

"Great work, people, it's really coming together. Let's take a ten minute break and please hold your questions until I return. Great work!"

She quickly trots over to Grandpa before she can be swamped by the most over-enthusiastic of the dancers. She gives him a hug and a kiss.

"I didn't expect to see you here," she says.

"I wouldn't miss it. I'd like to tell you it looks great, but I have no idea what is happening. In any case, you look great, and they all seem to love what you're doing."

Tommy turns a chair around to sit facing him.

"I'm happy with it. It's going well, and I'm glad I volunteered."

"And the fella?"

"Trouble. At least I think so. Grandpa, something happened the other night."

"Did he do something?"

"No, no, nothing like that. He's been wonderful. It's me—actually us, the Pastors."

"Oh, that. You mean it's me, *the* Pastor."

"It's never been an issue like this before, and I don't know what to do."

"Have you spoken to your parents about it?"

"No, I'm concerned it will upset them and I don't want that, not at Christmas, when everyone is together."

"Look, I know you have to get back to the dancing, but I'd like you to come by and tell me more about it."

"We have a rehearsal Sunday afternoon at 2:00. Can I come by at noon?"

"That's perfect. I'll treat you to lunch. Tell everyone I'm looking forward to their visit on Christmas Eve. Now go back to your rehearsal, my angel."

"I love you, Grandpa."

She heads back to the waiting throng and Tommaso nods at Marcus. Marcus comes to return him to his room. The rest of the rehearsal goes without incident. Scotty has been wracking his brain looking for the right thing to say to avoid creepiness and awkwardness, while Tommy has been planning her escape route in an attempt to avoid the same. As the crowd disburses, Marcus wheels in a tray with three mugs and a carafe. He catches Tommy near the door.

"Where do you think you're going, young lady?"

"I, um...."

"Don't even try it. Come, sit down and take your medicine."

"You know, you and my grandfather are quite a pair."

"You mean that we both care about you?"

"I was thinking more like demon wizards."

"It's a gift. Yo, Scotty, leave the chairs."

Scotty comes over and joins them at the table. Marcus pours three hot chocolates from the carafe.

"Great rehearsal, Tommy," says Scotty.

It sounds even more awkward aloud than it did in his head. He shakes his head and turns to Marcus.

"Can you toss an oxycodone in mine, please?"

"Make mine a double," says Tommy.

Everyone laughs which breaks some of the ice, but before Scotty can launch his plan for another date, Marcus jumps in.

"Tommy, do you have plans tomorrow morning?"

She is caught off guard, because she was trying to word a polite rejection in her head.

"Uh, no, I don't think so."

"Why don't you come to Mountainside Park? Scotty, Carter, and I have our last flag football game of the season at 10:30. It's supposed to be sunny and pretty nice out. We can all go out to lunch afterward."

"Um...I..."

"We could use your help. We need someone to take a few pictures for the newsletter. You can use my camera."

"Okay, I guess...sure, why not. It sounds like fun. Mountainside Park, where the pool is?"

"Yeah, right next to the pool."

"All right, I probably should be on my way. Thanks for the hot chocolate, and I'll see you in the morning."

She makes her way to the door. After she leaves, Scotty turns to Marcus.

"What the hell was that?"

"I was saving your ass, *again*."

"I mean the newsletter. We don't have a newsletter."

"She was waffling. It closed the deal."

"I think my brain is going to explode. Please explain."

"You were gonna ask her out again."

"True, but you chumped me off."

"She was gonna say no."

"We'll never know, will we?"

"Exactly. She wanted to say yes, but was probably going to say no, so why take the chance? Now you're still in the game."

"She said yes to you, not me."

"Wrong. When she left, she thanked me for the hot chocolate, then distinctly turned to you and said 'I'll see you in the morning.'"

"If that's the case, why are you so convinced that she was going to say no?"

"She likes you."

"Why are you doing this to me?"

"No, she likes you a lot, enough to keep you from getting involved in a complex relationship."

"By saying no?"

"Exactly."

"Complex how?"

"I haven't figured that out yet."

"I think I'd like some drugs now, please."

"Let's clean up and go home, asshole."

Saturday, Dec 22nd
~ Montclair ~

Tommy parks her car and looks in the mirror. She sighs and removes the beret. After a pause, she puts it back on, takes a deep breath, and walks over to the field. Scotty, Marcus, and Carter are chatting on the sidelines when she arrives.

"Hey, I'm glad you could come," says Scotty.

"Well, it's a perfect day for it," she says.

Marcus hands her a camera.

"Very simple, just aim and click."

She takes it and looks it over. She removes the glove on her shutter finger and motions the three of them to stand together. They pose smiling. She takes the picture, checks to see that it came out, and nods.

"Piece of cake," she says. "So what do you need pictures of?"

"Just a few random shots for the church bulletin," says Marcus. "This is a church league and we wrap up this week. It's pretty laid back. There are no playoffs, just a bunch of guys trying to maintain their youth."

"I like the beret," says Carter. "It's *sassy.*"

Marcus shoots him a look, but before he can say anything, a whistle blows and they move to the field.

"Good luck!" says Tommy.

As they move to the end of the field to receive the kickoff, Carter notices a group of four gigantic men on the sideline near their opponents.

"Damn, who the hell are those dudes?" he asks. "They weren't with the team the first time we played them."

Marcus fields the kickoff and runs out of bounds after a modest gain. As they huddle for their first offensive play, the four giants walk onto the field and line up in front of the ball. The smallest of them is six foot two and 280 pounds. Marcus moves to the quarterback position and nods to Carter. He has no idea where these guys came from, but expects an all-out blitz. The nod to Carter is to confirm that he acknowledges that he is the safety valve and needs to be ready for a short pass. Marcus barks out a few signals and takes the snap.

The giants do not blitz. They do not even rush the quarterback. Marcus darts around the right side and streaks down the sideline. Since there is little resistance, Scotty runs ahead to block and they both continue unmolested into the end zone. When they turn back to the field, they see the giants getting up off of a pile. They seem to be throwing a few knees and elbows as they get up. As the giants move toward the sideline, they notice Carter on the ground where the pile was. They run over to him to find him moaning.

"Oh, fuck me," he says.

Scotty looks toward the other bench. They look as confused as everyone else. The giants are long gone from the field and halfway to the parking lot.

"I told you to stay away from that Cherisse," says Marcus. "Can you get up?"

"I don't think anything's broken, but I got the message. I trust the team can carry on without me."

They lead him gingerly to the sideline and sit him down on a cooler. His lip is split and he already has some puffiness around his left eye.

Tommy runs over to Scotty and puts her hand on his shoulder.

"What the hell was that? I don't know a lot about football, but I'm pretty sure that's illegal. Is he hurt?"

"Mostly his pride, I suspect," says Scotty. "It's a long story."

"He'll be okay," says Marcus, "but he's done for today."

"Laid back league, you said?" asks Tommy. "Should I take him somewhere, like maybe a hospital?"

She pulls her coat tightly around herself.

"You know what?" says Scotty. "Why don't you take him ahead to lunch. This way you can get a table and get out of the cold. Carter can direct you. We'll wrap this up and be along in about 45 minutes."

"Whatever you say, but if he passes out or spits up blood, I'm taking him to the hospital."

"Fair enough. I'll see you in a little while, then."

They help Carter up and he limps toward the parking lot with Tommy.

Carter slowly slides into a booth at White Castle. It's early, but the place is already bustling with the usual variety of patrons. Tommy looks around nervously and sits across from him.

"Not what you expected?" he asks.

"Not in any way. I've somehow avoided the White Castle experience. What an odd mix of people. I figured we'd be going to a diner, or…well, something. Let me get you something to drink for now. Do you suppose they have coffee, here?"

"I assume so, but it's never come up before. I'll have a Coke if you don't mind. You order on that line and pick up over there."

Tommy manages to get a Coke and a coffee and returns to the table.

"I'm not sure I've ever seen such a variety of piercings and tattoos."

"Try coming after midnight, when the real characters come out."

Carter is holding his drink against his eye.

"I've never met anyone with the first name Carter," says Tommy. "Is it a family name?"

"Slave name."

"Oh, sorry!"

"No, psych. I'm just trying to be funny. My father gave it to me."

"Ooh, you're evil."

"Seriously, the day I was born, Gary Carter of the Mets hit two home runs. My father was three things; a Mets fan, a dog, and a bum. I seem to have inherited the first two. My mother wanted to name me Malcolm, after Malcolm X. My father breezed in, filled out the form naming me Carter, and disappeared."

"Disappeared? Now I know you are kidding me."

"Sorry about before, but this story is true, and I don't mean he disappeared for the weekend. No one has seen him since. Technically, since my eyes weren't open yet, I never saw him."

"And your mother?"

"Oh, she raised me right. Of course, she does hate the Mets."

"I can imagine. Do you mind if I ask you what the hell happened at the game?"

"Let's see. How I can put this. I recently went fishing for salmon in a smaller bear's stream. It seems that the smaller bear had four rather large friends who he got to suggest that I fish elsewhere."

"And why didn't your...um...*bear* friends intervene?"

"Technically they did. They discouraged me from fishing there in the first place, but I have no doubt that if these bears persisted, my bears would have protected me."

"The code of the wild?"

"I suppose. My problem is, I just can't get me enough salmon."

They both laugh.

"I am amazed at how you three look out for each other."

"They are both fiercely loyal and honest. Scotty has the biggest heart of anyone I've ever met."

"Well, to be honest, speaking of myself, that type of friendship is outside my experience."

"In my experience, it may be a gender thing. On TV, women all have friends just like the men, but I've seen very little of that in real life."

"Well, I'm happy to discuss gender issues, but we may need to be here long enough for me to meet the midnight crowd."

"I'll take that as a warning, and thank you for using more subtlety than those who administered my last warning. I do have one gender question, however. Humor me—why is it, to me at least, that women seems so humorless compared to men?"

"I suppose it's another example of the unwritten rules that influence how women act, or are supposed to act, or think that they're supposed to act."

"Men have rules too, don't they?"

"Yes, but less, no, different consequences. Let's say Louis C.K. and Sarah Silverman tell the same joke. Make it a raw, borderline offensive joke. Do you react the same way?"

"I'll take the fifth for now. How about this one? A guy goes to a football game in a wheelchair to get in free. What's your immediate reaction?"

"Offense. No, I think disgust is probably about right."

"Yet, it's a true story from when Marcus started at the rehab hospital. The Jets give free tickets to the patients, which is odd if you think about it, but a patient gets a couple of tickets and asks Marcus if he wants them because he can't go. Marcus throws a wheelchair in his car, and calls Scotty and invites him to the game. He picks up Scotty who sees the wheelchair, but doesn't think anything of it, since he knows where Marcus works. They get to the stadium and Marcus drives all the way up to the handicapped parking. Eventually, Scotty figures out the scam, but they're already there, so they agree to switch at halftime."

"You're serious?"

"Yeah, they were kids. They had to sit with all the war vets. They learned a lot, got embarrassed, but didn't hurt anyone. It was an experience, an adventure. I think it's a great story. I told it at a Toastmasters meeting. The men loved it, and the women were all, 'Well I *never,*' like every stuffy broad in The Three Stooges."

"Stuffy broad? I'll have to look that up in one of my textbooks. In any case, now I think the story is cute, since I can't stop picturing Scotty stuck in the chair."

"Speak of the devil."

Scotty and Marcus walk in.

"I see that you lived," says Marcus. "Did we learn anything at school today?"

Carter hands Marcus a couple of twenties.

"Yeah, I learned the usual. You were right and I was wrong. Happy?"

"Happy about what? I was already right before you got your ass kicked. I take no satisfaction in you being too dumb to listen."

"Just order for me, please. Get me the usual. No, make it onion rings instead of fries."

"We'll order, wash up, and then pick up the food," says Scotty. "What can we get you, Tommy?"

"I guess I'll have a cheeseburger and a Coke," she says.

"What? You've never been to White Castle before?" asks Scotty.

"I don't understand. How do you know that?" she says.

"Never mind. Marcus, we have a newcomer here. Order the 'newbie special.'"

They return in ten minutes with an extremely large bag filled with a couple of dozen small boxes containing a variety of food items that all smell like onions. They take turns explaining to Tommy the "Buy 'em by the sack" philosophy of White Castle, along with the history and culture of the restaurant.

"So every bistro and burger joint with sliders on the menu is ripping off White Castle?" asks Tommy.

"Essentially, yes," says Scotty, "but not accurately. Sliders were named for the grease, not the size."

"And before being called sliders, they were called 'rat burgers' or 'murder burgers,'" adds Carter.

"Well, it's certainly been a culinary experience. I found the 'surf and turf' particularly interesting. It's prepared somewhat differently from the one at the Ritz Carlton. I'm just hoping to have a contact with Scotty one day that does not include nausea."

"What you are experiencing," says Carter, "might be *love.*"

Marcus elbows Carter in his already sore ribs causing Carter to groan. He gets up and grabs Carter by the shoulder dragging him out of the booth.

"I think I should get this one to a doctor," says Marcus. "Tommy, would you mind bringing Scotty home?"

Tommy smiles.

"Not at all. Thanks for lunch and the 'education,'" she says.

Carter croaks out, "I go quietly into that good night."

After they leave, Scotty moves across to the other side of the table.

"That's not necessary," says Tommy.

"I just wanted to avoid any awkwardness. Marcus and Carter have been insulating me for the past few days, to keep me from…well…we look out for each other."

"I can see that, and I think it's special. I think I'm ready to give it another try, if you'd like to."

"I very much would like to. How about dinner, or something easier on the stomach?"

"Dinner would be wonderful, but I'm pretty tied up with Christmas for the next few days. How about Wednesday, the 26th?"

"That would be perfect. May I look for something we can do before dinner as well?"

"Sure, call me. I'll reserve the day."

Scotty cleans the table and they head for the door, both smiling brightly.

Sunday, Dec 23rd
~ West Orange ~

Tommaso Pastor is reading the paper when Marcus walks in.

"Good morning, Mr. Pastor. Are you going to rehearsal today?"

"God no, to watch a bunch of old bags and young fags prance around? I'd rather have more physical therapy. My granddaughter is going to stop by beforehand."

"Any progress on the other thing?"

"No, and as a matter of fact, it's gotten worse…maybe a lot worse. I need to make a phone call, but I don't want to go through your switchboard. Can you help me?"

Well, first of all, I don't think we use switchboards anymore, but you're welcome to use my cell phone as long as it won't get me rubbed out."

"I'm less worried about my people than I am about the Feds. Once they take an interest, they never let go. If you got in Dutch with us, it would be over and done with quickly, one way or another."

"That's good to know. I'm sure, however that the Feds wouldn't be tapping our phones."

"Don't be naïve, Marcus. They have an endless supply of your tax dollars and an endless hard-on for high profile arrests, even if they never result in a conviction. Anyway, it will be safe to use your phone. I call a clean number, and then get called back from a different clean number."

"Obviously I'm new at this, but how do you know that your contact isn't under surveillance by law enforcement?"

"Because I didn't survive 70 years as a criminal by being a moron. My contact *is* in law enforcement."

"So you rig the game?"

"I prefer 'my game, my rules.' If the other players never get the rules, that's their problem. Now show me how this goddamn phone works."

Tommaso punches in a number and hangs up. In less than a minute, the phone rings. Marcus hits the appropriate button and hands the phone back to Tommaso. Marcus turns to leave, but Tommaso raises a finger indicating that he should wait. Tommaso listens to the call but says nothing. In a minute, he turns off the phone and hands it to Marcus.

"Bad news?" asks Marcus.

"Very bad. My Plan A just went out the window and I don't yet have a Plan B."

"Anything I can do?"

"It may come to that, but for now, I must think."

At that moment, Tommy lightly raps on the door as she sticks her head in the room.

"Hello, Marcus," she says. "Is my grandfather allowed to have guests?"

"Anytime for my Tommasina," says Grandpa with a smile.

"Hey, Tommy," says Marcus. "I'm off to finish making the rounds. I'll see you at rehearsal."

Tommy moves toward the bed and hugs her grandfather.

"How are you, sweetheart? I enjoyed your rehearsal the other day," he says.

"You don't need to be polite, Grandpa. I know that it must have looked like complete chaos to you. You were there to check on me. Oh, and I'm quite fine, thank you."

"Now who is being polite? I'll admit that the dancing was not my cup of tea, but you were happy, and that's what I came to see. On the other hand, I know that you are not 'quite fine.' Please tell me what's troubling you."

"Well, even though it's evident that you somehow already know, here goes. I had a…well, not exactly a date, but a few…um…"

"Friendly meetings?"

"Okay, friendly meetings with this fellow—"

"Scotty."

"Jesus, Grandpa! Give me a chance!"

"Well, I am 82. I don't have forever."

"Oh, you're hilarious. Yes, Scotty. The bottom line is that I like him and there may be something there, and for the first time ever, being a Pastor has come up."

"Have you spoken to your mother? She has been through this."

"No, she was really more in Scotty's position. I'd talk to Dad, but he is swamped with some end-of-the-year crisis at work."

"I'll tell you what. Your young man seems quite special and I know that he is very interested in you just by the way he looked at you. You focus on that. Obviously separating my business from family has always been an issue, but I expect that to change for the better. Give me a few days to think about it and put some things into motion. For now, the best advice I can give you is never to change who you are. It's unfair to you and unfair to him. Do you understand?"

"I think I do, Grandpa."

"May I discuss this with your father before you mention it to him?"

"I don't see why not. Are you coming to rehearsal?"

"Not today, sweetheart. It reminds me too much of your grandmother, or actually, you remind me of her."

"I can think of no higher compliment, Grandpa. Thanks for listening."

Sunday, Dec 23rd
~ Cedar Grove ~

Elmo is driving his father's Land Rover up Pompton Avenue toward Bellino's Nursery. Pep is in the passenger seat playing with the radio. He's cycling through the preset stations.

"Oldies, oldies, NPR, Ooh, classic rock, another rock, what the hell is this? Metal? Can you picture Pop listening to hair bands?" says Pep.

"Not really. He came to all of my football games wearing a suit and tie."

"I think I remember him wearing a sport jacket to the beach once."

"I must have been at camp. I don't think I ever saw Pop at the beach."

"What are we picking up that requires both of us, anyway?"

"Just a couple of wreaths and poinsettias. Mom wanted us out of the house so she could wrap gifts. We're supposed to get lunch, too. Any suggestions?"

"What was the diner we used to go to after your games?"

"Tick Tock, over on Route 3. It's not far. Wanna go there?"

"If you don't mind. I used to feel like such a big shot going there after the games."

"Good for you. I actually played in them and look where I am now...babysitting my kid brother and doing errands for my mommy."

Pep is taken aback by the bitterness in his brother's voice. Before he can think of a response, Elmo pulls into the entrance to the nursery and parks. Without a word, he gets out of the car. Pep joins him and they head inside the nursery building. Elmo gives his name to the kid behind the counter and tells him that they are picking up an order. The kid shuffles into the back and brings out three poinsettias. Even to Pep they seem pretty small and unhealthy.

"What the hell are these?" says Elmo.

The clerk gives Elmo the stink eye, but before he can respond, an older gentleman in an apron comes out of the back room. He looks at Elmo and then at the plants.

"Leo, you got the wrong ones. Can you go in the back and bring the big ones on the left hand side?" he says.

"But—," says Leo.

"Leo, *please!* Just do as I ask, for once."

Leo finally breaks his stare at Elmo and heads into the back. He brings out three fuller poinsettias and places them on the counter.

"My apologies, Elmo, he's new," says Mr. Bellino.

"Fine, whatever. We pick out two wreaths from out front?"

Elmo picks up two of the plants.

"Of course, Elmo. Take whatever you need."

"Hi, Mr. Bellino," says Pep.

Mr. Bellino gives a wan wave but never diverts his eyes from Elmo. Pep picks up the remaining plant and follows Elmo out the door. They put the plants in the back of the SUV. Elmo grabs two wreaths off of the stand and puts them in as well. They both get into the car.

"What the hell was that?" asks Pep.

"What was what?"

"Mr. Bellino, he was petrified of you."

"You think? Good. His plants are shit."

"You don't understand, Elmo. He was afraid of *you*."

"No, Pep, *you* don't understand. That part is what it is. I'm a Pastor, and he's not. I know it and he knows it. I'm not saying it's good or bad, just that it is."

"But doesn't that bother you?"

"Come on, kid. Grow up. It doesn't matter whether I'm bothered or not. You think a lion is bothered when he eats a zebra? This is business. The Pastors have been buying from Bellino's for, I dunno, like, 50 years. He gets a good customer and we get, um, let's say more attentive service. You think this is from fear? Who do you think Bellino goes to when he needs a business loan, or when his kid gets busted for pot? Who gets the drainage fixed on his street? This is fucking commerce."

"I'm confused. Then why were you so short with him?"

"Why? Did you see those plants he was selling? I wasn't pissed because he gave *us* shitty plants. I'm pissed because he's selling shitty plants. Some other dope, who's not a Pastor, is gonna walk in there, and walk out with shit. That never happened at Bellino's. That place used to be beautiful."

Elmo's voice cracks, slightly.

"Dude, they're just plants."

"Wrong, smart guy. His kids didn't want to stay in the business and it's gone to shit."

"To be fair, his daughter is a doctor, and his sons are a dentist and a lawyer, I think."

"Right. A great business that put his kids through school is now an embarrassment with goons like Leo running the place. Now people are going to have to buy their plants at fucking Wal-Mart. Who is that good for, huh, smart guy?"

Elmo pulls off of Route 3 into the Tick Tock Diner parking lot. They go inside and the hostess seats them in a booth. They both order and wash up.

"This place hasn't changed much," says Pep.

"Well something's changed. I used to be a big shot here."

"I'll say. I was in middle school, and I got such a rush coming here after your games."

"Everybody loves the quarterback."

"It wasn't like that for me. I hated football, and I hated football players even more. What impressed me was your leadership. Everyone looked up to you."

"Well, that ends fast once the games end."

"You think too little of yourself. You taught me plenty about commerce today."

A grey-haired man walks over to the table.

"Elmo Pastor…is that you?" says the man.

"Mr. Nick, it's nice to see you. I don't know if you remember my brother, Pep."

Nick holds his hand at table level.

"Not since he was this big. It's been a while. Are you having a reunion?"

"What do you mean?"

"Dale Hankins, your tight end, just came in and sat at the counter."

Confused, Elmo turns to look, but does not see Dale. Pep points out the window and they watch Dale get into his car and drive off. Mr. Nick wishes them well and leaves.

"That was odd," says Pep. "He didn't say hello or get any food."

"Odder than you think. He was also at Bellino's."

"You saw him?"

Robert O'Connell

"No, but I saw the car. Who else would be enough of a douchebag to have a vanity plate of FIVE-OH?"

Sunday, Dec 23rd
~ West Orange ~

Scotty is arranging the tables and chairs when Tommy walks into the Rec Room.

"You're early," he says.

"I wanted to beat the crowd. I can't stay late today, family dinner on Sundays. You mentioned something about scheduling dinner for the two of us later in the week?"

"Yes, I was hoping you'd be available Wednesday evening. You don't celebrate Boxing Day, I hope."

"No we're Roman Catholics, not the church of England. Have you been watching Downton Abbey?"

"No, but I would like to choose a place that you would like."

"How about Merola's in Montclair? It's kind of a home game for me, but you might as well get the full Pastor experience."

"Well, I'm intrigued. Can I pick you up at—"

"Make it 6:00, and I'll take care of a reservation."

"Wow, that was easy. Since I'm on a roll, let me plow forward. I would like to take you into the City on Thursday. This is, of course, assuming that we survive dinner on Wednesday."

"That would be lovely. We can discuss it on Wednesday."

They are interrupted by a woman in a feathered hat and a leotard with leg warmers.

"Off to work," says Tommy.

She turns toward the woman.

"How can I help you, Mrs. Silver?"

"Good afternoon, dear. I wanted to catch you before the Wasserman boys get here."

"You mean Lew and Stew?"

"Yes, I know they can come on a little strong. They're on my condo board at the Claremont Towers."

"They live in the Towers?" asks Scotty.

"Sure, and they're on the upper floors, too. The two of them are loaded from their investment company, even in this economy," says Mrs. Silver.

"Hmm," says Scotty, "I wouldn't have guessed—"

"From their obnoxious outfits?" says Mrs. Silver. "You should see what their wives wear, Oy!"

"Wives?" says Scotty.

"Excuse me," says Tommy, "but we need to get started. Was there something specific, Mrs. Silver?"

"I just don't want you to let the boys push you around," she says.

"Well, thank you, Mrs. Silver," says Tommy. "I think I can handle them."

"Well you should also know that I myself danced on Broadway," Mrs. Silver continues. "It was where I met my Solly, may he rest in peace. I thought I might make a few suggestions…"

Tommy looks toward Scotty in exasperation, but he just smiles, gives a little wave, and heads over to his place at the boombox.

Monday, Dec 24th
~ Newark ~

Alex Gersten is sitting at his desk in the Essex County Prosecutor's Office. He has a large stack of files on his desk. A middle-aged woman in a business dress pokes her head in.

"There's a walk-in here to see you," she says.

"Jesus, Millie, it's Christmas Eve for God's sake. When am I supposed to get some work done? And what happened to the intercom?"

"First of all, you never answer when I call. Second, you don't celebrate Christmas and will probably be here tomorrow anyway. Lastly, he said he's a detective."

"Sorry, Millie, I'm just swamped. Send him in."

Millie leaves and returns a minute later to show Dale Hankins into the office. Alex cannot place him right away, but it finally comes to him.

"Hawkins, is it? Have a seat."

Dale stands and holds out his hand, but Alex ignores him.

"It's Hankins, sir. Dale Hankins, I'm a detec—"

"Yeah, I remember. Sorry, but I'm on kind of a deadline here. What can I do for you? I don't recall any cases I have with you."

"No, sir, it's not a current case. I mean I hope to someday—"

"Sorry, Hankins, can you get to the point?"

"Oh, yeah, sure, well, when we met the other day, you mentioned the Pastors, specifically Robert."

"And?"

"And that I should keep an eye on them."

"That was a figure of speech, you know, like keep them on your radar."

"Oh."

"I mean that as law enforcement professionals, it would be nice if we you knew what the bad guys were up to occasionally."

"Yeah, I get it. So I used to play football with Elmo Pastor, Robert's son."

"So?"

"So I think he might be up to something."

"Like what? Wait, what did you do?"

"I followed him around for a few days. On my own time, of course."

Alex rubs his head in frustration.

"Okay, what did you see?"

"Well, first, he hangs around with this mope Donny Manzetti. He's got a lot of juvie stuff. He works in a garage—"

"Wait. Let me get this straight. You took it upon yourself to follow people who are not currently part of an investigation, with no orders from your superiors or department. You looked up records with no cause, all because I said, at a party, to keep your eyes open, all after being a detective for a week?"

"Uh, yeah, I guess so. Well, it wasn't quite a week."

"Let me give you some advice, kid. The wheels of justice move slowly, but they do move. While I appreciate your initiative, we do *not* need any cowboys going out of their way to grease the tracks, so to speak. That type of work usually ends up in lost cases and, sometimes, dead cowboys. Here is my card. If you find something legitimate, *call* me. Otherwise, focus on doing the jobs you are assigned and learning from the veteran officers. Some of them might be a little slow moving or even lazy, but they are all alive to solve more crimes and to catch more bad guys."

Alex stares at Dale. Dale finally realizes that the conversation is over. He stands and gives Alex a demonstrative wink.

"I read you loud and clear. I know *exactly* what you need."

Dale leaves the office grinning. Alex just shakes his head in disbelief.

Monday, Dec 24th
~ West Orange ~

"I appreciate you doing this for me," says Tommaso.

Marcus is arranging chairs around a couple of tables facing the old man's bed.

"It's a fair deal. You funded the holiday party the staff is having later."

"They deserve it. This is a shitty type of work and you get a lot out of them. Well, other than that kid with the headphones."

"You won't see that again. We had a sit-down. There's still pride out there if you look for it."

"You're not afraid to break the rules."

"For them, not you."

"Did you get me the clothes I asked for?"

"Yes, sir. I'll help you get dressed in a minute."

"My son is coming before the rest of the family. You remember the call I made yesterday?"

"Of course, bad news."

"Yes. I told you about the old Don, Enrico Pizzoli, and that he was a vicious leader who consolidated the North Jersey family."

"Right, but now his son is the Don."

"Yes, Anthony. He's as rational as his father was emotional. He introduced, with my help, business models and computers and moved us onto Wall Street. Peace was kept by better profits, diversification, and legitimate business."

"And the bad news?"

"Anthony is unwell. Very unwell. He's not even 60 and he may not make it there. My sources say that his son Rico is ready to take over."

"Your sources. The phone call?"

"Yes."

"So what's the problem?"

"It's Rico. He's a sociopath, worse than his grandfather. And he's paranoid, as well. There have been discussions about it among the family, but no one expected it to be critical so soon."

"So forgive me for seeming dense, but what effect does this have on you?"

"Me? None. I'll be gone soon one way or the other. I'm worried for my son. He's not a soldier and Rico hates people smarter than him, which includes pretty much everyone. Rico will see him as a threat. Now, I have no way to get to Anthony."

Marcus helps Tommaso get dressed for Christmas Eve dinner. Robert walks in and greets Marcus. Tommaso gives Marcus a nod and he leaves the room. Robert leans in and kisses his father on the cheek.

"Papa, you look great. Where'd you get the outfit?"

"I had Marcus pick it up for me."

Tommaso tosses his head toward the door where Marcus just exited. Robert looks mildly surprised and shrugs.

"So, you wanted me to come early. What's on your mind?"

"I assume that you've heard about Anthony."

"Heard what? Papa, I've been swamped with the regulatory changes."

"Jesus, Robert. You need to be more tuned in."

"Papa, I know that you have your contacts, but trust me. Everything is fine. It's not like the old days. I think being cooped up here has made you a little paranoid."

"That paranoia has kept us safe for a long time. Obviously you are unaware of Anthony's health problems."

"What? You heard he has the flu? Papa, it's going around. I'm sure he'll be fine."

"Not the flu, Robert. He is seriously ill, and we foolishly have no succession plan in place. Are you ready for that psychopath Rico to take over?"

"Relax, Papa. That's years away. I plan for both of us to be retired by then."

"I'm not worried about me. I'm finished either way. It's you that I am worried about. Rico is old school, or at least thinks he is. He doesn't believe in retirement plans."

"Jesus, Papa. You're getting pretty worked up. I'll look into it, okay?"

"I just don't want it to affect Ramona or the kids. My biggest regret is not—"

He chokes up and Robert takes his hand.

"I know, Papa. I know. Ramona is strong. I know she deserves better, but we're in this as one. As for the kids—"

"It's already touching them."

"What do you mean?"

"Talk to Elmo. He's, how should I put this, confused about his future."

"I'm aware of that. Ramona and I are working on it."

"Don't wait too long. And then there's Tommisina..."

"Tommisina? What? How is that—"

"Ask her how her date at the Town Hall went a few days ago."

"Damn it, Papa. How do you...never mind. I'll talk to her."

There is a commotion in the hall and Ramona, Tommy, Elmo, and Pep come in carrying several bags. There are hugs and kisses and a wonderful-looking fish dinner from Martucci's. There are gifts as well. The family sits down to a traditional Christmas Eve dinner, or as close as you can get in a room in a rehab hospital. Gifts are exchanged and they sit down for a dessert of tiramisu and cannoli. Robert gets a phone call and steps out of the room, waving for the others to continue without him. He comes back a few minutes later looking concerned.

"Is everything all right?" asks Ramona.

Robert looks at his father.

"I'm not sure," he says. "Anthony Pizzoli just suffered a massive stroke."

Monday, Dec 24th
~ Newark ~

Scotty and Marcus park on the street and head for Hope Baptist Church. It's a few minutes past 7:00 PM.

"Thanks for inviting me," says Scotty. "Christmas is a weird time for me."

"No biggie. I came mostly to hear Miss Carrie's daughter sing. From what I understand, it's some sort of a candlelight ceremony. It won't be anything like Carter's church."

"That's a relief. When we went to his nephew's christening, I was somewhat unprepared for the laying of hands and the hypnotic music."

"It was a first for me, too. When the big lady next to me 'got the spirit,' she flung off her glasses and knocked over the chair. I thought she was going to take me with her to the other side."

"I figured that you were used to that sort of thing until I saw your face. I like how the sisterhood stood by with towels to cover the legs of the women who fainted, and the younger girls would fan them."

"It was pretty crazy, but this is pretty sedate. The choir is amazing."

I'm glad it's early at least. Tommy and her family go to Midnight Mass. You'd think the Catholics would want their kids in bed early on Christmas Eve. They have a live manger with real animals, I think."

"Yeah, well, I don't think too many people want to be out in this neighborhood after midnight, even on Christmas."

"It's too bad. I can't believe that my grandmother grew up near here."

As they walk into the foyer, Carrie Parker sees Marcus and greets him. He introduces Scotty and she points out where Marcus' mother is sitting. They head into the church. It is a simple building with an altar in front of an organ surrounded by tiers on both sides for the choir. There are candles all around the front and sides of the sanctuary. Scotty gives Mrs. Walker a hug and sits in between her and Marcus. The crowd quiets when the choir files in wearing satiny robes of purple with yellow trim. Ranisha Parker takes her place in front of a microphone next to the organ. Mrs. Walker leans forward and turns toward Marcus.

"That's Carrie Parker's daughter. She sings like an angel," she whispers.

"Yeah, I know, Ma."

"You should talk to her."

"Ma, she's a child."

"Your daddy was older than me."

"Yeah, and when did you last see him?"

Scotty elbows Marcus and Marcus just shakes his head.

"Would you listen to the way that boy talks to his mother, in God's house, no less," says Mrs. Walker.

Scotty smiles at her and they sit through the service. Dozens of children wearing white come down the aisle to light the candles while the choir sings a series of hymns. The choir sounds amazing and the scouting report on Ranisha was, if anything, understated. After the service, the three of them move toward a relatively quiet corner.

"Ma, do you need a ride home?" asks Marcus.

"No, baby, I'm going to walk with some friends from the choir once they get out of their robes."

"I just don't want you going alone."

"I can take care of myself, but I assure you that I will not be alone. Scotty, tell me how you are doing. Do you have a girl, honey?"

"Work is good and I actually do have a date with a new girl in a couple of days," says Scotty.

"Well, I hope it works out, honey. I have a couple of your students living in my complex. They always tell me how much they love your class."

"Well, thanks, and it was great to see you. Have a Merry Christmas, Mrs. Walker."

"Well, you are always welcome to come by with Marcus."

"Thanks, but I'm going to help out Carter. He has his family coming over tomorrow."

She hugs and kisses both of them and they head for the car. Marcus pulls in front of their apartment, turns, and looks at Scotty.

"Aren't you coming in?" asks Scotty.

"I have to run an errand...for a friend."

"On Christmas Eve? I know you're not meeting a woman, because you'd have a better story."

"Carter will be home from his side job in a few. He'll tuck you in if I'm not back in time."

"That's it. That's what all the mystery is about."

"What the hell are you talking about?"

"You're him. You're Santa Claus. That's how he gets through Detroit and South Central and Harlem in the middle of the night. Santa is black, and you are him."

"You're so stupid. Get the hell out of the car."

They both are laughing as Marcus drives off.

Monday, Dec 24th
~ Montclair ~

The Pastor family exits Robert's Land Rover and heads for the entrance of St. Bartholomew Church. Tommy, Elmo, and Pep walk ahead to see the live nativity. Pep runs into a few friends and they chat as they wander through the crowd. Robert and Ramona hang back several yards.

"I'll say a prayer for Anthony, as he has always been good to us, but it seems odd to be in a church praying for a crime boss," says Ramona. "What is this going to mean for us?"

Robert is pleased to hear her use the plural pronoun. He knows they are a team, but it's always nice to receive a little reinforcement. He has her arm, but instinctively pulls her closer.

"Well," says Robert, "if we get struck by lightning, it won't be because of you. I will be praying for us, not Anthony. His son Rico is a real loose cannon. I begged Anthony to put things in place, but he always put it off."

"Can you handle the situation?"

"I hope so, but I wish I were more confident. There are a lot of variables. I'm kicking myself for not getting out sooner. I had planned to be out by now, but with the economic downturn, Anthony needed me, and quite frankly, I got greedy. I wanted better financial security."

"Don't be hard on yourself, honey. We talked at the time and agreed on this course."

"That's the problem. I only looked at the money. With Rico, retirement may not be an option. I'll never forgive myself if I put you and the kids through hardship of any kind. Plus, we haven't dealt with Elmo yet. Rico's crazy, but not stupid. I wouldn't put it past him to use Elmo to control me."

"That's something that I would not let happen."

"Ro, you are the best thing that has ever happened to me. Well, you and the kids. But, Papa has told me stories…well, let's get through Christmas, and I'll get to work on this."

"Just don't keep anything from me. Maybe Anthony will pull through."

"It doesn't look good, but I promise to keep you in the loop, baby."

After the service, they are heading for home.

"You know, it would be nice for the three of you to go to church once without causing a scene," says Ramona.

"He started it," says Pep.

Pep is in the middle of the back seat and he elbows Elmo who is on his left. While Elmo and Pep are having a fake slap fight, Tommy holds her fist as close as she can to Pep's cheek without touching it.

"Check out these lights," she says.

Pep turns to look, smashing his face into her fist.

"You got snuck!" she says as they begin a slap fight.

"Left turn!" shouts Elmo, as he leans hard to his right shoving Pep into Tommy with fake centrifugal force.

"Right turn!" shouts Tommy, as she pushes back the other way.

"Middle turn!" is shouted in unison by Elmo and Tommy as they both plow into Pep. Ramona is smiling, but notices that Robert is not paying attention and is rather deep in thought. She reaches over and rubs his arm.

When they arrive home, they notice a large shopping bag by the front door. Robert instinctively waves them back behind him as he peers inside.

"They're presents...from Papa! How the hell does he..." mutters Robert, shaking his head.

Tuesday, Dec 25th
~ Glen Ridge ~

Tommy smiles as she reads the Merry Christmas text from Scotty. The Pastors are all in their pajamas and robes. Ramona hands Robert a cup of coffee and they all begin opening their gifts and taking pictures. It is a relatively sedate holiday, but Ramona is in all her glory, directing both the order of the gift opening and the picture taking.

"Where is the bag from Grandpa?" asks Pep.

"Oh, my!" says Ramona, "I almost forgot."

She gets the bag from near the front door and hands out the packages, one for each of them. The cards are all signed in Grandpa's hand, so he did not farm this task out over the phone.

"I still can't figure out how he manages some of the things he does," says Robert.

He is turning his package over in his hands.

"Maybe he's been faking this whole time," says Ramona. "I wouldn't put it past the old wizard."

"Holy shit!" says Elmo. "Are these real?"

He is holding up a pair of diamond and gold cufflinks that were in his package.

"Yes, they are," says Robert. "They were his favorite, and he only wore them on special occasions. You should feel honored."

"I do, Pop," says Elmo. "He told me he'd let me pick out a set. Jeez, I don't even have any shirts that use cufflinks."

"We'll have to go shopping," says Ramona. "Pep, what did you get?"

Pep opens his package and holds up a pair of driving gloves. This is met with oohs and aahs from everyone.

"Those are hand sewn lambskin from Italy," says Robert, "also his favorite."

Pep slides his hands into them and models them.

"My God!" he says. "I know I'll never hear the end of this, but these feel so good that I feel like my hands are up a lamb's ass right now."

Robert is beginning to feel a sense of foreboding about the theme of these gifts, wondering if his father is literally cleaning house in anticipation of something. Without waiting for Ramona's direction, he opens his gift from Grandpa. He opens a little velvet box and pulls out a key.

"What the hell?" he says.

"You don't know what it's for?" asks Ramona.

"Maybe it's a car," says Elmo.

"Ooh, maybe a boat!" says Pep.

"No," says Robert, "it's definitely a safety deposit box, but where it is and what's inside it, I haven't a clue. Ro, open yours."

She looks at him, somewhat confused, but after a pause, opens her gift. It is a classic diamond necklace that has never been, and never will be, out of style. Ramona gasps.

"Oh my God!" she says, holding her hand to her chest. "This is the one from her wedding picture. You said it was gone!"

Robert shrugs.

"I assumed it was," he says. "I never saw it, myself, ever. He had gotten rid of her jewelry after she passed, or at least I thought he did."

"This must be worth nearly a hundred thousand dollars," says Ramona. "Maybe the key is to remind you to put it somewhere safe."

"Unlikely. If you recall, this stuff was just sitting out by the front door last night," says Robert. "Tommy, you're the last one."

Tommy slowly opens her package and finds a ring box. She opens it and gasps. She turns it around to show everybody.

"His pinky ring," says Robert. "I have never, not for one day in the entirety of my 56 years, seen him without it."

"Robert," asks Ramona, "what do you think it means?"

Robert shakes his head blankly. The others look at each other blankly. Tommy puts the ring on her slender middle finger and looks at it.

Robert O'Connell

"Never change who you are," she says.

Tuesday, Dec 25th
~ Montclair ~

"I'm off to my family," says Marcus. "I'll see you guys at 4:30 at the shelter. Merry Christmas, Mrs. Jackson, Rosa."

He slips on his coat and rubs the head of Carter's one-and-a-half year old nephew as he heads for the door.

"Later, little man," says Marcus.

"See?" says Carter, "he won't even call him by his name. Why would you want to name your son Faruki?"

Scotty is assembling a small basketball hoop that Carter bought for his nephew. He looks over at Mrs. Jackson and they both shake their heads.

"Here we go," says Scotty.

"Every holiday," says Mrs. Jackson.

"Who do you know from Africa?" says Carter. "Our people are from Virginia. Moms named you after Rosa Parks. Can't you find any role models here?"

"She wanted me to name him Thurgood," says Rosa. "Could you imagine how long he'd last in our neighborhood being called Thurgood?"

"But Faruki? He's gonna end up on a no fly list."

"Faruki means judicious. It's actually an homage to Justice Marshall."

"Then why didn't you just call him Marshall?"

"Enough, you two," says Mrs. Jackson. "Faruki's gonna test his new toy."

Scotty hands Faruki the small rubber ball. He picks him up and holds him in front of the basket.

"Okay, Faruki, you know what to do," says Scotty.

Faruki lets the ball go. It hits the front of the rim and rolls off.

In unison, Scotty and Mrs. Jackson say, "Just like Uncle Carter."

"Damn," says Carter, "my own mother."

Everyone laughs.

"What time is Darnell coming?" asks Scotty.

"His shift ends at noon, so I expect him about 1:00," says Rosa. "There shouldn't be any traffic today."

"So dinner at 2:00 is okay?" asks Scotty. "I need to get the turkey in the oven."

"Isn't it considered cannibalism for Darnell to eat turkey?" cracks Carter.

"Mama, make him stop," says Rosa.

"Carter, you leave that boy alone," says Mrs. Jackson.

"Moms, he's failed at everything he's ever done other than impregnating my sister," he says. "He won't even do the right thing by marrying her."

"I believe he did successfully get through the Police Academy once he was diagnosed and got a handle on his dyslexia," says Mrs. Jackson.

"Yeah, and Scotty was a big help to him, which is more than I can say about my own big brother," adds Rosa.

"I'm just looking out for you and 'half-pint' here," says Carter, handing his nephew the ball.

"Well, he's coming around and I expect you to be nice today," says Mrs. Jackson. "Besides, it's Christmas."

"Yeah," says Scotty, "having a cop in the family might come in handy someday."

Faruki attempts a dunk. It ricochets off the back of the rim and rolls to where Carter is sitting on the floor.

"Damn," says Carter. "Is dyslexia hereditary?"

Tuesday, Dec 25th
~ Upper Montclair ~

Robert and Elmo are walking through the grounds of the Immaculate Conception Cemetery. They find the grave of Marie Pastor, whose headstone reads "Loving Wife and Mother 1932-1974." Robert kneels and crosses himself. After a few minutes, he moves away some of the leaves that have accumulated. The headstone and plot are wide enough to accommodate another body, obviously for Grandpa. There is a marble bench at the foot of the grave. Robert sits on it and motions for Elmo to do the same.

"Thanks for coming with me, son."

"No problem, Pop, but how come we took two cars?"

"I need to go see your Grandpa after."

"I can go with you, Pop. It's about the key, right? I want to know the story, too. Hey, why are there years, but no dates on her tombstone? All the others have dates."

"Grandpa didn't want it. Your grandmother died on her 42nd birthday. I guess he felt that it seemed too, I don't know, tragic, maybe, as if breast cancer wasn't tragic enough. God, I was a senior in high school. Your Grandpa was lost. He threw himself into his work. We barely spoke, and soon I went off to college. I was sullen and remote. You know, I think that's what attracted your mother to me. She thought I was this sensitive soul like Billy Joel or Bruce Springsteen. Jesus, I was in a fog until I met her."

"And why is there a bench here? I don't see any other graves with anything like it."

"I think he used to come here and sit for hours at a time. He would drag me here every time I had an accomplishment. He would even take pictures."

"Pictures? What do you mean, like with a camera?"

"Yup, it's an Italian thing, I guess. Do you know that we came here before my high school graduation? Cap and gown and all. He sat on that bench and took pictures of me next to the headstone. I have no idea what he did with them, or if he even had them developed. Sometimes I think he just wanted to share the experiences with her."

Robert removes his handkerchief and wipes his eyes. Elmo awkwardly pats his father on the back.

"I wish you kids could have known her," he says. "I wish that your mother could have known her. Hell, I wish that I could have known her better. God, I was just a kid, younger than Pep is now."

"Um, so, can I come with you to see Grandpa?"

Robert blows his nose and puts away his handkerchief. He turns to Elmo.

"Elmo. I appreciate you coming here with me. I really do, but I have business to discuss with your grandfather."

"But Pop, you said you would talk to him about me."

"Son, I said I would, and I will."

"But I want to be like you and like Grandpa. And what about the key? Maybe I can help. Maybe I already know something about it."

"What are you talking about? Did you go back there to talk to him about the business?"

"No, Pop, I mean, I was going to, but I didn't. I just…overheard some stuff."

Robert is confused and is beginning to wonder if his father is beginning to lose his faculties.

"Elmo, I'm going to tell you something that no one on the planet knows other than me and your Grandpa, and now you. As my mother lay dying, she called him over to her bed. She said to him, 'Keep him out of it. It's all I ask. Keep him out of it.' It was the last thing she said to anyone. It was her dying wish and the biggest regret of your grandfather's life that he failed to keep this promise to her. I know what you want, and I need you to know what is at stake here. I need you to hang on and give me the time to work this all out. Can I count on you, son?"

Elmo looks to the ground.

"Yes, Pop. You can count on me."

Tuesday, Dec 25th
~ West Orange ~

Robert strides into his father's room and pulls up a chair next to the bed. He sees Charles Barkley on the screen, but the sound is off. Tommaso reaches for the remote to shut off the television.

"Why is the sound off?" asks Robert. "Do you need me to fix it?"

"No, I can't stand listening to them. This guy, every time he speaks, they all laugh hysterically, and I can't understand a word he's saying. I'm not sure they can either. I'll admit that he's funny to look at. By the way, Merry Christmas, Robert."

"You too, Papa. I just came from the cemetery. I said a prayer for you."

"Was your wife with you?"

"Don't start, Papa. We've got bigger problems. Elmo came with me."

"I just think that that it's her place to go with you. Elmo is a loyal son. She could learn from him."

"Look, Papa. Ramona never even met Mama, and she doesn't like the cemetery. If I'm okay with it, then—"

"So I guess I shouldn't expect her at my funeral."

"Papa, I didn't come here to argue, at least not about this. And if you don't like Ramona, why did you give her Mama's necklace?"

"First of all, I adore Ramona. She's the best thing that ever happened to you. Second, what I do with my things is my business. The cemetery thing is about you, not her, but I wouldn't expect you to understand."

"Papa, that code of yours is archaic and obsolete. Anyway, what was up with the gifts? It looks like you are, um, preparing for something. Should I be worried?"

"No, son, I'm not going senile and I'm not depressed, either. I've had a lot of time to think in here, and it was just time. I put a lot of thought into it."

"Well, they were all extremely moved by the gesture, which brings me to my gift."

"The key."

"Yes, Papa, I assume it's your 'retirement plan?'"

"In a way. Let me work up to that. First of all, my condition here is improving, but more slowly than expected. The damage from a 60-year-old gunshot wound is causing some problems. It makes an artificial hip impossible. Know this, however. I intend to walk out of here and live a long life."

"Okay. Do you have any news on Anthony's condition?"

"How would I know that?"

"Come on, Papa, I don't know how, but you find out before his doctors do."

"Okay, the last I heard, he was alive, but barely. No speech, extensive paralysis, they don't know about brain damage yet. Rico expects him to die, but for now, is willing to let nature take its course. I do not think his patience will last long."

"Seriously? What would be the rush? No one will contest his ascension. All he would do is piss off the traditionalists. There's no gain in that."

"Robert, the kid is not all there. He's crazy paranoid. Without his father to reign him in, the walls are closing in on him. He's just like Enrico in this way."

"Come on, Papa. Times are different, now."

"Robert, I've seen it, and you are his biggest threat."

"Me? How?"

"You control things with numbers and words, not fists or bullets. Rico can't understand it, so he immediately doesn't trust it. I guarantee you that he even knows that you're here talking to me. If I didn't put it out there that I was near the end, we'd already have heard from him."

"What? You did what? Papa, I think that it's you who's paranoid."

"Robert! I need you to listen to me. This is how it works. I'm not saying that you are naïve, but you've had it different from me, and you had my protection. I know you thought of getting out. Believe me, I'm sorry that you didn't move sooner, but with Rico, it's a whole new ballgame."

·"Jesus, Papa. This is a bad time, with the banking regulations and…Elmo. Papa, what about Elmo?"

"Robert, I was on the fence about Elmo, but I've thought about it, and your mother was right. I failed her and you and I do not intend to let it happen again. I am putting a plan in place, but I need some more time."

"So tell me about the key, Papa."

"Okay, you mentioned a 'retirement plan.' Some people in the business have tried to keep some dirt on those in charge as leverage in case they fell out of favor, or just wanted out. Unfortunately, this is like keeping nitroglycerin in the trunk of your car on a bumpy road. It's just as likely to blow up in your own face. It also flies in the face of *omertà*. Someone like Enrico, and now, I suppose, Rico, would go up in flames before they let themselves be leveraged."

Robert holds up the key.

"So what's in this box?"

"Nothing, actually."

"I don't get it, Papa."

"Basically, I'm hedging my bets. Something is going to happen, sooner or later. I have two goals. One, to protect you, and two, to protect your family."

"What about you?"

"Oh, I have no intention of sacrificing myself in some heroic gesture, but at my age…well, let's just say that my long term well-being is a lower priority to me when compared to the rest of you."

"Fair enough, Papa, but it's still a priority to me."

"Fair enough. Anyway, I need to keep Rico off balance for a few days. I have a few secrets left, but nothing that can be linked to you. What about the will?"

"Excuse me?"

"The will. Anthony's estate. You're his lawyer, aren't you?"

"Yes, I am, but it's public knowledge. Anthony has made no secret about the succession of the family."

"There's a sister, correct?"

"Yes, but she disowned the family and moved to San Francisco. She married a poet. They live on love, from what I understand. The will leaves her one million dollars, which I fully expect she will throw in the ocean or donate to feral cats. She can't help us."

"No, if she even looks to the east, Rico would have her killed anyway."

"Jesus, Papa."

"I'm not joking. I wish I were. This is what we're dealing with. I don't know if the will is of any use, but I do know that power is the only useful leverage against Rico. It's the only thing he can't rationalize dying for. Where are the copies?"

"Of the will? In my office, and in a safety deposit box, in Anthony's name."

"Where?"

"Downtown, in my building, unless he moved it."

"Interesting. See if you can find out. Be subtle. Rico will find out anyway, but don't be too obvious."

"Papa, you're scaring me. Why poke the bear? If he's as nuts as you say, you won't be able to control him through his paranoia."

"Not control…delay. If he's confident, he'll do what he wants. If he's confused, he'll try to work it out. Since he's incapable of trust, he has no consigliere. He may come to see you, however."

"I was afraid of that as well."

"Just be completely honest. That will drive him off the deep end. He's looking for duplicity, since that he can shoot at. Yes, honesty is just the thing to confuse him."

"Or drive him off the deep end."

"No choice, we're already on the pier, son."

"I suppose so. Well, I'll be in touch."

"Merry Christmas, son, and no telephones."

"Merry Christmas, indeed."

Wednesday, Dec 26th
~ Glen Ridge ~

Tommy is on her bed fiddling with her computer. Pep walks in carrying a plate.

"Hey, Sis. Would you like a Pop Tart?"

"What kind?"

"Red inside, with white icing and sparkles, or brown."

Tommy looks up.

"How do you know it's red inside?"

"I started that one."

"Brown it is, then. Thanks."

He hands her the plate and she puts it on the bed next to her. Pep sits on her desk chair and swivels to face her.

"Whatcha doin'?" he asks.

"Email, Facebook, anything to distract me from my work. I actually hate doing research."

"Odd, coming from a PhD candidate."

"Well, I really want to teach, but this is part of the path. Unfortunately, it has little to do with teaching skills."

"If the TAs I have at MIT are any indication, I'd have to agree."

"It's sad, actually. Most of my classmates hate teaching and would cut each other's throats to get into an R1 university. I can see that you're highly interested in this. What's the matter? Is the cable out?"

"Har har. I just wanted to talk."

"You're worried about Grandpa?"

"Yeah, I guess. You don't think he's getting his affairs in order, do you?"

"I see where you're coming from, but I don't think so. I think he's trying to send us all a message."

"What message?"

"It's different for each of us. You heard Elmo. He actually had discussed the cufflinks with Grandpa. And mine, too. And Mom, I'd guess that was him accepting— no—acknowledging her as the matriarch of the family. The key thing, I don't get at all, but it certainly got Dad's attention."

"So what about the gloves? I don't know what to make of it."

"Look, Pep, I'm only guessing here, but I'm sure you can talk to Grandpa about it."

"I intend to, but I would appreciate hearing your thoughts."

"Okay, I would say acceptance."

"How so?"

"Well, look at it this way. Grandpa wants to give you a gift, and he wants it to be personal. What does he do? Things that are personal to him wouldn't likely resonate with you and vice versa. He wants you to know that he both loves you *and* accepts you for who you are. He picked something that he cherished that you would cherish as well."

"What if I felt he was being patronizing?"

"Patronizing would be an argyle sweater vest that he hated. He took the chance that you were smart enough to recognize that the thought about the gift was the actual gift itself and that the fact that you love beautiful gloves is a bonus."

"That's beautiful, Sis. I wonder why everyone thinks that you're such a cynical bitch."

Tommy picks up a stuffed elephant off the bed and flings it at Pep, who is laughing.

"Rajah, kill!" she says. "You know, I've actually been thinking about that, and Grandpa's gift has been a factor."

"Go on, Doctor Feelgood."

"During my abortive date the other day, I was letting myself be controlled by outside forces. Actually, most of them were inside forces screaming at me to bail because of a little adversity. I guess I was letting the way I was, or at least believed that I was perceived by others, to dictate how I acted. I spoke to Grandpa about it, and he had some simple advice, which I didn't get right away."

"Plastic surgery?"

"I'm serious, Pep."

"Sorry."

"I didn't get it until he sent me the ring. Being myself includes deciding who I want to be on my terms, not anyone else's."

"So you're seeing the guy again? I'm surprised with you going back to Boston in a week."

"I like him, plain and simple. He might make me happy, and I deserve to be happy. Happiness is worth working for, and I gain nothing by giving up because of outside circumstances."

She holds up her hand to show him that she is wearing the ring.

"Wow, that's deep, Sis. I don't know if I'm ready for so much change. Can't you just keep being a bitch to me?"

Tommy lowers all of her fingers except the middle one with the ring on it.

"Happy?"

Wednesday, Dec 26th
~ Montclair ~

Robert is working at his desk when a voice comes through the intercom. "Mr. Pastor, there's—"

The door opens suddenly and in walks Rico Pizzoli. He is alone and strides in toward the two chairs in front of the desk. He pulls one closer, sits in it, and puts his feet up on Robert's desk. This is clearly for show, but is so awkward that Robert nearly bursts out laughing. He keeps his cool, however, as he knows that Rico is testing him. He assures his secretary that security will not be needed.

"Rico, it's good to see you. I see that you do not have an appointment, something of which your father always gave me the courtesy, but I believe I can give you a few minutes."

"Why thanks, Robby. You got some nice office here in my bank."

"Well, Rico, to be accurate, this bank is owned by a consortium of investors, which is part of a larger investment conglomerate. As a member of the board of directors, I am well aware of your family's, er, your father's rather large stake in the company."

Rico leans forward and points at Robert.

"I don't need any of your legal mumbo jumbo to know what's mine, Robby."

"I suppose not, but the legal mumbo jumbo, as you say, is useful in *keeping* what's yours. Again, unless there have been any further developments, I assume we are talking about your father's assets for the moment."

Rico eyes him coolly.

"For the moment, yeah," he says, "but I want to ensure a smooth transition when, or rather *if*, something happens."

"While my oath as a licensed attorney in this state precludes me from discussing any details, I can assure you that all is in order for any eventuality."

"Meaning?"

"Meaning that your succession is assured."

"It had better be. You know, my father put a lot of faith in you—"

"And I trust he still does."

"Yeah, well, I'm not so trusting, Robby. You and your old man have gotten fat off my family for years and I'm keeping an eye on you two. I know you went to visit him yesterday."

If this is meant to shock Robert, he gives nothing away.

"Of course. Who could consider himself a good son and not visit his ailing father on Christmas Day? I'm sure that you were by Anthony's bedside as well."

Rico reddens at this.

"Never mind me, Robby. There's gonna be some oversight going on in here once I'm in charge. You're not the only lawyer or bean counter in the phone book, y'know."

"Very true. I have a copy of the Yellow Pages here that is at your disposal should you need it. Keep in however, that oversight and auditing will reveal your secrets as well. There is a delicacy to this type of work that you cannot find in the phone book.. As I recall, we also helped you with some legal difficulties in the past. Something involving prostitutes, I believe?"

Rico is visibly angry now. He takes a moment and leans back in his chair.

"What about Elmo?"

Robert is trying to keep cool, but knows that he is beginning to show strain.

"What *about* Elmo?"

"I hear he's looking for a little help finding his way in the world. You know, I'm gonna need some new *blood*, if you know what I mean."

Robert grips the arms of his chair tightly and leans forward.

"Let me make this clear," he says. "My family is off limits."

"We're all family here, Robby, or don't you get that? I just wanted to see you without the legalese or any smooth talk. I think I got what I came for."

Rico gets up and walks out the door. Robert leans back and lets out a breath. He stares at the ceiling for a few minutes to slow down his heart rate. He is furious at himself for losing his cool. He puts his hands over his face and begins to gently sob.

Wednesday, Dec 26th
~ Glen Ridge ~

Scotty pulls in front of the Pastor home at 5:40. He's typically early and his anxiety about this date pushes him even earlier. Pep, who has been watching his sister pace the living room since 5:30, looks out the window and spots the car idling out front. He informs Tommy who verifies his identity. She takes a deep breath, slips on her coat and heads outside. Scotty is trying to wipe the sweat off of his hands when she taps on the window, giving him a start. He hops out and rushes to open the door for her, but when he gets to the passenger side, finds it locked. Since the car is running, he has to run back around to the driver's side to hit the unlock button, then sprints back around to open her door. She originally reaches for the door when it unlocks, but backs off and waits when she realizes what is happening. She smiles at his chivalry and gets in the car.

They take the short trip to Merola's and Scotty parks in their back lot. This time, she waits for him to open her door and they walk into the restaurant. There are already several people waiting for tables, both in the foyer and at the bar. Tommy walks right through the crowd and makes eye contact with the maître d'. Without a moment's hesitation, he leads Tommy to a small table for two in the corner of the dining room.

"Signorina Pastor," he says, "it is so good to have you back."

"Grazie, Carlo, it's good to see you as well."

Carlo nods to Scotty who nods blankly in return. Carlo turns quickly and strides away.

"Wow," says Scotty, "I take it that you've been here before."

"I practically grew up here. My family are regulars. It seems that my dad somehow managed to marry the only full-blooded Italian woman who cannot cook. Two to three times a week was not unusual growing up."

"But the way you breezed through the crowd...I must admit, it was pretty badass."

"Well, my family has kind of a special relationship with the restaurant."

"You don't own it, do you?"

"No, ownership is too strong a word. Let's see, not connected. Patron, I guess, would be most apt."

"Like an investor?"

Again, not so much. The restaurant has more invested in my family. This table, for example, is pretty much on constant reserve for my family."

"What? The place is packed on a Wednesday. How can they justify—"

"The cachet. People come here specifically for that reason. This place didn't draw flies before my father became involved."

"Well, so much for my business degree. I would have advised them to put two booths in this spot and to replace Carlo with a hostess/runner system."

"That's part of the reason I brought you here. My world is somewhat different from what you are used to. Not drastically so, but I learned recently that it is important to both of us that I be myself."

"You're referring to our first date?"

"Partially, though I would prefer to think of this as our first date. You were with someone else then, someone who was too focused on being someone else."

"I think I know what you mean. Even though your situation has some rather specific trappings, what you describe is not uncommon. The first date is probably the ruination of some potentially great relationships. Maybe we should invent a dating site where all first dates don't count. I guess to some extent, that's what speed dating is about."

"Trust me, five minutes is more than enough time to torpedo a relationship. What about masks for the first date?"

"Ooh, how about a mask of who we're trying to be?"

"And who would you be on a first date?"

"Cary Grant, or maybe George Clooney if she looks too young to know who Cary is."

"It's funny, but I like this Scotty better. I would find Cary Grant unobtainable. It's funny how we take on that type of persona when we are trying to connect."

"We?"

"Oh, yes, I've tried to be Grace Kelly, Audrey Hepburn, and Eleanor Roosevelt all rolled into one. Ick, right?"

"Well, I can see the Grace Kelly, particularly when you allowed me to open your door for you when I was racing around my car like an idiot."

"You noticed. My mother will be quite pleased with herself."

"And, you probably are unaware that Eleanor Roosevelt is quite simply the Patron Saint of my people. It's actually quite a turn on."

"It looks like I may need to trade in my beret for a coal miner's helmet."

"Yowzah! Hey, I notice that no one has been to the table yet."

"Stop talking."

"What?"

Tommy puts her fingers to her lips. Scotty shrugs and stops talking. Within five seconds a waiter appears with a menu for Scotty, water, bread, olive oil, wine glasses, and some small plates. He leaves as quickly as he arrived. Scotty looks stunned for a few seconds and begins to laugh.

"What, may I ask, is so funny?" asks Tommy.

"I'm sorry. It reminded me of a cartoon, where everything happens in fast motion. What the hell was that?"

"It's called attentive service. But there's something else amusing you, isn't there?"

"You are very perceptive. I'm embarrassed to say it, but the waiter is a dead ringer for the guy that Grover is always tormenting as a waiter on Sesame Street."

"Except for the blue skin, er, felt, I suppose."

"So you've noticed this. The mustache, the bald head, the eyebrows, and even the eyes. He might even be the same height."

"So much for Cary Grant. I can see that you have more questions."

"What if you come here and don't want to talk? Does the meal last only five minutes?"

"No, they are expert at pacing and at not interrupting, always around, but never in sight. Anything else?"

"Okay, why one menu, and why are there no prices?"

"Okay, one at a time. I haven't opened a menu here since I was about 12. I just tell them what I want and they bring it, whether it's on the menu or not."

"You're not serious."

"Yes, I am. During one of my rebellious phases, I came here with three school friends. We ordered tacos and hot dogs. Somehow they were back here in fifteen minutes with all of the food we ordered. Of course, this resulted in my mother giving me a two hour lesson in grace and manners."

"How did she find out?"

"Probably one of her friends saw us. I guarantee you that no one in the restaurant said a word."

"So if I order, say, potato latkes, they would bring them?"

"Would George Clooney do that?"

"Maybe George Carlin. What about the prices?"

"Our money is no good here."

"I don't understand. Is your family paying for this? I'm not comforta—"

"No, our money is actually no good here. They won't take it, not in any form. My father is not paying for this. No one is."

"Okay, Tommy, I'm starting to freak out a little here. I have taken a few courses in Economics and Finance. This business model does not make sense."

"That's the deal here for patrons and their family."

"How many patrons does this place have?"

"I believe that would be one."

"Your father."

"Yup."

"So how is the veal in this joint?"

"If you're asking to test me, then I will inform you that I personally do not eat veal, but also don't make value judgments about those who do. If you just want to know, I hear it is outstanding. My father eats it often."

"I just never get to eat it. I had it as a kid and liked it, but it's been a long time."

"Just keep in mind that the calf gains nothing from this."

"If it's as good as you say, then the calf did not suffer needlessly."

"Oh, I doubt there was any suffering. Just two hollow points in the back of the skull. Pop! Pop!"

"Okay, I guess we've both passed the sick humor test. We appear to be compatibly horrible people."

They order and as mentioned, the meal is perfectly paced. It is also perfectly prepared and seasoned. Tommy has a glass of red wine with dinner, but Scotty turns over his glass indicating that he is not having any. The waiter looks at Tommy as he removes the wineglass. She shakes her head and he shrugs conspiratorially. They have a wonderful meal and wonderful conversation. After the meal, the waiter brings one tiramisu with two forks and two cups of espresso.

"Did we order this?" asks Scotty.

"It's part of the whole experience. No one will be offended if you don't have any. You also can order a different beverage."

"My only concern is you being offended if I eat it all. As for the espresso, I don't think I can take the waiter's disappointment if I don't man up."

Suddenly, when Carlo is distracted by a large party, Dale Hankins walks in and stops by the table.

"Hey, Scotty," he says, "I see that you are moving up in the world. This place is pretty hefty for a teacher."

Almost instantly, Carlo is beside Dale. Behind Carlo is a heretofore unseen waiter who is probably six foot seven and 260 pounds. His jacket can barely contain his arms.

"I am sorry, sir, but this section is reserved for our guests, and I do not see a reservation in your name."

"I didn't give you my name," says Dale.

"Nevertheless, sir, I must ask you to leave this establishment."

"I'm with the police."

"Very good, sir. Allow me to take you over to the table of your Chief. I'm quite sure he would like to congratulate you on your manners."

Dale looks at Carlo and his associate. He gives them a contemptuous look and heads for the exit.

"My apologies, signorina," says Carlo, with a slight bow of his head.

"I'm guessing that none of this sort of thing ever shows up on Yelp or Urban Spoon," says Scotty.

Tommy laughs and takes a taste of the tiramisu.

"You are a good sport," she says. "I'll give you that. Here's the big question. Have you been scared off, or are we still on for tomorrow?"

"If you think this will scare me off, you don't know who you're dealing with. I'd do this just for the story, although,

I assume Dale's visit was no coincidence. I doubt he was watching *me*."

"Don't sell yourself short. He couldn't be the first closeted homosexual to be attracted to you to the point of trying to ruin your dinner with a beautiful woman. I hear Clooney gets that all the time."

"What do I know? I think Eleanor Roosevelt was hot."

"Touché."

"So now, what do we do? Do I leave a tip? Take a blood oath?"

"Just stand up. You'll be impressed."

Scotty nods and stands up. Immediately the waiter arrives to pull out Tommy's seat. In one motion he hands her coat to Scotty so he may put it on her. He stands aside and gives a little bow. They head for the exit and get in the car.

"Oh, my God!" he says. "That was choreographed like a stage play. I had a great time. Can you meet me in Town Center tomorrow at 10:40? I want to catch the 10:55 #87 bus to the City. Your father doesn't own the bus line, does he?"

"No, I'm afraid we'll need tickets. I had a great time as well. I hope that your detective friend didn't freak you out."

"Please, I was already freaked out by the curlicues made out of butter. If he shows up in Manhattan, I might get worried."

Scotty pulls in front of her house and she waits for him to walk around to her side. He opens her door and walks her up the walk.

"Tomorrow, then," he says.

"I can't wait," she says.

They share a nice kiss before she waves and goes inside. Scotty pulls into a space in his apartment lot. When he puts the car in park, he realizes that he doesn't even remember walking to the car or driving home.

Wednesday, Dec 26th
~ Clifton ~

Elmo and Donny are sitting in a booth in Shorty's.

"Who's this guy you want me to meet?" asks Elmo.

"Don't worry about it. I met him through Hoosmanian when he came to install some equipment is the garage. He's gonna help us out."

"Look Donny, about that. I've been thinking—"

"Hold up, he's here."

A guy walks in wearing a blue work shirt. The shirt has an American flag patch sewn on one arm, the Trident Alarm logo on the left side of his chest and the name Vinny stitched on the right. Donny waves him over to the table.

"Hey, Vinny, glad you could swing by. This is the guy, uh, Frank, I was talking to you about. How about a beer?"

"Bud Light," says Vinny.

He slides in next to Elmo and shakes his hand. It takes Elmo a second to realize that Donny called him Frank as an alias. He wishes they had discussed this. He has no idea what to call Donny. Donny returns with three beers and sits down. He turns to Elmo.

"As you can see, Vinny here works for an alarm company. It's the same alarm company that installed the system in a certain building that we have an interest in."

"Sure, uh…dude," says Elmo. "Uh, how does it work?"

Vinny leans in and lowers his voice.

"It's a grand to get you in the building, and two grand if you want to get into the bank. To get into the boxes from there, you'll need something more powerful than I can get, but you should be able to punch the locks once inside."

"Powerful?" asks Elmo. "You mean explosives?"

"Don't worry about that," says Donny. "I know a guy."

"But, Don—"

"I said I'd handle it, *Frank*."

"Hey, that's up to you guys," says Vinny. "You know what service I provide, you know how much, and you know how to reach me."

Vinny finishes his beer, burps, stands, and heads for the door.

"Thanks for almost using my real name, E," says Donny. "Jeez, you gotta get with the program."

"Look, Donny. I don't know about this. Explosives? That sounds dangerous. And two grand? I don't have that kind of scratch lying around."

"Didn't you just get some diamond cufflinks for Christmas? E, we can't wait any longer. This is what you call an investment. This is our ticket in."

"I gotta think about this, Donny."

"Well think fast. I've already taken some risk here. Jeez, we only got a few days left."

"Donny, I think I'm being followed."

"Followed where? You haven't done anything illegal. Just the same, let's get out of here."

Elmo pays the tab and they head to Donny's car. They head back to Essex County, but see no sign of a tail. They pass a series of dark parking lots in an industrial area. Behind one of the buildings there is a work van parked with its lights off. Inside, Vinny is on a cell phone.

"Yes, sir, this is Agent DeLuca. Remember that chop shop investigation in Bloomfield? Yes, sir. That's the one. I was contacted by one of the grease monkeys looking for some alarm breaching expertise…Yes, strictly small time, but I thought it might lead to something…Well, it seems to involve a bank, so it might be federal…Yes, I know, sir…Yes, thank you, sir, but there's more. I just met another player and I think it was Elmo Pastor…That's what I thought, sir. I'll certainly keep you informed."

Wednesday, Dec 26th
~ Glen Ridge ~

Ramona walks into Robert's home office next to their bedroom. She's in her nightgown and robe.

"Robert. Is everything all right? You never work like this, certainly not when the kids are home. What's the matter, honey? My, you're still in your work clothes."

"It's just a bad time. I did loosen my tie a few hours ago."

Ramona opens her robe to reveal a lacy silk white night gown.

"Do you remember this?"

She smiles and moves behind him.

"Let me help you with that, big boy."

She reaches around his neck and pulls his tie through the knot. She puts it on her own neck and twirls it like a boa. She is channeling Mae West.

"Hey, why don't you come up and see me sometime?"

He smiles wanly.

"Something is wrong, isn't it?" she asks.

"Sorry, babe. I'm working out a few things. Tell me about the kids."

"Okay. Your daughter had what appeared to be a successful date with her dance coordinator. She didn't say much, but she was walking on air and she's seeing him tomorrow."

"For rehearsal?"

Ramona pulls up the side chair and sits down. She spins Robert toward her and picks up his feet one by one and removes his shoes. She places his feet on her lap and begins to massage them.

"No. The final rehearsal is on Sunday. They have Christmas week off. They're taking the bus into the City. She went right up to her room, but my spy said they kissed at the door."

"Pep. He should be less nosy. Ooh, that feels good. Your spy didn't mention who kissed whom, did he?"

"Clearly, he should be less nosy. I believe he described it as mutual, not too long, not too short, in all, quite romantic."

"And what's he up to?"

"He's at a sleepover with the girls. You know, the usual suspects from band. Janine's mother is fine with it, but I don't know. It just seems so...odd to me."

"How are you doing with all of that?"

"I'm trying. Honestly, I'm embarrassed. Not by him, I don't mean. I mean by myself. I must admit that you have been much more accepting than I have. I'm actually a little surprised, with you growing up with your father and the whole 'family' thing. And your father, he's been amazing. Who saw that coming?"

"I suppose maybe we were all hoping that someone else would scream or cry, and it would all go away, like a big family secret. I guess maybe Papa and I have enough secrets at work. You'll get there, baby."

"At this point, I'm more worried about Elmo. Tonight, he came home and went right to his room. He looked upset, Robert."

Robert looks away slightly, but enough for Ramona to take notice.

"There is something," she says. "Robert, what are you keeping from me?"

"I'm worried about him too, babe. You know that he's been itching to join the business. I talked to Papa and we seem to be on the same page. We've both talked to Elmo, but we can't seem to connect with him. He's lost, and I'm having trouble reaching him. I've even considered counseling, and you know how we Pastors feel about that. Who would he see? I don't think there are career counselors for gangsters."

"What are we going to do, honey? I've only ever asked one thing of you."

"I know."

"You *must* keep him out of it."

"I KNOW. I'm sorry, babe. I'll figure it out."

"I trust you, Robert. Now please come to bed."

"May I have my tie back, please?"

Ramona stuffs it in the top of her night gown, stands and heads for the bedroom.

"I seem to have misplaced it. Maybe you can help me look for it."

He smiles, stands, and turns off his lamp.

"Woman, do I have to do everything around here?"

Thursday, Dec 27th
~ Montclair ~

"Have a good time, Sis."

Pep pulls away after dropping off Tommy in Town Center. She looks around for Scotty, but doesn't see him. She is wondering whether she should have worn a heavier coat and decides to revisit her mother's "fashion over function" argument when she gets home. She watches a black limousine pull up to the curb. Tommy is surprised to see Carter get out in his uniform. He walks around to the rear curbside door, opens it and smiles.

"M'Lady, if you please."

"Why, thank you, sir."

She gets in the car and is surprised to find no one else inside. Carter closes the door and gets in the driver's seat. He pulls away from the curb.

"Carter, I'm confused. Where—"

"In a moment, madam."

In a few blocks he pulls over to the curb in front of a Dunkin' Donuts. Scotty walks out carrying a tray of coffee and a bag. He gets in the back with Tommy.

"Surprise!" he says.

He hands a coffee into the front to Carter. He hands a coffee and the bag to Tommy.

"There are creamers, sugar, and artificial sweeteners in there. I didn't know what you wanted. After the espresso last night, I assume you like it strong."

"Well, I must admit that the espressos were decaf. I know that it's sacrilege, but I would still be up if I had regular last night."

"Then I guess the reason I couldn't sleep last night was because I was thinking about you," he says.

Carter is unable to stifle a chuckle. Tommy joins in.

"I'm sorry," says Carter, "am I gonna need to close the privacy window?"

"Keep it open," says Tommy. "I may need an escape route. What's this all about, anyway?"

"It seems that Carter has a job in Manhattan today and he offered to give us the royal treatment, which he was willing to do in exchange for a cup of coffee."

"How sweet," says Tommy.

Carter holds up his cup.

"Five sugars, baby."

"You know what I mean," she says. "So how does your job work?"

"My company does any type of driving like airport runs, proms, and such. We also drive around a lot of visiting dignitaries and celebs. I get a lot of that detail because, quite frankly, I'm the best. The hours suck, but the tips can be very good, and I'm learning the business."

"I assume you do less yakking to the paying clients," says Scotty.

"The customer is always right, sir," says Carter, "but since you are a fucking freeloading stowaway piece of shit motherfucker, I'll talk as much as I want...sir."

Tommy is laughing hysterically.

"So, who have you had in your car that I would know?" she asks.

"Barbara Walters, Oliver North, Mark Cuban...dozens, really."

"Who was the best?" she asks.

"Julie Andrews, definitely," says Carter, with no hesitation. "I know it sounds obvious, but she was as sweet as you can imagine, every bit the lady. I guess if you play enough princesses—"

"And the worst?"

"That's tougher. Some are just quiet, like you don't exist. I've had a few dicks, who blame you for the traffic or the size of the car, as though I could change that. Oh, wait. Definitely Rick James. He asked me where he could score drugs."

"Seriously? Was he joking?"

"I considered that, but I see that as worse. It stereotypes me and threatens my livelihood. In any case, he's in hell, now, probably in upper management."

"Carter, I have some bad news for you," she says. "People aren't all bad. I saw a talk show with the African-American detective from Law and Order—"

"Jesse L. Martin? I'm a fan."

"Yes, and he said he got into performing through an arts program for inner-city children in Buffalo."

"So?"

"He said the program was created by Rick James."

"Scotty, if your girl here is about to tell me that Julie Andrews cheats on her taxes, or had a love child with the Duke of Windsor, please ask her to keep it to herself."

Their laughter dies out when the privacy window reaches the top of the track. Carter picks up his coffee.

"Just you and me, kid."

Thursday, Dec 27th
~ West Orange ~

Tommaso is finishing his lunch when Rico Pizzoli walks into his room.

"Ooh, Jell-O," says Rico. "Is this what it's come to? I could have my chef stop by and bring you a few cannolis if you would like. We should have a few left over after my party."

"First of all, it's not canollis, it's cannoli. The plural is the same as the singular. Second, how could the son of Anthony Pizzoli have so little respect for anything?"

"You geezers and your respect, you make me sick. You've forgotten what it means. You don't earn respect. You *own* respect. And I own it all now."

"So there's been a change in your father's condition? I heard there was still some hope."

"Hope for what? Even if he lives, he's done for. Maybe we'll set him up in here, next to you. You can yammer about the old days while he drools on himself."

Marcus walks in the door with a clipboard, sees Rico, and turns toward Tommaso. Tommaso looks him off with a barely perceptible twitch of his head, but Marcus gets the message. He looks at the clipboard, scratches his head, and walks out the door.

"Stupid nigger help. Most of them don't even speak English," says Tommaso.

He stifles the guilt he feels, knowing that Marcus is listening. Marcus is fiddling with some food trays right outside the door so he can hear much of what is being said.

"Still feisty as ever, huh, old man?"

"Old man. You know your father still calls me Mr. Pastor."

"That ship has sailed, *old man*. You aren't likely to hear him speak again after the stroke, and you sure as hell won't hear it from me."

"And the party you speak of? Is this to dance on his grave, or possibly even before he passes?"

Rico ignores him and walks over to pick up Tommaso's cane. He is disappointed when Tommaso shows no reaction.

"Wolfman. That's what I'll call you. Like a cheesy old black and white movie."

"Get on with it, Rico. What do you want?"

"Want? I don't want anything from you, Wolfman. What would I need from a bedridden old man?"

"You realize that the reason I am in this bed is that I took a bullet meant for your grandfather. You wouldn't be here, if it weren't for me."

"Ancient history, Wolfman. You milked that for 60 years. It's time to move on."

"So why come here to taunt me?"

"It's your son, Wolfie. He makes me nervous. Just a little nervous, mind you, but who needs stress in these difficult times?"

"Robert has been nothing but loyal to your family, including you, as I recall. He also has helped your family make a lot of money over the years."

"I always felt that my father gave him too much freedom. Plus, he's the only other person who can influence those other chicken-shit fat cats leeching off of the Pizzoli name."

"That's your problem, Rico. Pizzoli is not just a name to them. It's a business model, a philosophy, if you will. It's no different from Warren Buffett, Richard Branson, or T. Boone Pickens. It's a brand now."

"I doubt they built their brands like my grandfather did."

"Don't kid yourself, Rico. Or their grandfathers did and they used that as a stake. That's right where you are now. You can be as big as them, but no, you've got to be a tough guy. In ten years you'll be dead or in a federal pen for sure. The thing is, how many people are you taking with you?"

"Ten years? At least I'll be outliving you. I guess I'll see you in hell. Just tell your son that I'm watching him. Oh, by the way, Wolfman, I know you've got a secret box somewhere. Just in case you were thinking about using it as a dirty bomb on me, know that that explosion will take out Robert as well. I might even throw in your grandson as a freebie."

Unlike Robert, Tommaso shows no reaction to this threat. Rico tosses the cane on top of Grandpa and strides out. Marcus turns away from Rico and buries his face in a chart. As soon as Rico turns the corner, Marcus goes into Tommaso's room.

"You okay?" he asks.

"Marcus, I want to apologize for before, what I said."

"Not necessary, Mr. Pastor. I don't like it, but I understand it. Words aren't hateful. People are hateful."

"Well, I've got a bellyful of hate for that little prick."

"I heard most of it. Anything I can do?"

"You've already done so much for me. Thank you again for helping me with the Christmas gifts. I wish that I could say that I won't need to call on you again. When can I get out of here?"

"I'd say two weeks on the outside, based on your chart, but I'm no doctor."

"I'll take your word over theirs. I need to think about this."

"It sounded pretty bad. It was tough for me to not come in here and strangle him myself."

"You did well, Marcus. Overreacting is how you give yourself away. I actually learned a few things from him."

"What, that he's a psychopath?"

"Actually, yes. While I already knew that about him, it gave me some insight into his strengths and weaknesses. From what you heard, what does he crave most?"

"Not money. I'd say control—no, wait. Power."

"Exactly. I don't know if I can use it, but it may be something I can bargain with."

"What else did you learn? I mean, that you didn't already know?" asks Marcus.

"We knew he was paranoid, and devoid of respect, but he's angry. Not for show angry, but something deeper."

"Maybe his father?"

"Maybe. He's also alone. He has soldiers, people beholden to him, but he seemed so alone."

"How does that help?"

"Again, I'm not sure it does, but he showed it, and it's more than we had."

"What's all this 'we' stuff?"

"Oh, sorry, Marcus. I didn't mean to involve you."

"I take it as a compliment."

"It's a compliment on you, Marcus."

"What about the key?. He must be watching you, your son, or both."

"Oh, I'm aware of that. That was all planned."

"You wanted him to know?"

"Not specifically…just testing his paranoia, and possibly setting up something for later if needed."

"Well, you've lost me now."

"Marcus, do you have any contacts at Holy Cross Hospital?"

"Where his father is?"

"Yes. I may need to arrange some things."

Thursday, Dec 27ᵗʰ
~ New York City ~

"I'm glad I wore comfortable shoes," says Tommy.

Tommy and Scotty are sitting on the floor in the Port Authority terminal waiting in line for the #67 bus back to Montclair.

"I hope it wasn't too much walking."

"Not at all. I am a dancer, as you know. My legs will be in great shape when I get back to Boston, but I wish I could say the same about my butt. Why don't they have chairs here?"

"They do, but it's better to be in the queue. From here, we can sit together. If we sit over there, we'll be strap hanging. It's a workday and it's after 4:30. I probably should've planned better."

"Don't be ridiculous. This is fine, and I really enjoyed the walk. It was sunny and mild, we got to see the tree and the skaters, and we had a nice lunch."

"I'm a sucker for the theatre district. My grandmother used to take me to shows all the time. We'd take the PATH when we were in Newark and the bus from Montclair.

We'd wait on line for half-price tickets. She couldn't sing a lick, but was always belting out show tunes at home, anyway."

"You miss her."

"Yeah, but her philosophy was to live every day to the fullest. When she was dying of heart disease, I sat with her in the hospital and asked her if she was scared of dying. I was 22 and just out of school. She told me that she was unafraid because she had made it her mission to do all of the things she wanted to do while she was able to."

"It's a good way to look at things."

"That's just it. It wasn't until a few years later that I realized that she was telling me what I needed to hear at the time. Even as she lay dying, she put my needs above hers. I was blown away. She was an educator until the very end."

"Scotty, are you trying to make me cry in front of all these people?"

"Sorry, but it looks like they're boarding. You can get weepy on the bus."

She slaps him on the arm as they get up and file onto the bus. They take a pair of seats in the middle of the bus. Scotty takes the window and Tommy sits on the aisle, but she leans on his shoulder.

"Nice," he says, "it looks like they cleaned up all the remnants of Hurricane Sandy in midtown."

"We were very lucky. We have a house on Long Beach Island."

"Lucky how? On the news it looked wiped out."

"We're in Harvey Cedars. We're on the ocean, but we had very large dunes compared to most of the rest of the shore. The dunes are gone, but our house is intact."

"Is that a nice area?"

"It's a *very* nice area, and we have a very nice house there. We usually spent all of August there growing up. My dad would come for long weekends."

"He would work during the week?"

"Yes, but he wasn't consumed by it. He came to every game, every recital. It's funny, he was always in a suit and tie, but he was there. Once he started getting his name in the paper, the other kids started calling him Dapper Dad, you know, like Gotti, the Dapper Don. I think that freaked him out a little, and maybe some of the parents, too. After that, he would slip into the back of the auditorium, or be standing way in the outfield."

"I guess that kind of goes with the territory."

"Maybe, but to me, I found him to be heroic."

"Well, as a Jew, I usually would go to Belmar or Point Pleasant, or occasionally to Seaside for the boardwalk."

"They're all pretty wiped out now, as far as I know."

"Man, the pier in Seaside that was destroyed, there used to be a spook house at the end. Marcus and I were down there one evening and he dragged me in there. Now, I absolutely *hate* being scared. Rides, dark spaces, slasher movies, you can have it all."

"And I suppose he challenged your manhood."

Flash Mob

"Of course, that's what dudes do. I also don't see very well in the dark. Anyway, we go in, and it's pretty placid, but all I want to do is get through it. Marcus, of course, is poking his hand through these holes in the maze and scaring the crap out of all these girls who are screaming their heads off. Near the end, there's a strobe light over a bridge over the ocean. You can hear the waves below and see them when the light blinks on. This, I can do without."

"You might actually be a wuss."

"Oh, it gets better. We get to the exit, and I'm quite content to leave, only Marcus wasn't satisfied and wants to walk through it backwards. So we get to the strobe bridge. I'm standing behind him in the middle and he is near the far end. He stops, because there is a dummy at that end, apparently to discourage just this sort of behavior."

"It wasn't a dummy, was it?"

"No, it wasn't. The guy in the outfit shouts 'boo' and here's what I see in the strobe: Click. Marcus running toward me in a panic. Click. I'm flat on my back, and I actually see the bottom of Marcus' shoes as he runs over me. Click. As I try to get off the deck, I see Marcus' heels turning the corner for the exit."

Tommy is laughing hysterically and some of the other commuters are giving her the evil eye.

"Please stop. I'm going to wet myself."

"I get out of the spook house to strangle him, but he's laughing so hard, he nearly choked on his own."

"I love that you have such close friends."

"They're the brothers I never had. Please have dinner at our place tomorrow."

"On one condition—I'd like you to have dinner at my house with my family on Saturday."

"Deal. When are you going back?"

"Don't spoil it, Scotty. I'm not ready to think about that."

Friday, Dec 28th
~ Bayonne ~

"Where are we goin' Donny?" says Elmo. "None of this looks familiar."

Donny and Elmo are driving through an industrial area of Bayonne.

"Don't worry about it," says Donny. "You got the cash, right?"

"Four hundred, but there's no way I can spring for the alarm guy. Besides, I got a better idea."

"The alarm thing smelled fishy to me, anyway. What's your idea?"

"The bank building is open until 3:00 on the 31st. We can go in at, say, 2:30 and hide out until the music starts. I know the place. I know where we can hide until security locks it down."

"Don't they have, like, motion detectors?"

"No, the building is like a hundred years old. Once we're in, we're good."

"Isn't there security at the door? You know, to get to the offices."

"I got that figured out, too. I got an ID. I worked there one summer. We go in together. I use the ID, and you sign in as my guest, using a fake name. You go out using my ID, that way, there's no more record that I'm there. Tell the guard you left something in your car, and then come right back flashing your guest pass."

"But then there won't be a sign-out for me."

"Yeah, but that's on a fake ID, so they'll just assume it's an error."

"Makes sense. How do you know it'll work? What if they check carefully?"

"They don't. I go in there to see my dad all the time. They don't even look up."

Donny pulls into a seedy self-storage facility. He drives his Nova to the third row and turns left toward the back. In the darkness, Elmo makes out another car at the end. Donny comes to a stop, about 50 yards away from the other car. Donny opens his door and gets out. He motions for Elmo to follow. They walk toward the other car and soon see a lone figure leaning against the rear quarter panel.

"You're not cops," says the man, "you gotta tell me."

"No cops," says Donny.

"Gotta hear it from both of you," says the man.

Donny looks at Elmo, and motions for him to speak.

"Oh, yeah," says Elmo, "we're not cops."

"Good enough," says the man, "let's see the four bills."

Elmo looks at Donny, and then takes the $400 out of his jacket pocket. He walks over and hands it to the man. The man lights a cigarette and in the brief flash of the match, gets a look at Elmo's face. The man reaches through his open car window and gets out a bag. He hands it to Elmo, who absently hands it to Donny. Donny reaches in the bag and pulls out a pistol. Elmo starts to gasp, but no sound comes out. Donny puts the gun back, and pulls out a second pistol.

"Ammo?" asks Donny.

"It's all there," says the man. "Now if you don't mind, it's time for you to leave."

Donny and Elmo get back in the Nova and take off. The man takes another drag on his cigarette and tosses the butt to the ground. He pulls out his cell phone and makes a call.

"Hey, it's me. I think I have something for your boss...No, for him, it's on the house. Just tell him that I'm behind him 100%...Yeah...I just sold a couple of pieces to some punk, but the guy he brought with him, I think it was the guy your boss was asking about...Yeah, red curly hair. That's the one."

Friday, Dec 28ᵗʰ
~ Montclair ~

"Carter, get the door," says Marcus.

Scotty and Marcus are scrambling around their small kitchen preparing dinner.

"Damn," says Carter, "I just sat down. They're showing Top Plays."

"Turn off that TV and let her in," says Scotty. "We're doing all the cooking. At least you can get your lazy-ass Toastmaster self over to the door and do something useful."

Carter turns off the television and heads to the door muttering.

"Yes, suh, Massa Scotty."

He opens the door and sees Tommy smiling and holding a gift bag.

"Welcome to the big house, Miss Pastor, Massa Scotty's been 'spectin' you'all. Please come in and allows this tired old body to takes your coat."

Tommy is momentarily taken aback, but Marcus pushes past him. He's wearing an apron.

"Don't listen to this fool. Welcome to our apartment."

He leads her in and gives her a peck on the cheek. Carter takes her coat. She looks around and sees Scotty in the kitchen and gives him a warm smile.

"Perfect timing," says Scotty, "dinner will be ready in about ten minutes. Carter will give you a tour if you'd like, assuming he's done with his minstrel show."

"I brought wine," she says. "You may want to stick it in the freezer if it's only going to be ten minutes."

Marcus takes the bottle and Carter directs her toward the bedrooms.

"It's not much, as you can see, but we all have our own space. This is my room and over here is Marcus'."

"It's so orderly. I mean, for guys. I mean, well, I've had nearly a dozen roommates over the years and they were all pigs. I assumed that guys would be worse."

"Scotty and I would probably be worse if it weren't for Marcus. He's kind of mental about cleanliness and germs. This is Scotty's bed, uh, I mean room."

"Very funny. May I freshen up and meet you in the dining room?"

"Absolutely, and if you want to snoop around, he keeps all of his porn in the bottom drawer."

She elbows him and heads into the bathroom. Carter has successfully amused himself.

Marcus is pulling bottles of salad dressing out of the refrigerator, and Scotty is bringing food to the table.

"Carter, fill the water glasses," says Scotty.

Tommy walks in and gives Scotty a nice kiss. He holds out a chair and she sits. Carter sits to her left and Scotty to her right, leaving Marcus the easiest access to the kitchen. Marcus hands the wine bottle to Carter. He also places two glasses next to him.

"Here, this is your area," says Scotty.

Carter looks at the bottle. He takes what looks like a Swiss army knife out of his pocket, pulls out the corkscrew, and proceeds to open the wine. He pours some into both of the glasses. He turns to Tommy.

"Would you like Tom or Jerry, my dear?" he asks.

"Tom would be fine," she says. "I always felt a little sorry for him. I love the jelly glasses."

"Sorry," says Marcus. "Scotty and I don't drink, and we have limited cabinet space. Don't worry, Carter drinks enough for all of us."

"It's unusual to find a teetotaling Scotsman," she says.

"A Jewish Scotsman is nearly as rare," says Carter, "but non-drinking Jews are pretty common."

He jabs his thumb toward Marcus.

"This one, however, lives by some sort of bizarre code. He doesn't eat pork, either. I think he might be Vulcan."

"Well, everything looks delicious. Thank you for going to all of this trouble," she says.

They pass the food around. There is a tossed salad, fried chicken strips, a bowl of brown rice with corn and some green leaves in it, and several condiments. A bell goes off in the kitchen and Marcus goes to retrieve a tray full of fresh biscuits.

"The rice is very good," says Tommy. "Is it your recipe?"

"It's actually a very old family recipe," says Marcus. "It was developed by a distant uncle of mine back in the South."

"I guess that explains the corn. What are the green leaves?"

"Those are collard greens," says Marcus. "Do you like them?"

"I believe I do."

Scotty picks up his napkin and holds it to his mouth. Carter has some biscuits on his side plate and is dipping them in a blob of syrup.

"This is another Southern tradition," says Carter. "My family has been having biscuits and syrup at family dinners for generations."

"I was wondering about that. This is so great. Southern fried chicken and all of this. It's wonderful for you to share your culture. May I try the syrup?"

"Absolutely," says Carter. "My aunt would be very proud."

He passes her the syrup, and she pours a little on her bread plate. When she puts the bottle down, her thumb uncovers the picture of a middle-aged black woman.

Tommy stares at it for a second and closed her eyes. Carter, Marcus, and Scotty all burst out laughing hysterically. Tommy bows her head.

"Aunt Jemima. I can't believe I fell for that. Can I assume that none of this was true?"

Marcus reaches over to the counter, grabs an empty box, and puts it on the table.

"Meet my Uncle Ben."

Carter is stomping on the floor.

"You might as well tell her the rest," says Scotty, gasping for breath.

"You mean there's more?" she asks. "Wait, let me guess…the collard greens?"

Marcus is slapping the table. He finally stops laughing enough to speak.

"Parsley," he says. "The leaves were fresh parsley, strictly for color. To be honest, I wouldn't know a collard green from a petunia."

"Well, at least you can't call me a racist," she says, "since I hate you all equally."

Later over coffee, they move to the sofas. It's a very short walk.

"No coffee for you, Marcus?" asks Tommy.

"Vulcan, remember?" says Carter.

"I hope you guys all like the warm weather," she says, "because you're all going to hell. You know, the worst part is the fact that I call myself an agent of change, and spend my time studying problems holed up in ivy covered walls, never experiencing real life. I realize what a fraud I am."

"Nonsense, Tommy," says Scotty. "I find your work interesting and important."

"It's not that. All of my internships were in offices and with intellectual types. We talk and talk, solving nothing, and then pat ourselves on the back. I never took the time to actually experience people."

"I've spent most of my life with those people," says Carter. "You ain't missing much."

"It's not that simple, Carter," says Marcus. "We've struggled to get out, but how many just don't get the breaks?"

"We made our breaks," says Carter.

"Some we did," says Marcus, "but not all. And how many more get help from people like Scotty, who's teaching in Newark? He doesn't have to work there."

"That's what I mean," says Tommy. "I've never walked the walk like Scotty. It's part of what I like about him."

"Well, what impresses me about you," says Scotty, "is that you are looking at building a better dike, while I'm just sticking my fingers in a few holes. Maybe together, we can do even greater things."

"Get a room," says Carter.

Saturday, Dec 29th
~ West Orange ~

"You could have used my phone," says Marcus.

He is handing Tommaso a cell phone.

"I appreciate that, Marcus, but I want to leave nothing to chance. Something is happening and I can't get out of this fucking bed. I'm getting piecemeal information about the locals, the Feds, and our adversaries."

"Well, your guy said this was the best burner you could get. I'm not going to be bumped off for 'knowing too much,' am I? This guy was pretty squirrelly, and you keep using plural pronouns. *Our* adversaries?"

"Again, I must apologize, Marcus. This has gone deeper than I could have predicted. I believe that both my son and my grandson may be in danger. Just say the word and you are out. Know, however, that I really could use your help, and that the protection of you and your friends is as important to me as that of my family."

"I'm in, sir, but not for you. My friend appears to be in love with your granddaughter and my loyalty to him, well, let's just say, you and I seem to follow a similar code."

"Fair enough, Marcus. You're a stand up guy."

"I'd say the same about you, but—"

"I'm a gangster?"

"Well, I was referring to your hip, but that works, too."

"Okay, close the door and get a pad and pencil for notes. We have a lot of calls to make, and I have to find out what the authorities know and what they think they know."

"That sounds tricky."

"Child's play. After that comes the tricky part. We need to get the dope on the Pizzolis."

Saturday, Dec 29th
~ Glen Ridge ~

Scotty checks his reflection in the window of the Pastor house. He had originally chosen a completely different outfit, but as usual, Carter and Marcus vetoed his choices and picked out something they felt to be more appropriate. They assured him that the corduroy jacket over the collarless cotton shirt and pressed khakis was very professorial. Scotty had originally picked out black and red in anticipation of dropping a meatball in his lap. He takes a deep breath and rings the doorbell. Tommy opens the door and steps out and gives him a kiss.

"Brr, it got cold," she says.

"I'll admit that I expected to be eating indoors, with your family."

"In a sec, I just wanted to prepare you. My mother and Pep will ask you a thousand personal questions. Elmo will be aloof, or ignore you completely, and—"

"Tommy, relax. I've eaten dinner before…with Jews. It can't be worse than that."

"Don't be so sure. My father is a very serious man, and he's been even more withdrawn lately. Don't be intimidated, and DON'T mention his work. Our dinners are not like the ones at your place."

"Now I am intimidated."

They go inside and Tommy introduces him around. He hands a box of candy to Ramona and is glad he passed on the flowers. The centerpiece on the table is probably four times the size and cost of what he had picked out. Robert walks into the room in jeans and a white cotton shirt with the sleeves turned up. Tommy does a double take and looks at her mother and at Pep. They are equally as surprised. Tommy cannot remember the last time she saw her father at a dinner in public or with guests without a tie and jacket. She can't ever remember seeing him in jeans. Robert gives Scotty a big smile and a firm handshake, even patting him on the shoulder with his other hand.

"It's great to meet you, Scotty," says Robert. "Let's all go into the dining room."

They walk in and Robert pulls out the chair nearest his end of the table on the left. Ramona points toward her usual seat at the other side of the table.

"Sit here tonight, honey, on this side. Pep won't mind, will, you, son?"

"No, Pop," says Pep.

He heads to the far end of the table. Robert is at the head of the table with Ramona to his left and Tommy to his right. Scotty is next to Tommy and across from Elmo. Pep is at the end across from Robert. Robert pours a glass of wine and tastes it. He stands and walks around the table filling glasses.

"I understand that you don't drink, Scotty. I know that Tommy expects me to glare at you with disapproval, but don't worry. You can toast with water. I read once that the association of alcohol with a toast has little to do with the beverage, only that spirits go hand and hand with special events."

Tommy looks to her mother. Robert has already said more than at any dinner in years. Ramona simply shrugs. Robert sits down and raises his glass.

"Scotty, welcome to our home," he says.

They all clink their glasses and drink. Ramona starts to rise to get the first course, but Robert takes her hand.

"Sit, let the boys handle it. Boys?"

Pep and Elmo head for the kitchen.

"So I hear you're a teacher..." says Robert.

When Pep and Elmo return with the salad and bread, they almost drop the bowls. Robert is still speaking.

"...although I am a finance guy by trade, I assume you have heard about my legal work, and who I work for."

"Yes, Mr. Pastor, I have," says Scotty.

"Unfortunately, I can't really discuss much of it, but I want to be honest with you."

"I appreciate that, sir. I do have some concerns, but also recognize that we come from very different cultures. Take the wine, for example. Tommy may have mentioned that I'm Jewish. I never actually met any of the McCalls. I never developed a taste for spirits. They weren't exactly discouraged, we just never had them around."

"Yet, many Italian children grow up with wine all around," says Robert. "I remember the first time my father gave me a taste. I was six. I almost choked on it, but I was so proud. It's a rite of passage for us."

Elmo and Pep are gesticulating at each other. Finally, Pep speaks.

"Pop, is everything alright?" he asks.

"Actually, no, now that you ask," says Robert, "I think that you and Elmo need to get the pasta course."

Robert winks at Pep, and now everyone, other than Robert and Scotty are shrugging at each other. Elmo and Pep head to the kitchen and return with several bowls. They continue with the pasta course and later move on to the main course of fish. Robert opens a bottle of white wine and pours for anyone who wants it.

"Elmo," says Scotty, "you went to Essex Catholic didn't you?"

"Yeah," says Elmo, "what of it?"

"I recognized you, as soon as I saw your red hair. I went to Montclair. When I was a senior, we played you and we were murdering you for two-and-a-half quarters. Your coach benched your starter and put you in and you were unstoppable. You were passing and running all over us. We only won because we blocked a kick late."

Elmo brightens.

"Yeah, everything worked. I was so scared that I didn't even run the plays that were called. I was running for my life. What position did you play?"

"Oh, I was playing, but not on the field. I was in the band."

"Tommy says you play football now."

"It's just a flag football church league. You should play with us next year. It's probably small-time for you, but it's fun."

By the time coffee and dessert come out, everyone is engaged and laughing.

"I brought a Catholic girl home for dinner once," says Scotty. "My grandfather calls me over and asks, 'so, what is she?' Well, I'm shocked and a little offended. My grandfather was the biggest pinko, left-wing, northeast liberal Jew on the planet. So I say, 'how can you ask that? All of a sudden she has to be Jewish?' and he says, 'Jewish, Christian, who cares? Is she a Democrat or a Republican?'"

Robert roars with laughter.

"With us it's the opposite. My father would ask, 'I know she's Italian, but what part of Italy is she from?'"

After dessert, everyone is helping to clean up.

"So, Mrs. Pastor," says Scotty, "I'd like to compliment you on a delicious dinner, but Tommy says that you don't cook much."

"I think you experienced the effect of my last attempt. No, I just never developed an interest in it. My specialty is making reservations. I have to be honest with you. Tommy is not much better. Pep is the chef in the family, and both Robert and Elmo are good with breakfast."

"I was on my own, pretty early, so I had to learn," says Scotty.

"Tommy told me about the dinner at your place. You and your friends are bad boys for teasing my baby. My first reaction was that something like that would never happen here."

"I don't believe that. We were all laughing the whole time."

"Yes, Scotty, we were. Thank you for that."

Later, Tommy puts on her coat to walk Scotty to his car.

"That was so weird," she says.

"I thought it was great. I like your family."

"I thought it was great, too. I'm just not sure it was my family."

"Well, I don't want you to catch cold before the flash mob. I'll see you at rehearsal tomorrow."

"Not so fast, Buster."

Tommy grabs Scotty and gives him a long and powerful kiss.

After he leaves, she goes inside. Everyone is in the front room.

"Everyone enjoy the show?" she asks.

"It was romantic," says Ramona. "I really like him."

"Yeah, he's okay," says Elmo. "I hope you didn't suck his entire face off."

"Let's get to the big issue," says Tommy. "What the hell happened to Dad?"

"Let me explain," says Robert. "I could see something different in you, when you talked about this young man. It made me think about change."

"You? Change?" says Pep. "This is more serious than I thought."

"Did you bombard him with personal questions?" asks Robert. "Did your mother laugh? Was Elmo engaged? Did I keep from scaring him off? Did Tommy get too hyper?"

"Okay," says Pep, "I get all that, but blue jeans? Jesus, Dad...baby steps!"

Tommy climbs in the chair and hugs her father.

"I'm glad you like him," she says. "Thank you."

Sunday, Dec 30th
~ Glen Ridge ~

"Elmo, I need you to take a ride with me," says Robert.

Ramona and Tommy are cleaning up from breakfast and Pep is bringing the perishables to the refrigerator.

"Okay, I guess," says Elmo. "Where are we going? Should I get Pep?"

"No, this is just for the two of us. I guess it's kind of a surprise."

"This isn't about Atlantic City is it?"

"No, son. It's your mother that wants you to stay for your sister's performance. If it were up to me, I'd be with you and Donny driving down to AC."

"Come on, Pop, you hate Donny."

"Hate is a little strong. I know he's had it rough. I just wish you influenced him more than the other way around. Your mother, however, does hate Donny."

They get their coats and head outside for the Land Rover. Robert pulls out of the driveway and heads south to Bloomfield Avenue.

"Elmo, I've been doing a lot of thinking lately, about a lot of things. I think it's time for a change, for both of us."

They are passing through Town Center. Elmo looks at the preparations for tomorrow's event. He also looks at the bank and sighs.

"What kind of changes?"

"I bought you something, something big. I should've consulted you first, but it seemed so obvious, once I thought about it."

"Something big? Pop, I'm happy with my car. I'm happy with everything you and Mom have gotten me."

"Elmo, we both know that you haven't been happy. Actually, Pep put the notion in my head. He cares about you very much. We all do."

"I know, Pop. I wish I could be more like you and him."

"Nonsense, son. That is my failing, not yours. You and I are different in many ways, but there is no better or worse. I promised that I'd help you find your path and I've let you down, not the other way around. Everything is changing. I'm looking into retirement, Elmo. Now that you three are out of the house, your mother is ready to start on new life, and I want to share it with her. God, even Tommy has a boyfriend. Talk about the winds of change."

"But nothing's changing for me, Pop."

Robert pulls into the parking lot of Bellino's Nursery. He waves his hand toward the window.

"Maybe we can start over. Elmo, I bought you this."

"What?"

"Bellino's. I bought you the nursery."

"I don't understand. Pop, you bought me a nursery? I don't get it?"

"Think about it, Elmo. You have a natural gift for this. You seem to know everything about plants. My guy almost destroyed our landscaping. You fixed it all like it was nothing. Your mother constantly is bragging how you saved her azaleas."

"But, Pop, a business? What do I know about running a business?"

"According to your brother, when he was here with you, you pointed out all the mistakes and came up with solutions to fix them. He was blown away. He called me at work to tell me about it. Is he wrong?"

"God, Pop, I don't know, I mean…I had some ideas. This place used to be so much better."

"And it can be better again. Look, son, this is a lot to take in, I know. Bellino is looking to sell. His kids don't want it, and he's had enough."

"I've noticed."

"Just give it some thought."

"But what about the money and all that?"

"Elmo, I said I was looking to retire. I'm sure not going to play golf and do jigsaw puzzles all day. I want you to consider hiring me, part-time, of course. I do have a fair amount of business knowledge. And your mother is looking for a new project. She can help you run the store, while you go out and build the landscape design business."

"You mean like laying sod and installing sprinklers?"

"No, I mean designing. You'll have workers to do all of that. You may have to supervise them at first."

"Management? Design? Gee, Pop. Do you think I can? Where would I find clients?"

"Elmo, I do know an awful lot of people with fancy yards and houses."

"God damn, Pop. I certainly didn't see this coming. It seems so crazy, but…can I think more about it?"

"Absolutely, son, I just want you to be happy doing what you like."

Sunday, Dec 30th
~ Glen Ridge ~

Scotty and Tommy walk into the Rec Room holding hands. The twins come running up to them, excitedly.

"I win! I win!" says one of them. "Pay up, Lew. I knew they'd get together!"

"Congratulations, Stew. I'll take Momma to the market on your two next turns. I blame you, for this."

He points at Scotty.

"Uh, sorry?" says Scotty. "What exactly was the bet?"

"We bet on who would be lucky enough to capture the heart of this sweet girl," says Stew, "and from the looks of it, I won!"

Scotty smiles at Tommy.

"And here I thought that I was the big winner," he says.

"And what did you bet on, Lew?" asks Tommy.

"My money was on his friend Marcus," says Lew. "I still think he'd be a better match for you."

"Oh, Lew," says Stew, "you're awful."

"I think I'd have to agree, Lew," says Scotty, "but you still might have been right about Marcus being the better catch. You have a good time with Momma."

Scotty gives Tommy a kiss and heads over to get the music set up. After a short but vigorous rehearsal, Tommy stands on a chair.

"Gather round, everyone," says Tommy. "A troupe is a group of people performing together as a team. When we met here, three weeks ago, we were just a group of people looking for an adventure, and an experience. I cannot tell you how much I have enjoyed this opportunity to work with you all on this project. You have all made amazing progress and you all have obviously practiced very hard. You are indeed now a troupe. Now comes the fun part. In two days, we get to show an audience how special you are. Unfortunately, our resident guests will not be able to join us on stage, but I trust they'll be with us in spirit."

The group applauds and the patients take their bows.

"The forecast looks perfect for Tuesday, but make sure you're prepared for anything. The single most important thing is to have fun. I can't wait to see you all there. You should all be very proud of what you have accomplished."

The group applauds. Lew and Stew shout out in together, "Let's hear it for Tommy!...Hip Hip Hurray!"

One of the ladies hands Tommy a bouquet of roses. Tommy begins to cry and looks at Scotty. He smiles from the back of the room and gives her a thumbs up.

Monday, Dec 31st
~ Montclair ~

"You boys are early," says Tommy, "about three and a half hours early."

She's talking to Lew and Stew, who are standing in the Town Center.

"We are just so excited," says one of them.

"Well, please calm yourselves. Go for a walk on Church Street, do some window shopping, take a valium for God's sake. A flash mob is supposed to be spontaneous. If you stand out here working on your steps—"

"I suppose you're right," says the other one. "Maybe we can practice in the parking lot."

"Trust me, you are both ready. The key is not to be *too* ready, if you know what I mean. Go find a program and plan the rest of the evening."

"Ooh, good idea," they say as one. "Let's go."

As they scurry off, Scotty walks up behind her and kisses her on the neck.

"Dale, be careful," she says, "Scotty is right over there."

"Oh, you're hilarious. And to think that I was going to treat you to coffee and a treat at the Bon Bon Café."

She turns and kisses him.

"Oh, it's you. That sounds like fun."

"I'd like to talk about the future."

"I guess it's time. I don't want this to end."

"You mean the flash mob, don't you?"

"No, I just want that to be over already. I've had just about enough of the twins. I mean us."

"I know. I just like to hear you say it. I don't want it to end either."

"Unfortunately, we both have to return to school in a few days," she says. "Quite frankly, you've disappointed me."

"How so?"

"I fully expected you to have screwed this up by now."

"Gee, it just eludes me how women can still earn so much less than men."

"It seems that many of us are attracted to assholes. Let me go talk to the deejay about the sound check and to confirm our cues. It looks crowded. Maybe you should go ahead and get us a table."

"Okay, Tommy. Don't be long."

He kisses her and heads up the street with a smile. His phone rings. He takes a look and sees that it's Marcus. He answers it.

"What's up, Bro?"

Monday, Dec 31st
~ West Orange ~

"Mr. Pastor, I can't support this," says Marcus. "You're not ready and you may lose your hip forever. This is not a wheelchair situation. This means bedridden, probably in constant pain."

"There's no other way, Marcus. I *must* do this. Things have gone sideways. I must protect my family. I know you understand."

"Swear to me, last resort."

"Marcus, you have my word."

"Shit. Okay, what do we do?"

"You said you had a friend with a limo. We'll need that. I need a wheelchair for the first stop, a Notary, I'll need a suit…"

"I'm a Notary."

"No bullshit, kid?"

"Yes, they needed one often here, so I went through the process. I figured it would come in handy one day. My stamp is in my car."

"Good thinking, a little extra income."

"Except I never charge anyone."

"That figures."

Tommaso turns on his electric razor and begins to shave using a small travel mirror. Marcus steps into the bathroom and calls Carter. He's relieved to find him at the apartment.

"That's right...All favors used up right now...no bullshit...listen to me. Get my grey suit and my black suit out of my closet...Yeah, socks and shoes, too. Two white shirts...yeah, the good ones...and ties...no color...as conservative as possible. Now, get on your uniform...Carter, life and death, I swear...this is no joke. On my mother's...Yes, get in the limo and jet over here to the rehab...Yes, speed is of the essence."

Marcus heads back into Tommaso's room.

"Miraculously, it's all set. Carter is on his way."

"Carter?"

"Yeah, what's wrong?"

"I'm getting senile, that's what's wrong. I assume that Carter is black?"

"Yeah, is that a problem?"

"Marone, sorry, but yes it is. I show up with a black driver, the whole thing is blown. Let me think. Call your friend Scotty."

"He's downtown with Tommy setting up the flash mob."

"We need him. He'll come and she'll understand…eventually."

"Maybe I can still get Carter to pick him up."

"No, we can't slow him down, and we might need the other car."

"Whatever you say."

Marcus calls Scotty and resorts to the code that has always been there and has never been used.

"It's on, Brother. Right now, at the rehab…and fast."

"That's it?" asks Grandpa. "I'm impressed. You're in the wrong business."

~~~~~~~~~~

30 minutes later, Carter strides in carrying a bundle of clothing.

"This had better be good," says Carter.

"Carter," says Marcus, "meet Mr. Pastor, Tommy's grandfather. Help me get him into the black suit."

"The grey," says Tommaso.

"I thought all you gangsters wore black," says Marcus.

"It would be my preference, but we need the black for the driver, and the grey is a much nicer suit."

"I know," says Marcus, "it was a graduation gift from my mother. I'd prefer that you didn't get any bullet holes in it."

"I'll try to take it in the face," says Tommaso. "Let's get moving."

"Can someone please tell me what the fuck is going on here?" asks Carter. "I'm the driver and I'm wearing black."

"Too much black," say Marcus and Tommaso together.

At that moment, Scotty walks in.

"Put on the black suit," says Tommaso. "Carter's outfit would be two sizes too big for him. Carter, do you have a hat?"

"In the car, sir," says Carter.

"He'll need that, too."

"Wait," says Marcus, "where's my suit?"

"You'll need the doctor outfit," says Tommaso.

"Scrubs," says Marcus, "and I'll get a white coat."

"Sorry, no white coat," says Tommaso.

"Let me guess," says Marcus. "I've got to be the nurse."

"Sorry, kid."

"Your organization has some serious motherfucking equal opportunity issues if you don't mind me saying so," says Carter. "I'm visiting your HR director in the morning."

"His office is in East Rutherford," says Tommaso, "and you may want to bring a shovel."

"I like him," says Carter.

"Good," says Tommaso, "I'm going to need your shoes. Marcus' are too small."

"Dag, Mr. Pastor," says Carter, "you're full of surprises. No wonder you're such a badass. You sure you're not one of us?"

"Carter," says Marcus, "this is serious. You got your sneakers in the car?"

"Always," says Carter.

"Get them and the hat," says Tommaso. "You may need them."

Scotty finishes getting dressed and helps Marcus get Tommaso in the chair. Marcus gets into a clean pair of scrubs. Carter returns and puts on his sneakers. Scotty puts on Marcus' shoes. Marcus puts on Scotty's sneakers. They help Tommaso into Carter's shoes.

"Carter," says Tommaso, "you'll need to distract the cops for us, get their attention off of the bank."

"How am I supposed to do that?" asks Carter.

"Take Scotty's car," says Marcus. "Stop home and get your leather coat and your skullcap. Pop the collar, so you look like Shaft."

"I am a bad mother…seriously? No takers?" asks Carter.

"This is serious," says Marcus. "Go in front of the jewelry store a half a block from the bank."

"How am I supposed to distract the cops?" asks Carter. "If I mess with the door or bust a window, I'll get arrested."

"Are you kidding me?" asks Scotty. "How long have you been black? In that outfit, you standing out front with your normal scowl will keep the cops' attention."

"That's it?" asks Carter.

"Almost," says Marcus. "Keep your phone where you can hear it. If you hear my ringtone, don't answer, just start running like you stole something."

"*What?*" asks Carter, "they'll chase me! They'll think I really stole something."

"But you didn't," says Marcus, "so they can't arrest you."

"No," says Carter, "but they can beat my ass."

"I like this plan," says Scotty.

"All right," says Grandpa, "let's get a move on. Carter, I appreciate what you are doing. I will fill in the rest of you on the way."

Monday, Dec 31st
~ Montclair ~

Donny checks his gun for the 27th time. He is pacing around Robert's office.

"Come on, Donny," says Elmo. "We shouldn't go through with this. We're gonna get caught, or maybe worse."

"Don't do the crime if you can't do the time, E. I've survived juvie, and once we're in, we've got protection. You told me your father specializes in getting made guys out of jams."

"But he's getting out, Donny. He won't be able to help us. We haven't done anything yet. We can sneak out once the hubbub starts and forget about it."

"Yeah, and what about your grandfather? You said he was desperate to get in that box."

"Donny, I don't even know what's in the box. Jeez, it could be empty for all I know. We got guns. We get caught, it's hard time."

"For me, maybe. Whadda you got to lose? A first-timer, with a super lawyer dad? You'll skate. I'm takin' all the risk here."

"What if the cops or the Feds are onto us? What if Rico Pizzoli finds out?"

"This will get us in with Rico. That's our ticket."

"Listen, Donny. My dad's got a plan for me and him. A business. I can talk to him. You can work with us."

"Are you batshit, E? Your dad hates my guts, thinks I'm a bad influence. Shit, he's right. Look at us. I can't be a bottom feeder for the rest of my life."

"You got him all wrong, Donny. And this won't be like the garage, workin' for the Armenians. You'd have a say with us."

"You're dreamin', E. Your dad wouldn't permit it. When are you gonna go make your own way?"

"You're a hard worker. Shit, you've been at it since you were twelve, Donny. You just need to get out of workin' for assholes."

"They're all assholes, E. This will just get us in with a better class of assholes."

Monday, Dec 31st
~ Glen Ridge ~

"Come on, Robert," says Ramona, "we want to get a good spot to see Tommy."

Ramona and Pep are waiting by the front door in their jackets wearing their First Night buttons. Robert walks in holding his phone to his ear.

"So he was there for 5 minutes, a half hour ago. Thanks, Benny."

He breaks the call, shakes his head, and looks at his wife.

"Ro, Elmo may be in trouble. I need to go down to the office separately."

"Oh, my God! Robert, what is it?"

"I'm not completely sure, but it could be bad. He did not go down to Atlantic City."

He turns to Pep and takes him by the shoulders.

"Peppino, I need you to stay by your mother's side, and I need you to watch your sister."

Pep stands a little taller.

"Absolutely, Pop, you can count on me."

"Robert, no!" cries Ramona.

"Honey, I need you to trust me."

He holds up two buttons.

"I hope that Elmo and I are right beside you for the show. Now *please*, trust me and go with Pep."

Monday, Dec 31st
~ Montclair ~

Alex Gersten and Dale Hankins are in a second floor office of Montclair Realty. There are four other men operating a variety of surveillance equipment. The building is directly across the street from the bank entrance.

"Let me introduce you to some people, Hankins. Dale, this is Alton McRae from the local Organized Crime Division of the FBI and his tech, Steve, and this is Wayne Markham from the SEC Investigative Division and his tech, Ernie, is it? Hankins originally brought this to my attention. I still don't see much, but you guys contacted me independently about something happening here today, so it's worth a look. Obviously anything involving the Pastors has the potential to be big, even if it's just the kid, Elmo. There's always the possibility of leverage."

"It's your jurisdiction, for now, Alex," says McRae. "We're primarily here to observe in case we get a nibble on something bigger."

"Fine," says Alex, "we don't move unless I say so. Hankins, you're new and ambitious, but don't try to be a hero. These things sometimes move slowly. Public safety is paramount. You have six officers assigned to you, but they also need to patrol normally. No one is to get spooked from a jumpy cop."

"Yes, sir," says Dale.

Dale heads to the door and tests his comm unit. Alex hears him and shakes his head. He hits a button on the console.

"We got you, Red Leader."

Dale hits the street and waves over the six uniformed officers.

"Okay, you know the drill. You two stay to the northeast of the bank and you two on the southeast side. Monitor the crowd and keep your eyes open for Elmo Pastor and his running buddy, Donny Manzetti. Don't look obvious and wait for my command. You two are directing away the traffic on the south side. Got it?"

There's some muttering.

"I said GOT IT?"

"Yes, sir," is heard from all.

Dale heads across from the bank and makes like he's reading a newspaper.

"Who the fuck put him in charge?" asks one of the officers.

"Look at him, fake reading the paper in the dark. Some detective work," says another.

~~~~~~~~~~

After about ten minutes, Carter walks into the Town Center, and heads toward the jewelry store. He almost runs right into Tommy, but is able to skirt around her undetected. He gets to his post, leans against a light pole, pops his collar, and pushes down his skullcap to just above his eyes.

~~~~~~~~

Ramona and Pep arrive at the venue and quickly find Tommy. Ramona puts on a brave face as to not distract Tommy from her production.

"Mom, something's happened to Scotty," says Tommy. "He was supposed to meet me at the café and never showed."

"Maybe he got tied up," says Ramona.

"No, we were already together. He went ahead to get a table."

"Are you sure he went to the right place?"

"He picked it. What could it mean? We were going to talk about the future."

"Relax, baby. I'll keep an eye out for him. Don't panic—he's a fine young man and I'm sure there's a logical explanation."

"Okay...I've got to get ready."

"Break a leg," says Pep.

~~~~~~~~

One of the officers notices Carter by the jeweler.

"Raffy, check out the guy by the jewelry store."

"What about him?"

"He's been there for more than 10 minutes."

"Maybe he's waiting for someone, or maybe he's one of the dancers."

"He's no dancer, I guarantee you that. The dancers are all fat broads and old queens. No, he's up to something."

"So call it in."

He contacts Dale on the radio and Dale looks over toward Carter. Dale passes the word onto Alex and agrees to reposition the northwest team closer to the jewelry store.

"Mike, Raffy, move over by the jeweler. I want you between him and the crowd," he says into his comm unit.

"Wrong comm, asshole," says Alex, into Dale's earpiece.

Dale uses his walkie-talkie and correctly moves his men.

~~~~~~~~~~

Robert walks toward the entrance to his building. He is pulling out his keys when a figure steps out of the shadows and stands between him and the door.

"Going somewhere, Robby?" asks Rico Pizzoli.

"Yes, Rico, I'm going to my office to pick up some papers. Please stand aside."

"Holy shit!" says Alex. "It's Robert Pastor. Who's the other guy? Fuck me, it's Rico Pizzoli. Please tell me you're recording. Can we get audio from here?"

"Got it," says Steve the tech, "but we'll lose it if they go inside."

"They won't go inside and risk getting arrested," says Alex.

"Only if they enter the bank," says Markham. "Pastor has an office in there and legally may enter. He may even have a legal right to the bank. He's on the Board of Directors."

"What are they up to?" says Alex.

"I don't think they're together. They seem to be arguing," says Steve.

~~~~~~~~~~

"You're not going near that box without me, Robby," says Rico.

"Will you shut up? They can legally listen in the street."

"If you turned to the cops—"

"When are you going to learn? They're *always* listening. Inside, they can't use anything, and as your attorney, I can't tell them anything even if I wanted to."

Rico waves his hand toward the door, and Robert unlocks the building.

"Just inside," says Rico, "and leave it unlocked. I've got men watching me and I don't trust you."

"It sounds like a power struggle with Anthony Pizzoli in the hospital," says Alex. "This could be epic. Is there any way to boost the signal? I don't care if it's legal or not."

"Not with this equipment and the glass doors," says Steve.

"Rico's got to be packing," says McRae. "We can get him on that."

"He's got a carry permit, so we can't touch him on that," says Alex, "We've got no choice but to wait."

~~~~~~~~~~~

"Go up to the roadblock," says Tommaso, "and open the back windows."

"Open?" asks Scotty. "They'll see you."

"That's the point."

Scotty looks for the window controls.

"Jesus, this console looks like a 747."

He finally finds the right button and lowers the windows.

Scotty rolls the limo up to the roadblock. He is met by two cops who wave him away.

"Just wait," says Tommaso.

There is a squawk of static on the officer's radio. He looks momentarily confused, but waves Scotty through.

"I can't believe that worked," says Marcus.

"Sorry, Bro," says Scotty. "I think I shit your suit."

He continues to the curb in front of the bank.

~~~~~~~~~~~

"We can talk now," says Robert.

"I don't want to talk," says Rico, "I want to know what you and your old man have hidden in the box."

"What box?"

"Now I know you're a fuckin' liar, Robby. You want to wait till Elmo gets here? You got about fifteen minutes. He's got a gun, you know. That's a dime. I can call him off."

"Elmo doesn't work for you."

"It's gonna be his only option in about fourteen minutes, Robby. Let's go open the box."

"Okay, you got me, Rico, but here's the thing: I'm the only one who can make your life miserable. Hell, I can produce so many wills alone that you'll be running your empire from probate court."

"Sorry, Robby, it's too late for that. I got Elmo, so I got you."

~~~~~~~~~

"Let's go, E. It's time," says Donny.

"Sorry, Donny. I'm begging you to trust my dad, and to trust me. I want a future."

"Sorry, amigo, I just can't. Good luck in the real world."

Donny heads toward the bank. Elmo opens his father's window and climbs out to the fire escape. He heads down to the back lot, forgetting that he still has a gun in his backpack.

~~~~~~~~~

"Okay, Rico, what do you want to leave Elmo alone?" asks Robert.

"You and I both know that ship has sailed. I can't trust you and I can't let you out without showing weakness...what the fuck?"

Robert follows Rico's gaze and sees his father walking up to the bank with two men, a black male nurse, and a rather short chauffeur. Robert is momentarily stunned. Scotty reaches and opens the door. He holds it in the open position. Marcus keeps his head down avoiding eye contact.

"Papa, what are you doing?" asks Robert.

~~~~~~~~~~

The mayor has finished his remarks and Tommy cues the deejay. New Year's Hayride begins and Tommy moves onto a platform and begins dancing. Every few beats, another bystander joins in to the lively music. It is going as planned. Ramona spots Elmo walking from the back parking lot toward the Town Center. One of the cops spots him and tells his partner. They start moving in, but are blocked by the crowd. Ramona looks at Pep and just begins dancing. She is not in step with the others, but starts dancing toward Elmo. Pep is about to follow her, but decides that his dad would want him to keep close to Tommy. Ramona reaches Elmo first and touches his arm.

"Mom!"

"Dance, Elmo!"

"What?"

"Elmo Pastor, you fucking start dancing now! Just do what I do."

Elmo is shocked, but begins to move to the music. Ramona draws Elmo away from the police. The police are momentarily confused and slow their pursuit. Tommy is dancing, but notices both her mother and Elmo doing a completely different number.

~~~~~~~~~~

Robert waves his father inside, but Tommaso shakes his head.

"You're too late, old man. Robby's gonna open my box now," says Rico.

"We got audio!" says Steve, from across the street.

"You're not getting shit," says Tommaso. "I own this bank now."

He holds up a document.

"Bullshit! My father is the majority shareholder," says Rico.

"He just sold it to me, dipshit. Here's the transfer of shares, all properly notarized."

Robert takes it from him.

"How, did you—" he says.

Alex looks at Markham.

"It this possible?" he asks.

Markham shrugs.

"It doesn't mean squat," says Rico. "I still got Elmo."

Suddenly, Donny runs into the lobby. He is momentarily confused by the crowd of people, but starts to reach for his gun. Scotty rushes him in a flash, but Donny swings the gun around and whacks Scotty just under the right eye, knocking him to the floor at Donny's feet. Marcus begins to move, but Grandpa puts his cane in his path causing him to hesitate. Donny doesn't know where to point his gun, but before he can, Scotty lifts his leg and thrusts one of Marcus' wingtips flush into Donny's balls. Donny crumbles to the ground in a heap. Robert rushes over to Donny and whispers in his ear.

"Where's Elmo?"

Donny is gasping for breath but croaks, "He's out."

Robert continues whispering.

"Decision time, Donny. I can help you. You can trust me. I'm doing this for Elmo. Pick a side."

"You, please," he gasps.

"Shit! Was that a gun?" asks Alex. "Is that Elmo?"

He pushes a button.

"All teams, go!"

Robert slides Donny's gun to Scotty, who puts it in his pocket. Dale arrives first. Marcus reaches into his pocket and speed dials Carter.

~~~~~~~~~~

Carter, who has been grooving to the music, looks at his phone.

"Shit," he says.

Carter breaks into a sprint toward the Town Center. The dance is almost over and Tommy sees Carter running toward her. She is rather shocked to see him dragged down by four cops. Luckily, the public venue saves him from a more severe roughing up, but he still has his face jammed into the sidewalk while being handcuffed.

~~~~~~~~~

When he sees the police, Elmo suddenly realizes that he is still carrying a gun.

"Mom, there's a gun in my backpack," he whispers.

"Slip it off while dancing," says Ramona.

She takes it, slips it onto her back to the music, and dances back over to Pep.

"Take Elmo home. No stops, no questions, and don't answer the door," she says.

Ramona briskly heads away from the crowd in the opposite direction of the bank.

~~~~~~~~~

Dale has only two officers as backup.

Robert turns to Dale.

"You seem to be in charge," he says. "I am an officer of the court. This individual assaulted my client in front of several witnesses. We intend to press charges and I demand that you make an arrest."

He points to Scotty.

"There he is, detective. I also believe that he has a gun."

Dale and both officers immediately draw on Scotty, who is still on the floor. He puts his hands up, but is otherwise too stunned to move. Dale removes the gun and once the adrenaline subsides, stares at his perp.

"Scotty?" asks Dale.

Dale radios Alex to ask what to do next. After a brief discussion, they can't think of anything else to do.

"Take in the two you have, and let the others go. We'll get statements later. They won't give up anything now," says Alex over the radio.

Alex turns to the group in the realty office.

"Shut it down. Happy fucking New Year."

He picks up a stapler and flings it across the room.

After the police take Scotty away, Tommaso and Marcus move inside the lobby and Robert locks the door.

~~~~~~~~~~

The flash mob is over. All of the dancers are high-fiving each other and talking about the exciting turn of events. Some thought it was actually part of the act. Tommy stands on her platform, but can't find any of her family. She sees another person being led to a squad car in handcuffs. The police turn the person to get him in the car. He has blood running down his face. She realizes that it's Scotty. Tommy begins sobbing uncontrollably.

~~~~~~~~~~

"What the fuck was that all about?" asks Rico, still stunned. "You people are fucking crazy."

Marcus is apt to agree at this point. Scotty is headed to jail, and almost certainly with Carter in the next cell. At least one of his suits is ruined, as well.

"Well, it seems that you lost Elmo," says Robert. "We are back at our original impasse."

"Fuck you! This means nothing," says Rico. "You're all dead, your whole crazy fucking family!"

"Calm down, Rico," says Tommaso. "You too, Robert. We all know what we want. Rico, you want the power, all of it."

"You're God damned right—"

Tommaso holds up his hand.

"The Pastors want out, completely. No strings, no holds, no insurance. This is impossible because it will make you look weak, and it will encourage other defections. Still, the idea appeals to you because you know that the Pastors will be a constant threat to your power. It would be much better for you if we all went away."

"Like I said, dead," says Rico.

"What if there was a way?" asks Tommaso.

"You just said, there is no way," says Rico.

"Maybe there is," says Tommaso. "What happened in the old days when a family member was, say, queer, as we used to call it."

"It would never happen, it would mean—"

"Exile, shunning, whatever you want to call it. A shame, so severe, that the family casts you out."

"Like what?" asks Rico. "None of you is queer. You all gonna go out and molest a kid or something? This gets crazier by the second."

"What if I could give you a reason?" asks Tommaso.

"Papa, what the hell are you talking about?" asks Robert.

"Give me the key, son."

"I don't have it," says Robert. "I assume Elmo took it."

From the floor, Donny snaps out of his haze.

"I got it."

He reaches into his pocket and hands it to Robert, who gives it to his father.

"Rico, what is in this box should interest you, but more important, may provide us a way out of our current stalemate."

Rico rubs his temples.

"Jesus...okay, old man. I can't stand this anymore, but just you and me."

"No!" says Robert.

Tommaso holds up his hand.

"It's okay, son. Take Donny. You need to go help Scotty and his friend. That was quick thinking on your part. I'm impressed."

Tommaso turns to Donny.

"Young man, my son saved you from a ten year stretch. Change your life…and cut your fucking hair."

"Thanks, Papa," says Robert. "Here, lock up when you leave."

He hands the keys to Marcus. Tommaso takes out the receipt for the transfer of the bank. He tears it in half, looks at Marcus, and flicks his head toward Rico. Marcus tosses Rico the keys.

"An act of good faith," says Tommaso.

He points his thumb at Marcus and says, "I need him to come help me."

They move slowly to the safety deposit box cage. It takes Rico a while to find the right keys. Eventually they get inside and get the box open. Marcus puts it on the table and steps aside. Tommaso motions for Rico to open it. He does and looks inside. He shuffles around some old papers and reads parts of the documents.

"Wait, so why am I looking at this shit?" asks Rico.

He turns to Tommaso, who just smiles. Rico looks confused and looks back at the papers.

"This is you?"

Tommaso nods.

Rico grabs the Wolfman's cane and swings it as hard as he can on the table, splintering it.

"You sick fuck! You got your wish. You and your nigger friend, get out of my sight!"

Marcus is surprised, but picks up the box and helps Tommaso out of the bank. Marcus calls the rehab center and gets one of the night orderlies to bring an ambulance. While they wait, Marcus makes Tommaso as comfortable as possible.

"You must be in tremendous pain," he says.

"I'll admit that I've been more comfortable. I think I may have shit your suit, as well."

Marcus laughs out loud.

"I could actually use a drink…and a nap. I know you're curious. Have a look. It's okay. Robert will take care of your friends. Tomorrow will be a brighter day."

Marcus looks through the documents.

"Well I'll be damned," he says.

Marcus pokes his head into Tommaso's room. He turns to Robert who's just outside the door.

"I think he's still out," says Marcus.

"If he's here to claim my body, tell him that I'm still alive," calls out Tommaso.

"I guess it's okay to go in," says Marcus.

Marcus, Robert, Ramona, Elmo, and Tommy walk in carrying bags from Dunkin' Donuts.

"What is that shit?" asks Grandpa. "I risk my life for you people and you bring food from a drive thru?"

"Happy New Year to you, too, Papa," says Ramona. "There's not a lot open today. Would you rather that I cooked?"

"Quick, pass me a donut," says Grandpa.

"How are you feeling, Papa?" asks Robert.

"Like I got hit by a truck," says Grandpa. "Marcus, what's the damage?"

"Your father might be the toughest son of a bitch I've ever seen," says Marcus. "He is, quite frankly, defying medical science. I think he'll be out of here in a week, right on schedule."

"Where are the others?" asks Grandpa.

"Donny's in our guest room," says Robert. "He's not completely ambulatory yet. Scotty and Carter are on their way. They are picking up the limo at impound."

"Already, and on a holiday?" asks Grandpa. "You must be some attorney. Remind me to hire you if I ever get in a jam."

"Just try to stay out of trouble for a few weeks," says Robert.

Carter and Scotty walk in. Carter has a pronounced mouse under his right eye from getting jammed onto the sidewalk by the police officers. Scotty has a large bruise on the left side of his face along with some stitches under his eye. He runs to Tommy and they embrace.

"Oh, my God," she says. "I was so worried when you disappeared yesterday, and then, when I saw you arrested, I just fell to pieces."

"Yeah, sorry, about that," he says. "It was kind of a blur. I'm still not sure about all of it."

He looks at Robert.

"Well, let's start at the beginning," says Grandpa. "Robert, if you will?"

"Okay," says Robert, "I got word that Elmo had been to the bank when he was supposed to be on his way to Atlantic City. Elmo and I have been having some issues, but I was hoping that we were passed that based on recent events. I guess my big secret was that I was trying to separate myself from the business, something I should have done earlier. Anthony Pizzoli's stroke was a big monkey wrench in that plan. Rico came to see me after his father's stroke, and it became obvious that I needed to get out."

"Can I jump in here, Pop?" asks Elmo.

"Sure, son."

"It's no secret that I've been having problems trying to figure some things out. I lost my confidence and what's worse, I lost my faith in my family. I'm sorry."

"We're here now, son," says Robert. "Go on."

"Well, I talked to Grandpa and Dad about getting into the business, but they advised me against it. I didn't understand it at the time, but they were right, only I overheard Grandpa and Marcus here talking."

"Marcus," says Grandpa, "can you believe with all the precautions we took, we got snooped by an amateur?"

"I heard about this important box in the bank and that Grandpa needed to get it before he could get out of here," says Elmo. "I mentioned it to Donny and, well, you know how that went."

"In the long run, it may have helped," says Grandpa. "When that idiot contacted the alarm guy, that was my man."

"Your man?" asks Robert. "What are you still doing with men?"

362

Flash Mob

"His father worked for us many years ago. He went up for a deuce to protect our interests but was killed in prison. It wasn't a hit, just a fight that got out of hand. Anyway, I've been watching out for his family ever since. His kid wanted to become an agent. I even pulled the strings to get him in the academy. He saw Elmo and thought I should know. I told him to tell his superiors."

"Why?" asks Robert.

"Rico came to visit me as well," says Grandpa. "I wanted the Feds close, just in case. They are easier to control when you know what they know."

"This is some crazy shit," says Carter.

"You have no idea, Carter," says Robert. "Okay, so once I find out that Elmo's in play, I head to the bank to put plans B, C, and D into place. I've got fake wills for the sister, for underbosses, and even for the Animal Shelter. I figure my best bet was to show Rico how dangerous I could be."

"Oh, Robert," says Ramona.

"Sorry, babe, but at that point, I was worried that it was me or Elmo. You'd have done the same."

"I suppose."

"Anyhow, Rico was way ahead of me and caught me entering the bank. At that point, his paranoia took over and Elmo and I were both cooked."

"Dad?" says Elmo.

"Yes, continue, Elmo," says Robert. "I'm curious what you and Donny were doing inside."

"Well," says Elmo, "we went in earlier. I used the ID scam so there'd be no record of us when the building closed for the day."

"It would've worked if I hadn't called the guard to verify when the building closed," says Robert. "That's why it's a high stress business. You just can't cover all the possibilities."

"Stress? What stress?" asks Carter. "I've been at it for a whole day and all that happened to me was my work vehicle was used in a crime, I got mugged by four cops, and I got sent to jail."

"At least your injury was on your good side," says Scotty. "Have you seen my profile mug shot?"

"Well," says Elmo, "Donny and I were hiding inside with a pretty vague plan to get the box after the noise began outside."

Pep turns to Tommy.

"Well at least he didn't blow off your performance to go to Atlantic City. He was there the whole time."

She makes a face at him.

"So I'm realizing what a mistake this is," says Elmo. "I mean, I should have known all along, but I guess I wasn't thinking straight. Well, Dad and I had a talk on Sunday, and, well, it made me feel good about myself for the first time in a long time and I liked the feeling. I really tried to talk Donny out of it and I realized how desperate he was and how I let myself be dragged down. He said I was a coward, but it wasn't like that. It's like I found a new strength, you know?"

Ramona comes over and hugs him.

Flash Mob

"I'm sorry, Mom," says Elmo.

Robert wipes his eyes.

"Okay," says Robert, "at this point, all hell breaks loose. Rico has me by the balls, and I assume Elmo is toast, as well. I was begging at this point, and then you show up, Papa. You looked ridiculous walking up with these two. I was convinced that we were all dead, but was strangely calmed when you arrived."

"We got very lucky," says Grandpa.

"That's when I saw Elmo," says Ramona. "I was so happy, but then I immediately saw the police draw a bead on him."

"It was surreal," says Pep, "she just started dancing with the flash mob. I thought she went crazy."

"I think I did, too," says Ramona.

"I went to follow her," says Pep, "but, you said to watch them both, and I figured you'd rather I stick with Tommy."

"You made the right call, Pep," says Robert.

"She grabbed me in the crowd," says Elmo, "and yells at me to dance. I was confused, but when she started cursing, I just did what she said."

"Cursing?" asks Pep. "What did she say?"

"It's too horrible to repeat," says Elmo. "All of a sudden, the cops jumped this guy, and I remember that I've got a gun in my backpack. Mom calmly took it, told Pep to take me home, and walked up the street."

"I saw some of this happening," says Tommy, "and I'm freaking out, but I'm in the middle of the dance. Remember that Scotty had disappeared on me earlier in the afternoon and I was already in a panic."

"That was my fault," says Grandpa. "I needed Scotty and Carter and had Marcus summon them. There was no time to explain. I can tell you that Scotty wouldn't shut up about what you were going to do to him."

"Slow down, Papa," says Robert. "Where did you come up with that bill of sale for the bank? That wouldn't have fooled anyone for long."

"I only had to convince Rico," says Grandpa, "and only long enough to keep him from killing us. It was actually damn near legit. We stopped at the hospital on the way and went to Anthony's room. That was actually his signature and it was properly notarized."

"By Marcus," says Robert, "and isn't Anthony in a coma?"

"Semi-conscious, to be accurate," says Marcus, "but I am a Notary and everything was done by the book. Mr. Pastor here was even kind enough to help his old friend hold the pen."

"I'm still a little foggy on my role," says Carter, "although, that could be the concussion talking."

"You played your part perfectly, Carter," says Grandpa. "Your timely dash had two benefits. It reduced by two thirds the number of officers that we had to deal with. We'd all have been arrested, if not shot, with six of them."

"And, you may have saved my Elmo," says Ramona. "We are forever in your debt."

"How did you draw away so many of them?" asks Robert.

"Just being my big, black, threatening looking self," says Carter. "Racial profiling, yay!"

"That sounds like one of your plans, Papa," says Robert.

"A healthy knowledge of human nature can be valuable," says Grandpa. "Before I continue, Ramona, what happened with the gun?"

"Well, my first goal was to get out of the area and distance myself from Elmo," she says. "I was going to dump it, but on all those detective shows, they can get fingerprints and DNA off of the bullets. I didn't want to take any chances, so I walked over to Merola's. Luckily the old man was there. He got Gino, you know, the giant, to take the gun and dispose of it properly. He then got me a cab and I went home."

Robert takes her hand and squeezes it.

"So," says Grandpa, "about this time, Donny comes running in with a gun. Scotty was on him in a flash, but Donny clipped him in the face and he went down."

"I had your back," says Marcus, "but Grandpa Pastor stopped me. I took a leap of faith that he knew this stuff better than me."

"It was more of a reflex than a plan," says Grandpa. "Rico said he had men in the area. At that point, I was just trying to minimize casualties."

"That's good to know," says Scotty, "and yet everyone seemed so nice at the family dinner."

"I told you it was an aberration," says Tommy.

"You came through like a champ, Scotty," says Grandpa. "You saved Donny for sure, and probably the rest of us."

"While I appreciate the kudos," says Scotty. "I'm still a little fuzzy about a few things. I haven't saved a lot of lives, but I would think that the proper response should be 'thank you,' not having me arrested. You even planted a gun on me. I mean, if you didn't want me dating your daughter—"

"Sorry about all of that," says Robert. "It was a spur of the moment thing. First of all, I knew I could get you out. It also gave me an opportunity to save Donny. I recently had a conversation with Elmo and realized that Donny still had the potential to not end up dead or in prison. Anything he does with his life from this point forward, he owes to you. Besides, it really freaked out Rico."

"It was both extremely clever and extremely noble, son," says Grandpa. "I'm proud of you. I'm proud of all of you. How did you get them out so fast, especially on a holiday?"

"I still have some powerful friends, Papa," says Robert. "I figured I'd better work fast while I still had them. Besides, as helpful as they were, these men are still amateurs. They didn't even know why we put them in the system. Carter is done, since running is not a crime, and Scotty, well, no witnesses came forward, and the cops had nothing. The gun will require an appearance, but he'll say he found it, and it will get tossed."

"I'll bet if Scotty and I switched places, the outcome would have been different," says Carter.

"No," says Robert, "I think you'd still both be out of jail. You'd just be dead."

Everyone laughs except Carter, who just shoots Robert with his finger.

"Well, Carter," says Grandpa, "I figured it would take more time to get your car out of impound. I assume you are in dutch with your employer. Tomorrow, I will call him and request your exclusive service for two weeks and at a considerable premium. I will also make sure that he knows that your customer service is responsible."

"Thank you, sir," says Carter. "Where would you like to go?"

"Me?" asks Grandpa. "Look at me. I'm not going anywhere. Take the two weeks off to do whatever you want. It's a paid vacation. As a matter of fact, Robert, don't we have some beachfront property in Marco Island? Why should he waste his vacation up here in the cold?"

"I'll take care of it, Papa," says Robert, "but aren't you forgetting something?"

"Oh, of course," says Grandpa. "Marcus, bring me the box."

Marcus picks the box up off of a table and hands it to Grandpa.

"First of all, I want to say that we are out, completely and safely. My biggest regret in life was failing to keep my son and his family out of my business. I know that this is thirty years too late, but I want my Marie to know that things are finally as they should be. Ramona, you and I haven't always seen eye to eye, but I could not have asked for a better partner for my son and a better mother for my grandchildren. I know that you never met my wife, but I can assure you that she would feel the same way about you. Peppino, I love you very much and unconditionally. Elmo, your father has given you a great gift. I have every confidence that you will do yourself proud."

"I will, Grandpa," says Elmo.

"As for you, Tommasina," says Grandpa, "my beautiful namesake, I can see when you look at Scotty that you care deeply about him. I know this is a new relationship, but I want you to know something. Scotty looks at you the same way that I looked at my Marie. Do not let petty obstacles stand in the way of love. Sometimes we are too smart for our own good."

"I understand, Grandpa," she says.

She holds Scotty tightly.

"Robert," says Grandpa, "you, too, must cherish your Ramona. I know that you are financially secure. Please find the life that your mother wished for you."

"Papa," says Robert, "I already feel like a weight has been lifted from me. We plan to enjoy each other. I think that we might even take cooking lessons together."

"Speak for yourself," says Ramona. "I have to help my son get his business up and running."

"I guess I can take up golf," says Robert. "Now, Papa, can you please share with us what is in the box?"

"Okay," says Grandpa, "here goes. You all know that I came to this country from Italy in 1942. I was 12 years old. When I got here, I was completely alone, and the story was that my family did not survive the war. This is mostly true."

"Mostly?" says Robert. "I'm confused."

Grandpa reaches into the box and pulls out a very old necklace with a locket. He hands it to Marcus who hands it to Robert.

"Open it," says Grandpa.

"It's a boy and a young woman," says Robert. "Is this you...and your mother?"

"It can't be him, Robby," says Ramona. "The woman is wearing a cross, but the boy is wearing a Jewish star, see?"

"It is me," says Grandpa, "and the woman is Rosalia Pastorini. She was my governess. I guess you'd call her a nanny today. I was born in what is now Poland, to Wladyslaw and Breine Olszewski, if I am pronouncing it correctly. She was of Austrian descent, and they were both Jews. He was a University Professor and she was a nurse. I was their only child and my given name is Oskar Moses Olszewski."

"I can't believe this," says Robert.

"Oy vey!" adds Carter.

"Here," says Grandpa. "I have the documentation to prove it."

Marcus hands Robert a folder.

"Most of this story was pieced together, so allow me to get through it," says Grandpa. "This part, I got from Rosalia before I left Italy. My father was a somewhat important scholar and travelled a lot, including to Italy. He met Rosalia at a University there and he hired her as my governess and as a research assistant, and she came back to Poland to help my mother. My father was apparently considered somewhat of a dissident, and when the Nazis rose in power, my parents thought I would be safer out of

Poland. They sent me with Rosalia to Italy, where my identity was a secret and I would be raised temporarily as part of her family. Of course, no one expected the war to reach the magnitude that it did. Keep in mind that I was only three-and-a-half years old when I left Poland. I have no recollection of any of this. I was raised as an Italian, went to Italian schools—basically, I became Tommaso Pastorini."

"This is incredible," says Robert.

Grandpa coughs and winces in pain. Marcus gives him some water and Grandpa nods that he is okay.

"In 1942, Italy was in chaos. Everyone was in danger. Rosalia's parents had a contact that could get her and me to America. She told me this story that I am now telling you, and she gave me this locket, which my parents had given her as a gift. When we got to the docks, the captain of the vessel demanded twice as much money than originally agreed to for the passage. Rosalia put me on the boat and went to find more money. All I know is that she never returned and the ship set sail. They had obviously forgotten about me. I hid in the hold for two weeks eating from the trash. When we arrived in New York, actually Hoboken, I got off the ship."

"Wait," says Ramona, "what about these papers?"

Grandpa holds up his hand.

"All will be explained, my dear," he says. "I knew no one in America and spoke no English. I heard some people speaking Italian at the docks and followed them. They tagged me as Pastor as a joke, like the people coming through Ellis Island, getting their name changed. They worked for Enrico Pizzoli, and that's how I got connected. I started by doing odd jobs for food and shelter. Eventually

Roberto Pizzoli took a shine to me, and here I am. Obviously, I couldn't tell anyone the truth. The Italians hated the Jews. They were enemies in the war and for control of the waterfront in Hoboken. I kept the locket hidden away from everyone, including Marie. She was a Pizzoli."

Robert holds up the papers.

"Let's jump ahead," says Grandpa. "When I turned seventy-five, you and Ramona treated me to a three week trip to Italy, remember?"

"Of course, Papa," says Ramona.

"Well, while I was there, I got a little bored drinking espresso at the local café, so I started poking around. It took a while, but I was actually able to find some of the grandchildren of the Pastorini's, Rosalia's parents. They knew who I was. Not the American me, but they knew of the boy that was sent to America. They thought Rosalia came across with me and wondered why she never contacted them after the war. Sadly, none of us ever found out what happened to her. They said that their parents assumed that my parents died in the camps, but no one could verify that, either."

"Um, if you are interested," says Scotty, "I may be able to help you with that. If nothing else, the Germans were meticulous record keepers. There are Jewish organizations that may be able to find them."

"Maybe when I get out of here, I'll take you up on that. I have a feeling that I will be seeing more of you. Anyway, we had a funeral service for Rosalia and in their family crypt, there was a box containing the papers you see here. I brought them back, added them to my secret box and pretty much forgot about it. When we took over the bank, I realized it was a problem, since I was too recognizable to get to it, and it still was dangerous."

"Dangerous how?" asks Ramona.

"For the same reason I was able to use it on Rico," says Grandpa. "It would be a tremendous betrayal to the Pizzoli's."

"Wait a second," says Carter. "These people hated Jews so much that they would banish you? If you pardon me asking, why wouldn't they just kill you?"

"I expect that Anthony may have. I married his sister and had the highest place of trust in the family. Rico, on the other hand, considers himself old school. With Rico, it was more about the shame than the betrayal. Also, Robert did a pretty good job in planting the seed that we could be a challenge to his authority. I guess it was a win-win."

"Win-win my ass," says Carter. "Who'd have thought it? I thought we had it tough."

"My people were slaves 3000 years before your people," says Scotty. "It seems we've made a few enemies along the way."

"Well," says Robert, "this changes a lot. I guess we'll get to it after some football and some sleep. I think it's time to go, everyone."

Scotty holds Tommy's hands.

"Okay, I'll come up to Boston on Martin Luther King weekend, and you come down for President's. We'll work on our respective spring breaks later."

"We have Patriot's Day in April," says Tommy.

Flash Mob

Eventually only Marcus and Grandpa are left.

"You've been awfully quiet," says Tommaso.

"Just taking it all in, Mr. Pastor," says Marcus. "It's been quite an adventure."

"It certainly has."

After a pause, Tommaso grins, claps his hands, and rubs them together.

"So, Marcus, what are we going to do today?"